RUNNING FROM STRANGERS

RUNNING FROM STRANGERS

C. C. HARRISON

FIVE STAR
A part of Gale, Cengage Learning

GALE
CENGAGE Learning·

Detroit • New York • San Francisco • New Haven, Conn • Waterville, Maine • London

GALE
CENGAGE Learning˙

LIBRARY OF CONGRESS CATALOGING-IN-PUBLICATION DATA

Harrison, C. C.
    Running from strangers / C. C. Harrison. — 1st ed.
        p. cm.
    ISBN-13: 978-1-59414-709-8 (alk. paper)
    ISBN-10: 1-59414-709-4 (alk. paper)
    1. Women social workers—Fiction. 2. Child welfare—Fiction.
3. Biologists—Fiction. 4. Wildlife photographers—Fiction. 5.
Colorado—Fiction. I. Title.
    PS3608.A7833R86 2008
    813'.6—dc22   2008019937

First Edition. First Printing: September 2008.
Published in 2008 in conjunction with Tekno Books.

Printed in the United States of America
1 2 3 4 5 6 7 12 11 10 09 08

ACKNOWLEDGMENTS

This book is dedicated to:
Child advocates everywhere who devote themselves to seeing
that all children have a warm place to sleep, good food to eat,
and someone to love and care for them

And to:
The wild horse herds in the American West, and the U.S.
Bureau of Land Management which nurtures and cares for
them

With special thanks to:
Mike Jensen, BLM Wild Horse Herd Manager, Mancos-
Dolores Ranger District, Dolores, Colorado

And with particular love to:
The wild horse herds that roam my land on Wild Horse Mesa,
San Luis, Colorado

Thanks a million to:
My agent, Pam Strickler.
My ever supportive daughter, Barbara.
Lena and Barbara, wonderful writers and friends.
John Helfers, Tiffany Schofield, Brittiany Koren, and all the
other talented folks at Five Star and Tekno.

C. C. Harrison
Anthem, Arizona

CHAPTER ONE

The neighbors were fighting again, their loud voices jolting Allie Hudson out of a sound sleep. She wanted to get up and close the window, but it seemed too much effort to kick free of the damp bed sheets twisted and tangled around her legs. Instead, she turned face down in the pillow and snaked her arm over to wrap it around Sammy's broad shoulders.

Only Sammy wasn't there anymore. He'd moved out, taking a television set and one of her credit cards with him. She groaned, remembering she hadn't yet called VISA to cancel that card, then peeked at the bedside clock and groaned again. In less than two hours, she was due in court to argue seven-year-old Davy Lopez's placement case.

No, she corrected herself. She didn't argue cases anymore. She wasn't allowed to. Her law license was under disciplinary suspension. A little matter of shoving her finger into the chest of the abusive ex-husband of her client when he lied during a child custody hearing.

"Well, he deserved it," she mumbled, knowing she'd gotten off easy. She could have been arrested for assault.

Now she was a Court Appointed Special Advocate, the guardian of the best interests of abused and neglected children in judicial proceedings. A comedown on the face of it, she supposed, especially financially, but infinitely more rewarding to her spirit.

She adored kids, and as a CASA she got to spend plenty of

one-on-one time with them, visiting in their foster homes, taking them to the movies, to the park, to the mall, to McDonald's. She got to know them. Came to love them.

Her heart swelled a little remembering how Davy's eyes had gone from disbelief to pure joy when she took him to the toy store last Christmas and told him to pick out a gift.

When she was a lawyer, the children were rarely more to her than a name and a faded photograph in the file. Her clients were their parents—irate, angry, determined to stick it to their spouses by demanding sole custody. Occasionally, she helped a disgruntled relative dutifully, if not willingly, take in the orphaned or abandoned child of a distant family member. Her Aunt Helen's sour face, disapproving and wrinkled as a prune, suddenly popped to mind. From the day the court placed five-year-old Allie on *her* doorstep, Aunt Helen's peevish expression had never softened.

Outside, the bickering grew louder, forcing Allie to give up the idea of sleep. Throwing back the covers, she got out of bed, closed the window, flipped on the light, went into the bathroom, then walked barefoot downstairs into the kitchen, catching her little toe on the doorjamb along the way.

"Oww! Ouch!"

She hopped on one foot, ouching and moaning, making a big deal of it until the throbbing stopped. People should holler more when they hurt themselves, she thought. It released the negative energy and freed the endorphins, making the pain go away faster.

She put the coffee on and waited impatiently for it to drip into the carafe. When it did, she filled a mug, added two teaspoons of sugar and a big glop of real cream—her only indulgence if she didn't count the half-gallon of coffee ice cream in the freezer—and carried it into the combination den and guest bedroom off the living room that she used as a home office.

She switched on her computer and clicked into her e-mail. Except for a keeping-in-touch message from her cousin in Greece, she deleted them all. Solicitations from credit counselors, loan officers, and online dating services—none of which she needed. Well, maybe the credit counselors, but not the dating services. She was a fool for love, but not that big a fool.

She took a sip of coffee, closed out her e-mail, and with a pleasant sense of expectancy, opened a web site.

Graphics filled the monitor, then one by one, a montage of photos flashed on the screen—panoramic views of mountain ranges, heavily forested wilderness, wild animals. Some of the animal shots were extreme close-ups. And then a name popped up, the name she'd whispered into her pillow a thousand times.

Beckwith Williams.

She propped her elbow, put her chin in her hand, and grinned. A big, warm feeling spread through her middle.

The web site had been updated with a more recent picture of him. The killer smile was the same, but his hair was longer now—below his shoulders, and sun-streaked. He was wearing khaki hiking shorts, and a red bandana wrapped around his forehead. Mirrored sunglasses hid his eyes. Shirtless, his stomach flat, his tanned arms and shoulders hard and muscled, he stood on a rock outcropping with his hands on his hips looking directly into the camera. Behind him were mountains and a brilliant wash of blue sky. He looked exactly like what he was—nature photographer, wildlife biologist, lover of wild things.

Adventurous. Untamed.

A loner.

He'd never married.

It crossed her mind to wonder who'd taken the picture.

She scrolled down the web page and clicked on the link that

described his research project with the Bureau of Land Management—a study of the wild mustang herd whose range extended onto Wild Horse Mesa adjacent to the William's family ranch in southwest Colorado. He was also photographing the animals for an upcoming article in *National Geographic*.

She read each word, though she could have recited them all from memory. Every detail of Beck's life was scorched into her brain, imprinted on her soul; she'd been following his web site for years. He was a piece of unfinished business of her heart, but one she'd have to live with, because it was her fault. After everything he'd done for her, she'd left him. He probably thought she was an ungrateful bitch.

If he thinks of me at all.

She felt a sad, sweet longing that was like an ache, and her eyes misted. She let some of the memories come into her mind, holding them away just a little, grieving the past that had led to this moment. Beck had loved her once, but after what happened, she knew he'd never forgive her.

She'd met him when she was thirteen, and had quickly gotten used to him always being there for her—covering for her, getting her out of jams, taking the blame. It wasn't that she didn't know there might be consequences to her actions; it was just that she somehow thought she might be able to skip over them. Beck was the only one who understood that she didn't deliberately get herself into those messes. Everyone else just thought she was wild.

She smiled to herself remembering how he'd tried to scold her, tried to be angry, but always ended up kissing her instead. She could have gotten away with murder—

"Stop it!" She said the words aloud, instantly silencing those ticking time bombs of memory.

She gave herself a mental shake, regretting the unfortunate choice of metaphor in her thoughts, and waved her hands as if to clear the air of the pictures in her mind so she didn't have to relive the hurt, the fear, the scorching pain that looking at the past always brought on. That achingly sad and glorious time, that pathetically confused period of her youth that seemed to have happened to someone else.

And then she did the same thing she always did . . . she touched her fingers to her lips in a kiss and pressed them to his picture on the monitor.

"I love you, Beck."

The familiar hole of sadness in her stomach opened up and pain, like fire, like licking flames, swept over her. A tear trickled down her face, and she tugged in a breath to check the sob.

What a mess I've made of my life.

She rose from the keyboard and hurried to the bathroom, stripping off her nightgown along the way. She turned on the shower and stepped in, letting the warm spray mix with the tears.

It was nearly eight when Allie pulled into the only vacant space in the Domestic Relations Judicial Complex parking lot, took the .38 she carried for protection in bad neighborhoods out of her purse, checked to make sure the safety was on, then put it in the center console. She noticed she was out of parking meter quarters—again!—and made a mental note to get some change. Exiting her ten-year-old Jeep Cherokee, she hefted the straps of her bag and a bulging leather briefcase onto her shoulder and headed for the Family Court Division entrance.

"Mornin', Allie." The elderly security screener at the door smiled in greeting, white teeth and white hair stark against her dark skin.

"Hey, Ruby. Gettin' any?" Allie teased as she deposited her belongings onto the metal detector conveyor belt.

"Nah. How about you?" Ruby opened Allie's purse and gave

it a cursory search, then pushed it through the scanner.

"Not much."

Ruby looked up in surprise. "What happened to Sammy? You run that man off already?"

"Tried not to, but he left anyway," Allie replied. "Thing is, he took a credit card and my extra TV with him."

"Men," said Ruby, feigning disgust. "You can't live with 'em, and you can't kill 'em." She finished checking Allie's briefcase and flashed another smile. "Have a good Memorial Day weekend."

"See you next fall, Ruby. I'm taking the summer off."

Allie picked up her bag and briefcase as they moved smoothly out the other side of the x-ray scanner, then turned left down the hallway leading to the Family Court waiting room, reminding herself to call VISA and report that credit card stolen.

God, I'm bad at picking men.

A parade of boyfriends had wandered through her life before she married Paul, some of whom she'd allowed to pause in her bed before realizing they weren't *the one.* Unfortunately, Paul Robbins hadn't been *the one,* either, only she didn't find that out until after she'd married him. That was all far enough in the past that she could think about him dispassionately now. But not about what he did.

Sammy, a slick piece of work with blue eyes from Denver, never had been a permanent fixture in her recent widowhood, just a distraction to keep her mind off the circumstances of Paul's death.

The Family Court waiting room, drab and institutional and depressing as hell, was stuffy, the air heavy with the smell of too many people in one place. Anger was like a living, breathing creature hovering overhead, a frightful thing eager to embed sharpened talons into troubled hearts. Fear and dejection had carved their initials on morose faces. Nobody was there because they wanted to be, not even the lawyers.

All the seats were taken, so she found a vacant spot against the faded pea-green wall and pressed into it, waiting with the others to be called into a hearing room. Babies in bulky infant carriers slept or cried. Toddlers fussed in strollers. Older kids ran around working off a sugar high or sat slumped in chairs, peering around the room looking confused and scared. Young mothers with fifty-dollar nail jobs and three-hundred-dollar hair extensions, who Allie knew would soon be telling a judge they had no money to buy food for their babies, argued or whispered into cell phones.

For good or for bad, at least these mothers came to court. Davy's parents hadn't shown up once.

Allie closed her eyes and dragged a long, steady breath. It's for the children, she reminded herself. I do this for the children, for they are the real victims, helpless to counter the abuse and neglect imposed on them by trusted adults. As a CASA, she was in a position to do something about it.

Unfortunately, she couldn't help them all, but for the children whose cases were assigned to her, she was vigilant in seeing they had a safe place to live, a warm bed, good food, and someone who gave a damn what happened to them. The strong must take care of the weak she told people who decried the misery quotient inherent in her work.

Someone called her name, and she looked up to see Diana Rameriz, the docket clerk, wending her way through the crowd toward her, waving to catch her attention. Sharply dressed in a well-cut suit and high heels that showed off her good legs, Diana looked agitated as she approached.

"What's wrong?" Allie asked.

Nervously, Diana wet her lips before answering. "Judge Emery's not here."

Allie tensed. "Why not? Where is she?" Jo-Jo Emery, family

court judge and close friend, was predictable and precise despite her heavy personal and professional schedule. It wasn't like her to be late.

"Nobody knows. When she didn't show up at her usual time, the office phoned her house, but there was no answer. I had to get another judge to substitute, and he wasn't happy to be called in on such short notice." Diana stopped speaking, but her lips were left slightly parted as if she had more to say.

"Oh?" Allie felt a tiny tug of apprehension. "Who is it?"

Diana averted her eyes a moment before saying the name on a rush of air. "Judge Berriman."

The news hit Allie like a soft blow to the chest. "Thornton Berriman?" she repeated, taken aback. " 'Bury Me' Berriman?"

He had earned that nickname, and was called it irreverently and secretly by the county's legal community, because of his disdain for lawyers who displeased him, rebuking and ridiculing them unconscionably. The offending lawyers left his courtroom humiliated, their clients often suffering the brunt of the judge's bad temper by receiving harsher sentences than might have been imposed by a different judge. He seemed to have an unlimited stockpile of axes to grind, and unfortunately, Allie would not be a stranger to him.

"Just thought I'd warn you," Diana said, and then she was gone.

Diana knew, as did everyone in the district, it was because of Judge Berriman that Allie no longer practiced law. It was in his courtroom that she'd experienced her major lapse in impulse control and, as her suspension records stated, abused the court's protocol by engaging in behavior unbecoming to an officer of the court. Berriman had cited her for contempt, and his complaint to the bar association resulted in her suspension. She had appealed, lost, and then applied for the CASA position.

That was a year ago, and she hadn't seen him since. He usually presided over big money divorce and high-profile custody trials, not temporary placement hearings such as the one about to be held for Davy Lopez. That was Jo-Jo Emery's domain, only now she wasn't here.

Allie scanned the crowd looking for the social worker who had initiated Davy's case, but Tiffany Day hadn't arrived. No surprise.

It was common knowledge that Tiffany, fresh out of Michigan State—the ink on her degree in social services administration still damp—saw her job as nothing more than a necessary stepping stone to bigger and better positions. Unfortunately, civil service personnel protections made it next to impossible to fire anyone, so Allie had to put up with her ineptness.

She was steeling herself for the encounter with Judge Berriman when the first cases were called. Anxiety constricted her chest as she filed into the hearing room with the others on the morning docket. In family court proceedings, especially dispositional hearings such as this, much of the formality, at least compared to a full blown trial, was dispensed with in the interest of expediency. There was no jury box; child placement hearings did not have juries. The room was smaller than most of the courtrooms in the hall of justice, but, thankfully, it had natural light pouring in from large windows set high on one wall.

Lawyers, social workers, and Child Protective Service officials sat around a crowded conference table that took up most of the floor space, while for Allie and the others—parents, guardians, grandparents, and assorted interested parties—it was standing room only around the perimeter.

She saw right away that Davy's parents weren't there, and Tiffany Day still hadn't shown up. No one cared enough about the little boy to be present. Except her.

"All rise," hailed the bailiff. "Honorable Judge Thornton Berriman presiding. Family Court, County of Macomb, State of Michigan."

Chairs scraped back and conversations were instantly terminated as everyone stood. The judge, wearing a scowl and looking prickly as barbed wire, entered the hearing room with an officious rustle of black robes. Sixtyish, and fit and trim, he had a full head of neatly combed white hair so resplendent it practically glowed. After he settled into a high-backed leather chair, the clerk intoned, "You may be seated," and everyone sat, noisily.

Judge Berriman shuffled through some papers, then lifted his head like an animal catching a scent and peered around the room, his eyes dark and flinty, throwing sparks. His gaze halted when it reached Allie, and his face pinched imperceptibly at the sight of her, as if passing judgment on her very existence.

She smoothed fidgeting fingers over her sleeked-back hair and tugged at the hem of what she now realized was a too-short skirt.

"Disposition for placement," announced the clerk into a microphone. "Emergency placement hearing for Davy Lopez. Alma Hudson, CASA. Case number oh-seven-dash-three-nine-seven."

Judge Berriman's expression remained stern. "I see you're first up, Miss Hudson."

Allie approached the bench, managing to keep the falter out of her step, and placed her case file on the lectern. "Good morning, Your Honor," she said, showing her teeth in a tentative smile, trying for charm and working up enough civility in her voice to cover the nervousness.

Ignoring her pleasantry, Judge Berriman shoved his glasses up the bridge of his nose and began reading the file handed to him by the clerk.

"Speak," he barked.

"Your Honor, this child was taken out of his home by Child Protective Services. The CPS investigation began when Davy's grade school principal called to say that Davy had been absent from school more times than he'd attended. When CPS social worker Tiffany Day arrived at the home, she found it filthy, well below health department standards, and the boy was home alone."

The judge was still reading, and Allie stopped, not sure he was listening. He snapped, "Go on," so she did.

"Miss Day helped him pack his things, then called the police and took him into protective custody. Davy was placed in a foster home, but due to a serious illness, the foster mother can no longer keep him. I respectfully request that another suitable foster home be found for him."

The judge took a moment longer to finish reading the social worker's report, pulled his glasses to the end of his nose, and lifted his eyebrows. "This seems like a simple matter," he said archly. "The boy's father works for the Church of Spiritual Light doing"—he read from the report—"odd jobs, maintaining the grounds, keeping the vehicles tuned and running. Mother stays home." He looked up. "I see no reason he shouldn't be there, too."

A slight panic swirled inside Allie. "Well . . ." she began, then quickly gathered her thoughts, choosing her words carefully.

"Actually, Your Honor, I have additional information that bears on this matter. As the Court Appointed Special Advocate for this child, I object to his return to a home filled with undesirable influences. It would not be in his best interest to live there. I've conducted my own home visitation and have an updated dispositional report."

She held it out to the bailiff, who took it and handed it off to the judge. After the judge read it, he glowered down at Allie.

"You're making some pretty serious allegations here for which there is no preponderance of evidence. I have no choice but to ignore them."

"But Your Honor—"

"The social worker's report indicates the home is clean and warm, there's food in the cupboards, and the parents have attended parenting classes."

Parenting classes? Allie seriously doubted that.

"Based on her investigation," Judge Berriman went on, "the caseworker feels the boy should be returned to his parents."

"But Your Honor, if I may continue."

He allowed her to, but reluctantly, and she hurried on before he changed his mind.

"I spoke to Judge Joanne Emery about this boy and his home situation. She has a copy of my investigational report—" Too late she snapped her mouth shut.

Judge Berriman stiffened. "You spoke to Judge Emery privately about this?" His tone was incredulous, and he was clearly offended. "Surely, you know it's against regulations to have private conversations with judges about matters that should only be addressed in open court."

"Yes, Your Honor, I do, but in this case I thought an exception might be made since the child would be so adversely affected if he were sent home." Her breathing had speeded up, but she stood her ground. Berriman stared at her silently, darkness churning behind his eyes.

"You don't like rules, do you, Miss Hudson?" he said at last. "You don't think they apply to you, do you? Are there any boundaries you respect?"

Without waiting for an answer, he rapped his gavel with a loud bang. "I hereby order Davy Lopez returned to his parents. Next case."

Her gasp carried traces of a laugh. "What?" She looked around to see if anyone else caught the humor. "Is this a joke?"

There was a collective intake of breath. In the silence that followed, the wall clock could be heard marking off the seconds. No one was looking at her except the judge, and he was seething with anger.

"It's no joke, Miss Hudson. I don't tell jokes. Davy Lopez is to be returned to his parents by the end of the day." He handed the file to his clerk who gave him another. "Next case."

"Wait a minute!"

Allie's heart was racing at a hard clip. Her hands shook, and she struggled to keep a tremble out of her voice. "Do you really expect me to return that boy to a home with an amphetamine popping father and a prostitute for a mother?"

The sound of the gavel cracked like a gunshot. Everyone in the room jumped.

"That's enough!"

Judge Berriman's eyes glared daggers. "There is no evidence for the allegations you are making, and if you don't watch yourself, young lady, you will be spending another thirty-six hours in jail for contempt, after which I intend to help you along a career path to more suitable employment."

An impulse rose in Allie's chest, but words didn't follow it. Her work was important to her, more important than anything she'd done in her life. She couldn't further jeopardize her job and the opportunity to help children who needed her. Acting in anger was not a smart idea. She took in a breath and released it slowly, trying to slow the beating of her heart.

"You will return that boy to his parents today, or I'll have the marshals pick him up and take him there. Is that clear?"

Clear enough. She was perspiring. Her underarms were soaked. Sweat ran down her side soaking her bra as she pictured how frightened Davy would be to see armed, uniformed marshals coming to take him out of the best home he'd ever known. She couldn't let that happen.

"Yes, Your Honor. I understand," she replied, gentling her voice. "I'll take him to his parents. It won't be necessary to call the marshals."

"By noon," he amended, arbitrarily shortening the deadline.

Blinking furiously, Allie made her way out of the courtroom. She ignored the sympathetic whispers that trailed in her wake, fully aware that behind the expressed collegiality was profound relief that it was she, and not they, who had been buried alive by Judge Thornton Berriman.

When she reached the waiting room, she dug her cell phone out of her bag and punched in a phone number.

"Come on, Jo-Jo, pick up," she grumbled through clenched teeth. A connection was made, and she took a breath to speak but stopped abruptly when the answering machine came on. Listening to the outgoing message, picturing her friend—fifty-ish, hair gone to grey, peace sign earrings jiggling when she moved her head—she waited for the beep.

"Jo-Jo, this is Allie. Where are you? Call me on my cell right away. Judge Berriman ordered Davy returned home. He had a report from Tiffany saying the parents had cleaned up their act. I'm supposed to pick Davy up from foster care and take him to his house now." She hesitated, wanting to say more, wanting to rant, but signed off. They could talk about it later. "Call me."

She closed the phone with a snap, then opened it again and called Tiffany's office. No answer. Tasting the hot edge of temper on her tongue, Allie left a stern message on voice mail, then shoved the phone back in her bag. *When I get my hands on you, there'll be hell to pay,* she promised silently.

In the parking lot, she unlocked the door of her Jeep and started to get in, then stepped down and reached around to rip the parking ticket from under the windshield wiper. Without looking at it, she threw it on the passenger side floor along with the others.

"Damshuckems," she said glumly.

It wasn't much of a curse, something she'd picked up in Key West when she heard a waitress in a clam bar say it after cutting her finger on a jagged clam shell. It struck Allie funny at the time and was the first good laugh she'd had since her husband died. Somehow the expression stuck.

But a real curse was called for here, so she gave the steering wheel a thump with her fist and let loose. "Shit," she began, then, "Dammit," and followed that up with every swear word she could think of.

Gloomily, she turned the key in the ignition, then sat with the motor running, watching pieces of paper trash swirl around the cracked asphalt. Thoughts chased each other in her brain. There must be something she could do.

Unable to think of anything, she shifted into gear, pressed the gas pedal, and turned left out of the parking lot, driving slowly toward the neighborhood where Davy lived with his foster family.

If only she could talk to Jo-Jo first.

Where was she anyway?

Tiffany Day, in a hurry, cleared out her desk. This was her last day with Child Protective Services. CPS just didn't know it yet.

Upon graduation from college, Tiffany had been accepted into a preferential hiring program whereby CPS agreed to pay her college loans in exchange for two years employment— *servitude!* she amended—with the county. Those two long years during which she had worked for near poverty-level wages were coming to an end as of now.

Technically, her two years weren't up until next Friday, but she had a week's vacation on the books and was taking it effective immediately. She was burned out, suffering the inevitable meltdown that came from dealing with county hard cases, from days spent knocking on doors of families who didn't want to see her, who pretended not to be home, who threatened and occasionally attacked her. They were families who saw her as someone who came to their house and took their children away. She wasn't welcome.

She pulled a stack of case files toward her, then opened them one at a time and inserted a written report describing a recent home visitation. That she hadn't actually visited the home was of no consequence to her. That each report showed a satisfactory child placement or recommendation for return to parents assured her a glowing employment reference when she applied for her next job.

Finishing that, she glanced at her desk calendar and noticed that the Davy Lopez placement hearing held an eight o'clock court docket slot. She'd missed it, but that was of no consequence to her, either.

Her phone rang, and flicking a guilty glance at the other mostly unoccupied cubicles in the room she ignored its insistent summons, just as she'd ignored all her calls that morning. Edgy and anxious to be away, she transferred personal items from her desk drawer to her handbag—breath mints, a lipstick, a mini-pad, then as an afterthought, she scooped up a handful of fine-point pens and dropped them in, too.

When the phone stopped ringing, she picked it up, touch-toned a number, and made a connection.

"Medora Detective Agency."

"Detective Medora, please. It's urgent."

After a brief moment, he came on the line. "Mark Medora here."

"Hey, Markie," she said, deliberately low and breathy.

"Hey, baby."

"Are we still on for dinner tonight?"

"That and more."

She smiled. "I'm leaving now."

"You really quit your job?"

"I told you I was going to."

"Okay. See you later."

"You'll see *all* of me later."

"I'm counting on it."

She hung up the phone, typed an e-mail to her supervisor saying she'd had a family emergency, then, after one last look at her ancient green metal desk and dinosaur of a computer, snapped her briefcase shut, slung the strap over her shoulder, and walked out the door and down the hallway, high heels clicking on the marble floor.

CHAPTER TWO

Allie steered the Jeep away from a small, timeworn house in a neighborhood that had once enjoyed middle-class status but was now gone to seed. Davy, buckled into the front passenger seat, sat quietly, staring straight ahead through the windshield. His frayed blue backpack was on his lap. In the backseat was a cardboard box with the rest of his belongings—clothes, a few toys, books, and an old Monopoly game. It broke her heart that everything the boy owned in the world fit into a tattered backpack and an apple box from Kroger's.

She glanced at him, and her heart tugged at his forlorn expression.

"I'm sorry this had to be so last minute. I wish I'd had time to talk to you, give you a chance to get used to it."

He nodded but didn't say anything, just tightened his grip on his backpack.

"Change is always hard, especially for kids. Grownups sometimes forget that."

"That's okay," he said, passively forgiving her and, by association, the entire grownup world.

"You've been in foster care for almost six months. That's a long time. The judge thought it best that you go home as soon as possible." She didn't want to tell him about the social worker's questionable report, about the pressures she and everyone else in the CPS system were under to get kids out of foster care faster in order to keep costs down.

Davy turned to look at her, his sad blue eyes focused on her face, probing. "I thought it only counted what *you* thought."

A spasm of guilt tightened in her chest and lingered there as she caught the undercurrent of accusation in his words. "Yes, well . . . That's true most of the time."

She contained a sigh, wanting to say more, but how could she explain so he'd understand it when she didn't understand it herself? The outrage inflicted on children by the idiocy of adults in the name of the law continued to astound her. No wonder he was confused and angry, though she could tell by his pinched expression he was stuffing the anger. That wasn't good.

She braked for a red light and slid a sideways glance in his direction, but he turned his head away and looked out at the sidewalk. His dark hair was tousled, in need of a trim. A cowlick stuck up in back. His navy blue nylon windbreaker was new; she'd bought it for him last week using her own money when the emergency funds approved by the county got stuck somewhere in the bureaucracy. The knees of his jeans were faded, the denim worn and thinned, and he was starting to outgrow them. It would soon be time for new sneakers, too.

Besides being beaten by his parents, he'd been the victim of weird punishments for behavior that to Allie was just little-boy stuff. He told her he'd been forced to kneel on grains of rice on the hard kitchen floor for an entire afternoon after he'd ac- cidentally let the screen door slam. He was yelled at and pushed around, except for the times he was ignored. His suffering was mental as well as physical, an unhealthy lack of nurturing, a dangerous absence of the kind of loving care every child needed, deserved, and should expect.

His father, uneducated, slow-thinking, a drifter who wandered in and out of jobs, wandered in and out of the family the same way. His mother used the money from turning tricks to buy groceries and pay the rent because most of the father's money, when he had any, went for drugs. They were both out of the house for hours, and sometimes days, at a time, and when they were around, they pretty much existed in a substance-induced stupor. Davy had spent more time alone than was good for a bright little boy. He was terribly lonely. Truancy had damaged his short education, and he had a lot of catching up to do in school.

The traffic signal changed, and Allie pressed on the accelerator, moving slowly along the narrow thoroughfare.

Her own father, an abusive drunk, had made her childhood a time of stomach-churning tension. The daily fights and slaps, barks and insults, had terrified her, but didn't cow her mother until he began withholding his meager paycheck from the family. When Allie was five, he left, taking that paycheck with him. The peace of mind that then flowed into their house made it worth it, even though her mother had to struggle and sacrifice to keep a roof over their heads. Six months later, her mother was gone, too, killed by a hit-and-run drunk driver. That's when she went to live with her grandmother's crotchety sister, the woman who insisted on being called Aunt Helen.

"I'll bet you're anxious to see your mom." Allie tried to make it sound like seeing his mother would be a good thing.

Davy's expression didn't change. "I just saw her," he said.

She cast a quick look. "You did? When?"

"Yesterday."

"What did she say?" Surprised, Allie wasn't aware either parent had ever bothered to visit their son at his foster home.

"Nothin'."

"Come on, Davy," she prodded gently. "What did she say?"

But he wasn't talking. She felt him slide deeper into guardedness, a characteristic common in abused children. Once or twice, he'd trusted her enough to confide in her, but she had a feeling that trust had been broken today.

His mother's unexpected visit was too unusual not to arouse curiosity, but she resisted the urge to push him for information. Instead, she acted as if it was of no consequence and hoped he'd tell her on his own. After a minute, he did.

"She said she was going away." There was no emotion in it. He said it with the same lack of inflection he might have used to announce the day of the week.

"For how long?"

Silence.

Holding the wheel with one hand, she reached out with the other to give his knee a playful shake. "Where did your mother say she was going?" she coaxed gently.

"I don't know," he said grumpily. "She came to say goodbye. She didn't say when she'd be back."

Goodbye? A wave of apprehension rumbled through Allie's chest. What would become of this child alone with a drugged-up father? She swore under her breath and tried Jo-Jo's number on the cell phone again.

Still no answer.

When she reached the intersection that led to the cluster of run-down homes where Davy's parents lived, she couldn't bring herself to take him there. On impulse, she swung a U-turn in a gas station, and headed back the way she'd come. She really had to talk to Jo-Jo first.

Davy looked around, and then at her. "Where are we going?"

"We're going to my house."

"But you said the judge said I had to go home."

"Do you want to go home?"

He frowned, considering. "I don't know," he said carefully. After a moment, he shook his head. "No. I don't think I want to."

He sat politely, hands in his lap, as if trying not to take up too much space in the car. Like most children in the family court system, he'd developed the ability to quickly assess a situation and his role in it, then melt quietly into the background. It was self-protective, a way of hiding in plain sight when he didn't understand what the adults around him were doing, which was most of the time.

Twenty minutes later and on the other side of town, Allie turned off the main drag and drove past three blocks of look-alike houses standing shoulder to shoulder along a leafy street.

"Okay, we're here."

Davy leaned forward and looked out the window as she pulled into her driveway. "Is this your house?"

"Yep."

"It's big."

Big and old-fashioned, with huge spreading trees and a wide grassy yard. She and Paul had bought it right after they were married, hoping to fill it with kids. After he died, she stayed on, trying hard to avoid the shadowy corners of grief with memories tucked into them.

Unlocking the door, she went inside, Davy following timidly. She planted him in front of the television in the den while she got back on the phone, leaving messages for Jo-Jo every place she could think of.

Allie paced, glancing at her watch, tracking the time, willing the phone to ring. After thirty minutes when Jo-Jo still hadn't called, she found herself at loose ends. A wistful sigh escaped her. She'd planned to spend the summer up north at her cottage on Saginaw Bay. The already packed suitcases beckoned from the foot of the stairs. She wished she were up north now, wearing a halter top and shorts, walking barefoot along the shore, breathing in the lake air, feeling the sun bathe away the chill of winter from her skin.

After trying Jo-Jo's number one more time, it occurred to her that Jo-Jo might have gone away for the Memorial Day weekend, though it wasn't like her to do that without telling anyone.

Restless, Allie checked the time again. A little after ten. If she left now, she could be at the cottage by one. She'd have the rest of the day, all of Saturday and Sunday, and most of Monday. She could talk to Jo-Jo on Monday night, and they'd be back in court Tuesday morning to straighten everything out. She could start her summer hiatus on Wednesday.

A burst of energy propelled her up the stairs to her bedroom where she kicked off her shoes, and stripped off her skirt and pantyhose. Clattering back down in jeans, tank top, and sandals, she called out.

"Come on, Davy. We're going up north."

Davy stared at her, but obediently switched off the television without comment.

What she was doing was against Child Protective Services regulations, but what the hell, who'll know? And come Tuesday, it won't matter anyway. Jo-Jo will reverse Berriman's order, and Davy will have a new placement.

She threw her bags in the back of the Jeep along with Davy's things, made sure he was buckled into his seat, then shifted into gear and headed to the tip of Michigan's thumb.

The cottage was on a narrow dirt road, through the woods, around a bend, and up a gently sloping hill screened by trees and shrubbery, well removed from the state highway and the village of Caseville farther up the shore near the state park. It was one of the older cottages on Sand Point, a narrow finger of land that jutted out of Michigan's thumb into the water with Saginaw Bay on the south shore and Lake Huron on the north.

Constructed of whitewashed cedar siding with a shake shingle roof, the cottage was small and compact, but its odd shape allowed every room to overlook the water. French doors led to a veranda of broken bricks with grass growing in the cracks, and beyond that, the broad green lawn ended in a sandy beach near the water's edge. The water was shallow in places; she could walk far out onto a sandbar and it would only be up to her knees.

The rooms had a seasonal feel to them, filled with peculiar oddments of furniture. There was a time she thought she might *feng shui* it, but in the end found she hardly spent enough time there to bother. After thinking about it, she decided she liked it just the way it was.

She had notified the phone company to turn on service for the summer, but they hadn't done it yet. Sand Point's remoteness made cell phone service spotty and undependable, and for a brief moment, she felt a cold prick of isolation.

After she unpacked—Davy had refused to take his things out of his backpack and apple box, choosing instead to stash them fully packed at the back of the closet—Allie drove them into town for a late lunch at the Bayshore Restaurant.

They took a table near the window, and the waitress, bone-thin and moving fast, came over with menus, turned over one of the mugs and splashed coffee into it. "I'll be back in a minute to take your order, hon," she said before bustling away in worn-down nurse's shoes.

Allie noticed a man in a booth along the wall, tanned, good-looking, wearing shorts and deck shoes. Automatically, she checked his left hand for a ring. There was none, and her gaze lingered a moment. He gave her a brief nod, a pleasant smile, then went back to reading his newspaper.

He probably thinks I'm married, she thought, and that Davy is my son.

She glanced at Davy and smothered the pinch of regret that always twisted at times like this. It could have been her son sitting there, hers and Beck's. He'd have his father's grey eyes and great sense of adventure, and they'd be spending the day together, a mother and son day of miniature golf and ice cream cones.

She jerked at Davy's touch. His hand rested lightly on her forearm. He'd asked her a question, but she hadn't heard. She stared at him while her thoughts cleared, and he asked it again.

"Can we? Can we, Allie? Can we go on that giant slide over there?" He pointed to the park across the street where kids, sitting on burlap bags, whooshed down a long wide metal slide. "I've never done it before." His voice was expectant, but his eyes were already taking on the glaze of disappointment.

She smiled at him, and ruffled his hair. "Sure. Sure, we can. Right after lunch."

Allie awoke the next morning to the sun streaming through sheer curtains, the scent of pine trees in the air, and the sound of waves sliding up the beach. Sunlight, splintered into mirror shards by a choppy wind teasing the surface of the water, sparkled on the bay. Far out from shore, fishermen cast lines from their boats. Life was good.

Allie and Davy swam, walked on the beach picking up stones and shells, went again to the giant slide and miniature golf park in town, then played Monopoly in front of the fireplace after dinner. Davy's Monopoly game didn't have the usual game pieces, and some were missing. The thimble was gone and so was the car. Instead, there was a button, a key, a speckled pebble, and a tiny plastic horse.

On Sunday, they watched sailboats, triangles of winged color blowing across the lake, then followed a footpath through birches and evergreens. It was quiet in the trees, their footsteps silent on the damp layer of duff covering the forest floor. Allie relaxed, feeling the tautness leave her limbs and muscles, and Davy began to let his guard down. He found a dead baby bird that had fallen out of its nest and held it out to show her.

"Ish," she said, and flinched. He gave her a withering girls-are-dumb look, then buried it under a tree.

That night after dinner, Davy fell into bed exhausted. Allie curled up in an overstuffed chair trying to read, but was unable to banish thoughts of the upcoming week and the unresolved issues surrounding Davy. Where was Jo-Jo?

The wind gusted outside, causing the trees to creak and groan. Lightning flashed far out over the water. A storm was lumbering in over the bay. If it rained tomorrow, they'd head home early, after lunch instead of waiting till evening. Maybe they should anyway, she considered, now having second thoughts about her impulsive decision to take Davy away.

Trees swayed in the wind and waves lapped on shore. She put her unread book aside and walked out onto the veranda, shivering a little in the cool breeze. At the edge of the clearing was a tarp-covered woodpile, an ax in the chopping block. As the wind picked up, whitecaps formed on the bay. She closed her eyes a moment, listening, clearing her mind, breathing in the cool air. A fine misty spray was blowing up from the surface of the water; she could feel it on her cheeks.

Suddenly something alerted her, and she looked toward the woods. A distinct movement several yards to her right. A shuffling sound in the undergrowth just beyond the woodpile, detectable only because she'd held her breath. She glanced around at hollows of shadow where watchers could hide, then hunched her shoulders against a chilly gust and shivered again. She went back inside, locking the doors and pulling the drapes closed, then crawled in bed and fell into an uneasy slumber.

At daybreak, she thought she heard a car negotiating the ruts and bumps of her driveway where it turned off the highway. Curious. She didn't get passersby here. No one would be visiting, especially at that hour. When the sound was not repeated, she drifted back to sleep only to be awakened again later by bullet-sized raindrops furiously pelting the roof and windows.

She got out of bed and padded barefoot across the cold floorboards to look out at the lake where swirling black clouds rolled over the water. A punishing wind churned waves that rose straight up from the turbulent surface then crashed loudly onto the beach. Rain, blowing sideways, mixed with the spray gusting up from the lake. On shore, trees swayed, and branches whipped and thrashed wildly. Suddenly, lightning bolted out of clouds that grew blacker and loomed closer.

"One hippopotamus, two hippopotamus." She recited the childish chant until interrupted by thunder crashing and rumbling somewhere out on the bay.

"Two miles away," Davy said. He had come to stand beside her at the French doors, his eyes lit with excitement, awed by the ferocious lake storm. "That lightning was only two miles away." He shivered a little in the morning chill and leaned against her. She put her arm around his shoulders.

"Guess we can't go to the slide today." The disappointment was evident in his voice.

"No, but I've got a great idea," she replied, giving his thin shoulders a squeeze. "How about I build a fire in the fireplace, and then after breakfast I let you beat me at Monopoly?"

He looked up at her and smiled. "Aren't you tired of losing?"

"Nope," she said, smoothing his sleep-ruffled hair. "I'm a glutton for punishment. Do you want pancakes or waffles?"

"What's a glutton?" he asked.

"It's someone who . . ." she began, then stopped, trying to think of a way to explain the concept of greedy excess to a child. "It's someone who can't get enough. Someone who deliberately overindulges," she finished uncertainly, frowning. He gave her a blank stare, his face expressionless.

"Never mind," she said. "Come on, pancakes or waffles? I

vote for pancakes."

"Me, too. Can you make those little ones like we had at the restaurant?" He formed a circle with his thumb and forefinger.

"They're called silver dollar pancakes, and yes, I can."

Davy climbed onto a stool at the breakfast counter, propped his elbow and rested his chin in his hand, watching her shake pancake mix into a bowl. "Do we have to go back today?"

"Yes, but we'll wait until the rain lets up." She measured out milk and cracked an egg. "The pavement gets slick and sometimes the roads wash out. We wouldn't want to have an accident or get stranded in the storm."

The quality of the silence that followed led her to glance at him. His eyes were downcast, his expression glum. She stirred the batter, heated the griddle, and waited for him to speak.

"Where will I go?" he asked finally. His bottom lip quivered, but his voice was steady.

"Tonight you'll stay at my house, but tomorrow we'll talk to the judge about finding you a new foster home."

He gave her a wary look. "So I won't have to go home like the judge said?"

She spooned pancake batter onto the hot griddle, wiped her hands on a towel, and turned to him. "We're going to talk to a different judge. A friend of mine." She cupped his cheek in a gentle hand, turning his head so he'd meet her eyes. "Don't worry," she said softly, trying to ease some of his anxiety. "You're going to be all right. I promise."

"Okay," he said, but Allie wasn't sure he trusted her anymore.

After breakfast, a lightning strike somewhere knocked the power out, so they ate cold pizza and sandwiches the rest of the day while Davy, who owned Boardwalk and Park Place and all the utilities, thoroughly trounced her at Monopoly.

By early evening, after one final furious surge, the storm relented. Despite a grind of distant thunder threatening further squalls, she packed the car and they left in a drizzle, the kind that got into the bones.

CHAPTER THREE

Traffic was heavy with weekenders heading home to the metropolitan areas from the north country, as she was now that the storm had abated. Headlights from her Jeep and the other cars cast watery reflections on the wet asphalt. Sheets of water thrown up from the pavement by tires of oncoming vehicles plastered her windshield. She gripped the steering wheel, braked lightly, and hung on, her heart in her throat, until the wipers cleared the glass and she could see clearly again.

She switched on the car radio, but there was only static, so she turned it off. Davy had fallen asleep, lulled into slumber by the hypnotic hiss of tires over the wet roadway. His face was slack, his head rolling slightly with the movement of the car. Without moving her eyes from the road, she took her cell phone out of her bag, flipped it open with her thumb, and dialed Jo Jo's number. Better fill her in on what happened in court on Friday, tell her she'd taken Davy up north. Still out of cellular range, the signal was too weak to make a connection.

A smidgen of disquiet over defying Judge Berriman's order stirred within, but Allie smothered it and pulled her thoughts together. In the end, it had worked out for the best, since Davy said his mother had gone away. Where? For how long? Yes, she reasoned, she'd made the right decision. Even so, she was at odds with herself.

A few miles north of Imlay City, she flicked on the radio again and this time picked up an AM station out of Port Huron.

The nine o'clock news was coming on, fading in and out of a background of crackly static. She started to turn the volume down, but stopped abruptly when she heard Jo-Jo's name. Holding in a breath, she went from shock to disbelief. The announcer was saying that Jo-Jo was dead!

The news report, devoid of details, merely stated that Judge Joanne Emery's car had skidded off the roadway and crashed into a culvert near her home.

"A passerby spotted the car at the bottom of the embankment this afternoon and called police," the newscaster intoned dispassionately. "Judge Emery had not been seen since court on Thursday and authorities suspect the accident happened either Thursday night or Friday morning. Judge Emery was pronounced dead at the scene."

Time slowed and blurred to freeze-frame motion as Allie pictured the narrow, winding road that led from the porte cochere of Jo-Jo's huge Victorian house to the hard-packed two-lane that connected with the highway. Something sharp turned in her chest at the thought of Jo-Jo lying there, dead or injured, for the past three days.

"And now for the weather. Thunderstorms continue to pound the metro area, causing widespread power and phone outages. Squalls are expected to continue through tomorrow."

Allie turned off the radio. A giant lump in her throat brought tears to her eyes. It didn't seem possible her friend was gone. Then apprehension carved through her grief. What would happen to Davy now? In her mind, Judge Berriman's face loomed, dour and forbidding. Defeated, she realized she had no choice now but to take Davy home to his father. Her punishment for contempt of court was bound to be severe. At the very least, she'd never work in the court system again.

She picked up her cell phone and with shaking fingers dialed her home telephone number to check the messages on her answering machine. Surely, someone had called her with news of Jo-Jo's death. After a couple of rings, she heard a faint hushing sound as of a distant sea, like someone had picked up and was listening. In the expanding silence, she said a surprised, "Hello?" But there was no reply, just another click, and then the silence of a disconnected call—the result, she guessed, of some glitch in her low-tech answering machine.

As she drove, she held the phone awkwardly in front of her over the steering wheel until she could see the backlighted screen, and then she quickly dialed again. This time the ringing was interrupted by grating static as lightning fractured the roiling sky. The storm had knocked out cell phone service again. Annoyed, she closed her phone.

A long hour later, the storm, struggling to keep itself alive with intermittent spits of rain and feeble rumbles of thunder, perished just as she pulled into her driveway. Davy was slumped in the passenger seat, lost in that deep, unfettered slumber that adults strive for but only children can achieve.

She slid the window down for air and left him where he was while she clicked free of her seatbelt and went to unlock the house. She'd make up the sofa for him in the spare room. Tuck him in. Carry the luggage in later.

She put her key in the door and reached her hand inside to the light switch. Only the lights didn't come on.

"Damshuckems. Electricity's out."

She mentally inventoried all the places she might have stashed emergency candles. Stepping lightly, using her hands to guide her in the dark, she headed for her office and the flashlight she kept in a drawer in her desk. That was when she heard the hum of the refrigerator kick in. The message light on the phone was blinking, too, and she realized with sudden bewilderment that the electricity wasn't out. Her heart began to hammer and a layer of gooseflesh rose on her arms. Entering her office, she saw the computer screen was lit and in its glow, that her office had been ransacked.

Pictures had been yanked from the wall and books pulled from shelves. Drawers hung open, file folders spilled their contents on the floor. Her eyes darted around the room. It didn't appear to be an act of vandalism, there was no anger in it. Rather, it seemed to be an orderly search, only nothing had been returned to its place.

The phone rang, and she jumped at the sound. Stepping over the mess, she stood over the answering machine and peered at the screen. The caller ID spelled out a name. Marie Lopez. Davy's mother.

Allie reached to answer it, but something—a faint creak in another part of the house—stopped her. With her hand hovering over the phone, the machine clicked on.

"Allie, it's Marie. Listen, girl. Take Davy and run. Just get out, you hear? Keep him safe. Take him away before it's too late. I'll explain later. Just run—"

Someone spoke harshly in the background. There was shuffling, the sound of a hand sliding over the receiver, Marie's muffled voice raised in anger, and then the call was cut off.

Allie stared at the blinking red light. Eleven other messages. The impulse to listen to them fought with the urge to heed Marie's warning and run. As she stood there, motionless, she thought she heard a sound, and waited for it to come again. It did. A car engine. Out front, out back—she couldn't tell.

Tiptoeing to the living room, she peeked out the window. Illumination from a streetlamp showed a car rolling by in the street, no lights, not fast, coasting, a faint tick-tick-tick emanating from the engine. It was a plain dark sedan, similar to the unmarked car her husband used to drive when he was on stakeout.

Then, because every sense was on alert, she heard the soft

step on the carpet overhead. Through the dimness, a shadow appeared at the top of the stairs. The shadow moved, then lurched down the steps. She took a step back, stumbled on the hassock, righted herself against the sofa table. A man was barreling toward her holding something in front of him, some kind of weapon.

Frantically, her hand swept the sofa table behind her, and her fingers closed around a heavy marble candlestick. She leaped forward and struck out at his head with all her strength.

He ducked away, but she connected with a glancing blow. He was falling, and suddenly she was on her way, moving fast, without thinking about it. Instinct, impulse, and fear for herself and for Davy all came together to propel her out the door and into the Jeep.

Panic exploded like a bomb in her chest. Shards of it wedged in her throat making her gasp for breath. Somehow, she managed to turn the key and floor the gas. Tires whined in protest as she burned rubber, reversing out the driveway into the street. She tromped the brake then shoved the shift into DRIVE. A split second before she accelerated again, something smashed into her peripheral vision and smacked against the side of the vehicle with a thump.

A man clung to the doorframe. He reached in through the open window and grabbed the steering wheel just as Allie's foot stomped the gas pedal. Thrown off balance by the sudden forward surge, he moved his hand from the steering wheel and clasped it over her face, covering her eyes, digging his fingers into the soft flesh of her cheeks. Frantically she jerked her head from side to side, trying to breathe, trying to see, and clamped her teeth down hard on his little finger.

He wrenched his hand free, and Allie's stomach roiled as she tasted blood. She swung the wheel, swerving the Jeep back and forth, trying to throw him off, but now he clutched the doorframe with both hands. His face was next to hers, but she didn't dare turn her head to look at him. He was swearing at her, calling her filthy names, and yelling obscenities that she could hear over the roar of the wind rushing through the open window.

Davy was awake, his arms thrashing out in fear and confusion, his hands reaching for something solid to grab as the Jeep lurched forward.

"Allie!" he cried out.

Daring to take one hand off the steering wheel, she tried to pry the man's fingers open and break his grip, forcing him off the side of the car. Instead, he made a quick grab, twisted his fist in her hair and yanked, banging her head against the door frame. It felt like her hair was being ripped out by the roots while at the same time lights burst behind her eyes.

She wailed with pain and reached for his eyes with her fingernails. She dug in hard and he jerked his head back with such force, his body was pulled away from the car and with a howl, he tumbled into the street.

"Allie!" Davy yelled again. His cheeks were wet with tears, his face red and puffy from crying.

Frantically damping down her panic, she directed all her concentration on driving. No time to console Davy now.

She passed a car going in the opposite direction. It was the same car that had driven by with its lights out, only now they came on as it braked and made a U-turn. She could feel her heart skipping, her arms trembling, her knees shaking, jerking up and down threatening to give out and cause her to lose control of the Jeep.

Then a horrible thought increased her alarm. He, whoever had been in her house, whoever was in that car, might have a gun.

"Get down," she said.

But Davy was frozen in place, one hand clasping her shoulder, the other braced against the door panel, his eyes wide with fright.

"Put your head down," she said, her voice hoarse. "Now!" She resisted the compulsion to take her hand off the steering wheel and reach over and push him down out of sight.

"What's wrong, Allie? What happened?" His voice was reedy with panic as he fought not to cry.

She didn't answer, her throat was dry, tight, her eyes riveted to the dark, wet street in front of her.

Davy twisted around straining against the seatbelt to look behind. "Is somebody after us?"

"Yes," she croaked.

"Who is it?" he asked, whimpering a little.

"I don't know! Now get down and stay down!"

Trembling, he did, clutching his backpack to his chest.

She kept her eyes on the rearview mirror driving as fast as she dared through residential streets. A traffic light was coming up and she prayed for the green. But no, it turned red as she sped through it, swinging a wide left. An oncoming van braked and swerved to avoid hitting her. Then cross traffic moved forward and other cars pulled in behind her. In the jumble of headlights, she couldn't tell which belonged to the sedan. She hoped it had been forced to stop at the light.

She caught the flash of a red and blue interstate sign, an arrow pointing straight ahead. More headlights amassed behind her, flooding her rearview mirror. Nervously she licked her lips, and looked from mirror to street to mirror. A car was changing lanes behind her, cutting in and out, coming closer, and her heart took a leap.

Traffic grew heavier as she approached the shopping mall, a sprawling town center of department stores and retail shops. Cars were snarled at the intersection leading into and out of the parking garage, further slowing the forward flow of traffic. The daylong rainstorm had apparently not kept shoppers away from huge holiday sales.

A surge of brake lights blazed in front of her filling the rain-misted air with a red glow as cars came to a complete stop. Instantly, she yanked the wheel to the right and swung into the mall, then wheeled quickly into the covered parking structure. Because of the late hour, more cars were coming out than were going in so her progress up the ramp was relatively unimpeded. Except she couldn't go more than ten miles an hour. When she tried to push it, her tires squealed on the turns.

With an uneasy glance at Davy, she opened the center console, took out her .38, and put it in her lap where she could reach it easily if she needed it. Davy's eyes grew round when he saw it.

"It's all right. Stay down," she told him, her voice steady. "We're fine." She hoped that was true.

A squeal of tires sounded from a car coming up the ramp behind her from a lower level, moving fast. Quickly, she switched off her lights and kept going, locking her hands on the steering wheel to keep them from shaking.

She headed for Neiman Marcus. She used to shop there when her paycheck was bigger, so she was familiar with its irregular shaped parking garage reached by a nearly hidden passageway just past the loading dock. Quickly, she turned into it.

Near the elevator, security vehicles, empty now, were parked behind the stair tower. Cringing at the telltale flash when she applied the brakes, she nudged the Jeep into the shadows next to the darkened security office and slumped down in her seat. She put her hand on her .38, put her cheek next to Davy's, and whispered. "Keep still."

He nodded.

She heard a car approach, but dared not raise her head to take a look. It rolled by slowly and she clearly heard the familiar tick-tick-tick in the engine.

Ohshitohshitohshit.

After a few seconds, she peeked over the dash, and saw a dark colored four-door sedan moving slowly away. Two men, their features indistinguishable in the dim lighting, sat forward in the front seat looking right and left. The car picked up speed on the ramp, tires squealing on the curve, then went out of sight on the upper level.

Allie sucked in a breath and counted ten, then sat up and started the Jeep. She quickly shifted into neutral and without revving the engine, let the Jeep roll forward, steering the wrong way down the entrance ramp, lights off, doubling back. When she reached ground level, she exited the parking structure on the far side where it led to a residential neighborhood and secondary streets.

Fewer cars here. She hung a right, then an immediate left into an alley. Another left, a right, and the freeway entrance was just up ahead. She swerved onto it, and accelerated into the passing lane, eyeing every car around her. No one paid attention. She slowed her breathing but kicked up her speed, and passed a hulking freight hauler. The sound of the diesel engine rumbled through the window.

On the open highway, she willed a calmness she didn't feel. A shiver slid up her spine as she remembered seeing her office torn apart, hearing Marie's voice on the phone. Davy was sitting up now, his eyes glittery. He had barely said a word, but she knew he was terrified.

"Look, Davy, I can't explain what's happening. At least not right now. Because I don't know yet. But your mother called—"

"Did you talk to her?" he cut in, his eyes bright and expectant.

"No, I didn't. She left a message. She wants me to take care of you until . . ." Allie remembered Marie's voice sharply cut off, the sounds of a struggle before the line went dead.

"Until later," Allie finished, trying not to let her own terror sound in her voice.

"Okay," he replied, nodding and adjusting his grip on the backpack in his lap.

Tough kid for seven, she thought. He didn't say anything else, and Allie couldn't think of anything comforting to add, so she drove in silence, keeping close watch on the rearview mirror.

Without consciously thinking about it, she found herself heading back to Caseville and the safety of the cottage, the place that had always been her refuge. After turning off the interstate, she took short cuts over the grid of unimproved farm roads, zigzagging north and west toward Sand Point. No traffic, no ominous headlights. She breathed easier. The Jeep ate up the miles and by the time she got there, it was midnight.

Turning into the narrow lane leading to the cottage, her headlights illuminated fresh tire tracks, ruts cut into the mud, and understanding washed over her in sickening waves. Through the trees, she could see lights on in the cottage. Someone had been there. Maybe was there now. Her muscles seized with terror, making it difficult to turn around and put the Jeep back on the highway.

Once she did, the hours ran together. She drove with fear in her heart, constantly scanning the road behind. Steering blindly, knowing only one place to go, compelled by a force she no longer attempted to comprehend, she drove, stopping only for gas and for rest when absolutely necessary.

CHAPTER FOUR

Two weeks later.

Beck Williams watched museum visitors, some balancing coffee and cookies in hand, make their way to the seating area, laying claim to the folding chairs set up nearest the front of the room for his lecture on wild horse herds.

He was always a little curious about the crowd that gathered for his presentations at the Cortez Cultural Center lecture series. They were a diverse representation of life in southwest Colorado—retirees, students, amateur photographers, wide-bodied old Navajo women beautiful in turquoise and silver. Occasionally, tourists, taking a break from their tour of Mesa Verde National Park, came in having read the speaker lineup in the *Things to Do* column of the local newspaper.

The woman at the back of the room didn't particularly stand out from the others, but he noticed her anyway. She was making no effort to claim a preferred seat up front, but instead hung back, finally settling herself and her little boy into chairs in the last row. There was something about her that held his gaze, though he was sure she wasn't someone he knew. Both she and the child were dressed rather poorly, even considering the casualness of the local lifestyle, which allowed that jeans, no matter how tattered, and boots, no matter how worn down, were welcome everywhere. In some strange way, their clothes didn't seem to belong to them. For one thing, they were filthy. For another, they didn't fit.

He was still lost in those thoughts when the audience broke into polite applause. The museum director, a thin, frail looking woman with pretty eyes but a sad turn around the mouth, had finished her introductory remarks and was looking at him expectantly. Quickly, Beck stepped to the lectern and cleared his throat, sweeping his gaze over the crowd, halting ever so fleetingly on the woman in the back row.

"I'm sure you're wondering," he began, "how a Special Forces operative came to be a reclusive wildlife biologist and nature photographer in the mountains of Colorado."

There were smiles, nods, and soft murmurs of agreement accompanied by a smattering of encouraging applause. Except from the woman in back. She sat still as stone, the hood of her jacket pulled forward, shadowing her features.

"Well, it's a long story, but I'll keep it short," he said. He ran the memories through his mind, skipping over the part about what drove him into the military in the first place. "One day, after years of undercover missions in the bleakest, roughest, baddest, most dangerous places in the Middle East, I looked down and there next to my boot was a flower struggling to survive in the harshest environment imaginable. It was pink and . . ."

A movement in back caught his eye. The woman in the oversized jacket had unwrapped a napkin and was handing the little boy some cookies and a muffin from the refreshment table. The sleepy-eyed boy took the food and ate hungrily. That child is starving, Beck thought, momentarily astonished.

"I, uh . . ." His words dried up, and he looked away from them, but quickly collected himself, and picked up his train of thought. "I decided then that I'd rather spend my time immersed in the beauty of nature, studying it, and learning all I could about the miracle of life." Rather than harboring an obsession with death, he thought, but didn't say.

Almost against his will, his eyes were drawn to the back of the room, and he stammered again as the next point in his printed outline dissolved from his brain leaving him speechless.

Something about that woman had captured his attention, drawing his gaze like a magnet. He couldn't stop looking her way. There was a hint of resemblance he couldn't fully grasp. It was almost, but not quite . . .

But then again, no. The hair was wrong. Spiky, yellow tufts poked out from under the hood of her jacket, not hair the color of autumn. Gripping the edges of the lectern, he dragged his concentration back to his audience.

"My interest in wilderness photography progressed naturally from my wildlife research." His mind blanked again, and he jumped ahead to cover it up. "Uh, let's look at some photos of my current project, the wild horse herd on Wild Horse Mesa."

The lights went down, and he flicked the switch that powered a computerized projector transmitting pictures to a portable screen attached to the wall. He managed to maintain his composure and go through the photos, explaining each one, though his mind continued to drift to the mysterious woman and her son. He cast a glance their way, and in the reflected light he could see that the boy had fallen asleep, his head pillowed on a backpack laid across his mother's lap. Resolutely, Beck turned his back and directed his pointer to the projection screen.

"Many of these mustangs are offspring of horses that were let loose by early miners after the gold played out in the late 1800s. Some go back further than that, descending from the horses ridden by early Spanish explorers." There were gentle murmurs of surprise mixed with a bit of awe from some of the members of the audience. Most non-Westerners weren't aware of this bit of history.

"The herds are facing some habitat danger now," Beck went

on, "so I'm analyzing the scope and condition of their range in a special project for the federal government. They have a mandate through the Bureau of Land Management to care for and maintain the herds in perpetuity."

He went through the photos, most of which he'd taken himself. When he finished, he turned off the projector and the room went dark. "If someone will get the lights, I'll be happy to answer any questions you might have."

As the lights came on, a forest of raised arms indicated there were quite a few questions, but they blurred in his vision as his eyes focused on the empty chairs at the back of the room where the woman and her son had been. Sometime during his program, they had slipped out.

Allie sat shivering on a bench at the edge of the ceremonial kiva outside the Cortez Cultural Center, under a shawl of shadows that fell from the newly leafed tree. It was two weeks after Memorial Day, but here between mountain and desert, the nights still carried a chill. Davy, too tired to keep his eyes open, curled up next to her asleep.

A shaky sigh escaped her. She should never have gone in there. Should never have come here.

But she'd had no other choice; Beck was the only one she could turn to. He'd protected her in the past, and though she'd since learned to take care of herself—she knew how to throw a punch and take a fall and use a gun—this was something different. This was some crazy combination of evil and insanity that had brought her here to sit in the dark in this strange town, too terrified to cry, too desperately miserable not to. This was something she didn't know how to handle, and now a child depended on her.

She felt helpless, like she was being swallowed whole.

She'd arrived at the cultural center an hour before Beck's

lecture was to begin, hoping that would be enough time to build up the courage she needed to approach him after all these years, but instead she had ducked behind the Anasazi pottery exhibit when he came in, her heart squeezing painfully. He'd walked in with the self-satisfied grace that comes from doing what you're good at, from being competent at what you've always wanted to do. Except for a few sharp edges, he looked exactly like he did in the pictures on his web site, exactly as she remembered him.

Later, during his lecture, their eyes had met for a flicker of a moment, and she'd found it impossible to move or draw breath. Had he recognized her? She thought she'd seen a spark of recollection in his eyes, but then he'd slanted his brows in a frown and looked away.

She caught back a sob that signaled the beginning of panic and steadied herself. The tough she could do, the impossible she'd always asked Beck to do, but she was foolish to think he'd help her now, when he obviously didn't know her anymore.

And how could he, in this shabby jacket she'd stolen from a coat rack in a diner at the state line, and her hair the way it was? Self-consciously, she plucked at the unruly spikes. She'd hacked at it with a manicure scissors, shearing it off at the base of her skull in back, then bleached it until it was dry and stiff like straw, hoping she wouldn't be recognized just before she and Davy hitched a ride with that trucker. When he'd dropped them at the truck stop in Cortez, no one paid attention to them.

The wind picked up, and she huddled Davy closer to her. She couldn't go back home, and there was nowhere else to go, so she waited, listening to the branches sway and creak overhead.

The shades of night had fallen fully by the time the heavy wooden door of the cultural center swung open and people ambled out. Allie straightened her shoulders and peered at them through the darkness, being careful to stay under cover of the shadows. One by one, cars started and drove away, and for a few awful moments, she thought she'd missed Beck, that he'd somehow left without her seeing him.

But suddenly, there he was, and a gasp jammed in her throat. He stopped on the sidewalk and glanced around, blew out a gust of air, then hunched his shoulders against the wind, and strode off toward Main Street. She waited until he rounded the corner, then, on a river of courage, she lifted the sleeping boy in her arms and followed.

Inside a motel room half a block from the cultural center, Beck threw the deadbolt, and yanked the night drapes over the window. There was no reason he could see for the agitation that had overtaken him and was now fueling his anxiety. But there it was, and only sheer force of will was able to control it. Why should he care so much about a down-and-out woman he didn't even know?

Maybe because there was a kid with her.

He shook his head to chase the thought away, then flopped on one of the two queen-size beds. Using the remote control, he turned on the television and clicked until he found the History Channel. He propped some pillows and tried to settle in, but he was uneasy, edgy.

It was unnerving how much that woman reminded him of Allie. He wished she and the boy had stayed. He'd felt the strongest urge to talk to her, find out what she was all about. He'd been disappointed beyond all reason when he saw that she was gone.

He shifted position, changed the channel to FoxNews, turned down the volume, and punched the pillows behind his head into a more comfortable nest.

Not a day had passed since Allie left that he hadn't thought of her. For a while, he'd hated her. Hated her for all the questions she'd left unanswered, for all the pain in his heart, for the unrelenting loneliness of his existence. From time to time, there'd been other women, some to spend the days with, some to pass the nights, but none of them had soothed his longing. He'd gone into the army hoping to die. There would have been mercy in it.

The sight of that woman in the cultural center had started him remembering things he wished he could forget. What went wrong, Allie? Did I need you too much? Did you need more?

His thoughts catapulted back in time. He was sixteen and Allie had just turned fourteen. She'd sneaked out to a party while her aunt worked a late shift at a restaurant in town where she tended bar and waited tables. At the party, mostly older kids from Pagosa Springs, a boy she'd just met coaxed her to drink too much beer, and began pawing her. Allie had phoned Beck, righteous anger in her voice. "Please come get me and take me home." He did, but not before he'd bloodied the other boy's nose.

They were late getting home, and Aunt Helen was waiting for them with stormy eyes. Beck was the one who got blamed, but he didn't mind. He would have gone to hell and back for her. He'd loved her that much. Damn it, maybe he still did.

The wind picked up, and grains of sand snicked against the windowpane. He thought he heard a knock but couldn't be sure. It might have been a random wind gust against the door, but then it came again, soft, deliberate. Instantly, years of military training kicked in, and he went on alert. Without making a sound, he slipped off the bed. Heart pounding, he backed up against the wall alongside the window, and tweaked the curtain aside with his finger just enough so he could see out. A bulky silhouette, dark and indistinguishable, stood by the door. After a moment, it moved, and a hand reached out and rapped lightly. It was the woman from the lecture, the one who'd sat in the back with the boy. What was she doing here?

Cautiously he stepped away from the window, released the deadbolt, and opened the door. The boy was in her arms, and when she lifted her head, moonlight drenched her face, revealing eyes bright with fear.

"Oh, Beck," Allie said. "I'm in so much trouble."

Her voice was half whisper, half rasp, the sound barely breaking through her lips. But he heard her, and it was self-protective reflex that made him take a step back, from the pain, from the past. The last time he'd heard that voice it was crooning into his ear, whispering sweetly, "Hurry back. I'll wait right here."

Afraid to look and afraid not to, he reached out a hand, needing to touch her to believe she was real.

"Allie?"

But it couldn't be her. Allie was a wild thing with coppery hair, and a husky laugh who walked as if she'd mow you down if you didn't get the hell out of her way. This woman was stooped and worn, her mouth a slash of misery cut into a haggard face. And she was holding a child.

When his hand touched solid flesh under the sleeve of the ratty jacket, she stumbled forward, the weight of the boy almost carrying her to the floor before he caught them both in his arms.

"Allie?"

He helped her to the couch and sat her down still clutching her little boy, then he slid to his knees in front of her peering closely at her face.

"Is it really you?"

"Yes," Allie breathed, "it's me."

His hand was shaking as he gently pushed the jacket hood back from her face, away from her head.

"Your . . . hair . . . What happened to your hair?" he asked remembering the rich, silky texture of it, the way it felt in his hands, on his face.

Choked with emotion, not knowing if he should curse her or kiss her, he slid his arms around her shoulders and tried to pull her close. It was then he thought again with some surprise of the child she was holding against her chest.

Her child? He pulled away, staggered to think it. But of course. It had been twelve years. She would have had other men. She was grown up now just as he was.

A stab of despair tore into his chest. *Was she married?*

The boy whimpered and stirred, and she loosened her arms from their protective embrace so she could look at the child's face. The gaze he returned was innocent, adoring, trusting, and when she spoke to him, her tone was infinitely tender.

"It's all right, Davy." She hugged him to her, resting her chin on the top of his head, closing her eyes in weary relief. "We're safe now."

Startled, Beck rocked back a little. "Safe?"

Her eyes flew open as the word choked out of him, her features dragged down by the harsh tone of it.

He looked at her and then at the boy. What does she mean? Just because he'd loved her once, did she expect him to take her in now, with someone else's child?

When her eyes widened with hurt, welling with tears, he instantly regretted those thoughts and the harsh tone of his voice, and he burned with the desire to take it back.

"It's okay if you hate me," she said softly, pleading, "but right now we need your help. Someone is after us. We're in danger and we ran. There was no one else we could go to. I thought that even if you couldn't forgive me, you'd protect us, the same way you protect wild animals in the forest."

Her eyes were blazing as she stared at him over the child's head. Strands of the boy's hair moved from her breath when she spoke. Raw hurt glittered in her gaze, and he knew he'd put it there. He flinched at the anguish in her face, the rebuke in her words.

Davy moved restlessly in her lap and said something unintelligible, his face muffled against her shoulder.

"It's okay, sweetheart," she whispered. "It'll be all right. You'll see."

Jealousy of her obvious bond with another man's child momentarily swelled in his chest, inhibiting his ability to breathe and speak. This could have been their child.

Despite a conspicuous effort to control them, her tears spilled over, and she held the boy close so he wouldn't see her crying. "We're just going to stay here tonight," she whispered to the child, glaring at Beck, daring him to deny them that. "Tomorrow I'll take care of everything."

Smoldering emotion, long buried in his heart, flared anew, washing over him in waves. Her closeness was like an opiate he couldn't—wouldn't—do without.

"No," Beck said, relenting. "I will. I'll take care of everything."

At that, he rose and gently took the boy from her, and after helping her undress him to his underwear, turned back the covers on one of the beds, and tucked him in, pulling the blankets up over his shoulders. Davy dropped back into slumber instantly.

Allie crossed the room and collapsed on the couch again, exhaling heavily, her hands falling limply into her lap.

The legs of her jeans and her sneakers were covered with red dust. He wondered how long she'd been walking, why she didn't have a car. The dun-colored jacket she was wearing looked like it came from the free box in Telluride. Threads hung where the buttons had once been. There were raw-looking scratches on her face, and that hair . . .

"But I want some answers," he said, his mind spinning. He had so many questions, he didn't know what to ask first. What was going on? Who are you running from? Why did you leave me?

"How did you find me?" he asked, instead. "How did you know where I'd be?"

She sighed wearily. "From the personal appearance schedule on your web site. Then I followed you here after you left the cultural center."

"On my web site?" Taken aback, he stared at her. For some reason her answer made him feel vulnerable and uncomfortable.

"Yes," she said. "I kept track of you that way. I . . . I wanted to know what you were doing, if you were okay."

An anger Beck didn't even know was building now took form. For years, he'd waited for a phone call that never came, a letter that never arrived, until finally, with quiet rage seething within, had hoped she would cease to exist for him. But it hadn't happened. Now, he resented the fact that she'd been able to keep track of his life through his web site when he hadn't a clue all those years where she was, or if she was okay.

Yet he wanted to take her in his arms and cry for the both of them, cry for all the time gone by, but something kept him from doing it, some self-protective instinct that shielded him against more hurt, more pain, more rejection.

"When they came after us," she went on, "I remembered you were speaking here. It was an automatic reaction to come, a panic decision, but not really a decision at all." She shook her head tiredly. "Oh, I don't know, Beck. It just sort of happened and . . . I had Davy with me, so that made it more urgent. I prayed we'd make it here before they found us again."

Suddenly, weariness overcame her, and her shoulders slumped. The lamp across the room cast a stingy light over her face, creating shadows that deepened the shallows under her eyes.

He'd been standing in the middle of the room, stunned, hardly knowing what to say or do, but now he walked to the couch and sat down beside her. She didn't resist when he lifted one of her hands in his. Her skin was dry and rough. Grime was embedded in the creases, and the once beautiful nails were jagged and broken. He held her hand as gently as if it were a rare, precious thing.

"You keep saying *they*, Allie? Who is after you? What's going on? You have to tell me."

She raised her other hand and put her fingers to her brow. With her fingertips, she gently rubbed her temple, and he could see just how badly she needed sleep.

"I guess tomorrow is soon enough," he said.

She looked up at him. "No, I'll tell you now," she said. Then her voice dropped in volume. "I'm asking for your help. You have a right to know."

CHAPTER FIVE

A dagger of guilt rose up and plunged itself into Allie's heart as she realized she might very well have brought the danger here to him. She winced inwardly. One more thing to beg forgiveness for.

Beck sat patiently beside her, stroking her hand. He was looking at her, waiting for her to begin. She met his eyes and saw that they were just as she remembered, soft pewter with dark blue streaks radiating from the pupils like sunbursts.

Where should she start? Would he believe her? She hardly believed it herself. Her mind whirled with confusion as she sought to find a starting point. Looking back over everything that had happened, she wasn't sure exactly where it all began.

"Two weeks ago. Friday before Memorial Day weekend," she said, though she was sure that some of it at least must have been set in motion long before that. "I was going to court—"

"Court?"

"Yes. I'm a child advocate. Davy is one of my cases. I'd asked for a hearing to prevent him from being returned to an unsuitable home with unfit parents."

Beck was staring at her with a surprised expression.

"What?" she said.

"Davy's not your son?"

She hesitated a moment before shaking her head no, though that didn't seem quite the truth. It felt like he was.

Beck's hand tightened around hers and held on. "Okay. Go on."

Words tumbled out as she told him what happened in court that day. Jo-Jo not showing up, Judge Berriman's order to take Davy home to his parents.

Tides of exhaustion engulfed her whole body, and she shivered with chill and fatigue. She wished she could get out of her filthy clothes, but all she had was what she was wearing. Her suitcase had been left behind when she and Davy were forced to escape out the bathroom window of a grungy motel in Omaha. Her Jeep was still there in the parking lot.

"So did you take Davy to his parents like the judge said?"

She looked sharply at Beck, and her thoughts filtered back to the terror of what happened later, but she stubbornly shoved the unsettling pictures out of her mind.

"Well, did you?" he persisted when she didn't answer right away.

Reluctant to look at him, she let her gaze drift to Davy asleep on the queen-sized bed, then shook her head. "Not exactly."

"What do you mean *not exactly?* What did you do?" He turned his hands, palms up in front of him, an exaggerated attitude of vexation. Lines of exasperation appeared between his brows. Both the gesture and the expression were familiar, taking Allie back to happier days when they were young and inseparable, and she could count on him always being right where she needed him to be.

She exhaled and shook her head. "I couldn't take him there. I wanted to talk to Jo-Jo first; she knew what kind of home it was. Only I couldn't get in touch with her. I assumed she'd gone away for the holiday like everyone else had, so I took Davy away with me for the weekend."

At this, Beck's mouth fell open, and he put his hands on the side of his head as if to keep it from exploding. "What? Why did you do that?"

She stiffened and her voice rose in injured indignation. "Because I hadn't been able to get in touch with Jo-Jo, and then Davy told me his mother had left town, and I couldn't find his father . . ." She didn't admit she hadn't looked for his father.

"And because it was the weekend, and the weather was nice, and I thought he deserved a little fun for a change." Maternal instinct firmed her spine as she defended her decision. "He has practically nothing to his name. Everything Davy owns fits into a beat up old backpack and a cardboard box." She withered inside as she realized he didn't even have the cardboard box anymore. It was in her car in the motel parking lot along with her suitcase.

Beck's face gradually softened. "All right. Then what?"

"And then I heard on the radio that Jo-Jo had been killed in a car accident."

Suddenly what little energy she had left slipped away. She slumped where she sat, her muscles weak from lack of sleep. She wondered if she'd ever be strong again. Beck's hand on her arm was warm, his touch gentle, and she caught his odor—like honey and leather.

Beck blew a low, breathy whistle. He looked at her for a long moment. There was movement behind the surface of his eyes, as if he were listening to some internal debate. "So, you . . ." he began, realization dawning on his face. "You took a child without permission?"

She nodded miserably and tears began to spill over. Beck got up, went into the bathroom, and brought out a handful of tissues. She gratefully accepted them, then wiped her face, and blew her nose.

"Are the authorities after you?" he asked when she'd collected herself. "Is that who you're running from?"

His expression was serious as he studied her face. The creases around his eyes had deepened. The pressure of his hand on her arm increased.

"I don't know," she answered, and shook her head warding off the question.

"What do you mean you don't know?" Frustration had seeped into his tone hinting at more than a little impatience. She couldn't blame him.

"I don't know," she said again. "Not for sure."

Her eyes fixed on every aspect of his face. What was he thinking? Did he believe her? A hard knot of regret was forming in her stomach. Now that she'd involved him, he deserved to know everything—what she found when she got home, Marie's phone call, why she ran.

Maybe she wouldn't have to tell him everything. Maybe the less he knew the better. All she really needed right now was a place where she and Davy would be safe for a while, a refuge, just for a few days. If only she could stop running until she regained her strength, until she was able to think clearly again, then they could move on. She could get a job, a place for them to live.

She glanced over at Davy as he murmured in his sleep. He cried out once, then settled down, breathing evenly.

Beck interlaced his fingers with hers in a familiar gesture that was infinitely comforting. She'd missed his touch. He sat staring at her, not moving, not speaking, but she could see tension in his jaw. The only sound was the wind whipping through the trees outside.

Weariness blanked her brain and drained the strength from her body. No, she decided, she wouldn't tell him the rest of it. Maybe there was no need to. In a couple of days, a week at the most, she and Davy would leave, and Beck could go back to his life of study and seclusion in the national forest.

But there was one thing she needed, and she needed it now.

"Would it be all right if I took a shower?" she asked.

Oh, Allie, what have you done? What have you gotten yourself into?

Understanding washed over Beck, reality settling into his gut like lead. She had kidnapped a child and taken him across state lines. No matter how she rationalized it, no matter what her reasons were, that's what she'd done and it was a crime. She was in serious trouble, and this time he couldn't make it go away by taking the blame.

Long seconds went by in silence. What had brought her to such desperation that she would do such a thing? He studied her face trying to discover her secrets, trying to imagine what events in her life had led to this.

He reached out and lightly gripped her chin. He had an overwhelming urge to kiss her breathless. Instead, he held it firmly so she'd be forced to look and listen.

"You have to take him back," he said with quiet authority.

Her eyes widened and instantly filled with fear. She pulled away and shook her head resolutely. "No."

"Listen to me, Allie. You can't take someone's child without permission. I know you didn't mean to kidnap him, but that's what you did and you have to take him back. After you explain everything to Child Protective Services, after you tell them your reasons, I'm sure it will all be straightened out."

"No," she said, more firmly this time. She met his eyes without flinching, and he recognized the determination in her expression. "I can't."

"Why?"

"Because I can't!" she shot back, pinning him with a look of the sorely betrayed. Their eyes locked and hers filled again with tears. She looked incredibly tired, on the edge. And unquestionably desperate. Why?

Allie rarely gave in to her emotions so completely that she cried. He couldn't remember ever seeing her weak and weepy. There'd been plenty of times he'd had to protect her, but not because she was afraid of things. It was because she wasn't afraid of anything.

But she was clearly afraid now.

He let go of her, went to his suitcase, and took out a clean tee shirt and freshly laundered drawstring pajama bottoms. "Here." He handed them to her, and motioned toward the bathroom. "Soap and shampoo are in there."

She thanked him and went into the bathroom. Soon he heard the shower running behind the closed door.

His eyes went to the sleeping child, and he wondered what kind of a hellish life the boy might have lived. He lacked that glow of health most properly nurtured little boys have. Poor kid. Of course, he'd help them, but not in the way she wanted. The best thing he could do for her was help her turn herself in, then stand by her through whatever legal consequences followed, see to it that she had the best defense lawyer possible and pay for it if necessary.

A terrible sorrow came over him. If only she hadn't gone away.

In minutes, she came out of the bathroom carrying her dirty clothes and dropped them in the corner. Her hair was wet, the harsh yellow color softened somewhat by the dampness. She'd tried to flatten it against her head with his comb; he could see the rake marks where she'd swept the unruly bangs off her forehead. Her heart-shaped face was scrubbed clean, the skin pink and glowing. It made her appear childlike, delicate and vulnerable.

Davy had kicked at his blankets, and she went to his bed to tuck in the covers. "Good-night," she whispered and lightly stroked her hand over his forehead. She straightened and looked meaningfully at Beck.

"Oh," he said after a moment, finally catching on. "You can take the other bed. I'll sleep on the couch."

She nodded.

His gaze lingered, and he wondered if she had a change of clothes. "Do you have a suitcase?" he asked.

She shook her head no. "But Davy has a backpack. It's outside." She paused. "I didn't know if you'd let us in, so I put it down outside the door. I'll get it."

Beck pulled an extra blanket and pillow from the closet shelf. "Tomorrow . . ." he began, shaking out the blanket and spreading it over the couch.

She turned to look at him, her hand on the doorknob. "Yes?"

His eyes swept her. Her toes peeked out from under his pajama bottoms where they puddled around her feet. Her breasts, small, round, and firm, riding high on her chest just as he remembered, gently rose and fell as she breathed. He could see the faint shadow of her nipples through the white fabric of his tee shirt.

"Tomorrow we'll see about getting you some clothes," he said.

She smiled thinly, opened the door, and leaned out to retrieve Davy's backpack. When she picked it up, the zipper gave way spilling its contents. Davy's Monopoly game, the box scarcely held together with tape and rubber bands, bounced out scattering game cards and playing pieces on the rug.

"It's Davy's favorite game," she said as she bent to pick it up. "And he's a whiz at it, too—"

Her voice broke off in mid-sentence as gunshots exploded the mirror above the dresser across the room, and a shower of mirror shards flew onto the bed where Davy was sleeping.

Allie shrieked, and Davy bolted upright, letting out a howl. He was covered with silvery splinters that glittered in his hair and on his outstretched arms. They slid off him when he scrambled out of bed. His eyes were wide with terror.

Allie, frantic, headed for Davy, but before she could reach him, Beck lunged, flinging an arm around her waist, grabbing Davy by the shoulder, and pulling them both to safety onto the floor between the beds where he covered them protectively with his body. After a moment that seemed to go on forever, Davy quieted down, and silence fell like all the air had been sucked from the earth.

"Stay down," Beck told a trembling Allie, pushing his hand hard on her head. Keeping near the floor, he looked around the end of the bed and out the open door.

"What the hell was that?" he said, his voice low.

"It's them," Allie whispered hoarsely, shaking uncontrollably. "It's them. I know it is. They've found us."

The room was dark, the bedside lamp having fallen to the floor in their duck for cover. Warily, Beck got up and walked to the door, but whoever had fired the shot had disappeared into the cavern of the nearly empty parking lot. A room door unlatched and opened a crack. Warily, a guest peeked out. Across the way, the night clerk, a pudgy Navajo teenager, was staring wide-eyed out the window of the brightly lit motel office.

Quickly, Beck closed the door, righted the lamp and switched it on, then sat on the edge of the bed. He picked up the phone and started dialing.

"Who are you calling?" Allie demanded shakily. She was still on the floor, holding Davy awkwardly on her lap, picking glass off, and trying to comfort him. He clung to her, but was looking at Beck, his eyes wide.

"The police, of course."

"NO!" she shrieked. "You can't do that!"

The rising panic in her voice caused him to put the phone

65

down and look at her in alarm. Fear, stark and vivid, glittered in her eyes.

"Please, Allie. You came to me for help, now let me help you. We have to report this."

"No," she repeated. This time the word was hoarse and raspy. "You can't call the police. They're part of it. They'll tell that I'm here."

"What are you talking about?" Beck asked. "They'll tell who?"

But she didn't answer. The color had drained from her face making her look ghostly and sick. No longer was she merely walking her usual fine edge. He feared she'd slipped over the edge, and if he did what she wanted, he'd be over the edge too. He was weighing his options, trying to decide if he should jump off the cliff with her. Not that he minded cliff jumping when necessary, but unlike Allie, he liked to know what was at the bottom.

Suddenly she stood up, set Davy on his feet, and hustled him to where Beck's suitcase lay open on the luggage stand.

"Here," she said grabbing up one of Beck's tee shirts and handing it to Davy. "Put this on."

Davy did as he was told, dragging it over his head and shoving his arms through the too-big armholes, glaring at Beck with a child's pouty mad look. The shirt hung below his knees making his thin shins look like sticks. His dark hair, badly in need of a wash, stuck out from his head where it had pressed up against the pillow while he slept.

Beck stood and held out a staying hand. "Wait a minute. What are you doing?"

"We're leaving," she said, earnest now, looking quickly around the room. "Come on, Davy, get your things. Hurry." Her gaze landed on Beck's car keys on the top of the dresser. She went for them, but Beck intercepted her, closing his hand around her wrist just as her fingers snatched up the key ring.

"No, Allie, don't. You can't leave like this. You can't run off into the night with no money, no clothes."

"Just watch me," she said defiantly, pulling and twisting her arm to break his grip. Her face was distorted with restrained rage.

Something sharp struck the small of Beck's back, the bony knees and flailing elbows of a seven-year-old boy. Caught off guard, Beck lurched forward, the breath knocked from his lungs.

"Leave her alone!" Davy yelled as he pounded furiously at Beck's head and shoulders. "Don't you hurt her. Leave her alone. I won't let you hurt her."

Beck released his grip on Allie's wrist, and doubled over, ducking his head, trying to disengage Davy without hurting him. Davy, tenacious, protective, hollering and kicking, continued to swing furiously, landing some sharp-knuckled blows that made Beck's ears ring.

Still holding the car keys, Allie wrapped an arm around Davy's waist and dragged him away. "Come on. We have to get out of here. Hurry. Get your backpack and let's go."

She went down on her knees to help him gather up the items that had fallen from his backpack when the zipper broke. Being careful of the jagged pieces of mirror embedded in the carpeting, Davy hurriedly began picking up Monopoly game cards and playing pieces, and tossing them into his bag.

"Leave the game. We have to go," Allie said.

"No," Davy insisted.

"Come on," she said, reaching for him. "We don't have time—"

"I want my game," he said stubbornly, pulling away from her to reach the last few pieces and throw them in the backpack.

Impatient, she took Davy's arm and reached for the door, but Beck placed the flat of his hand against it holding it shut.

"Allie, be reasonable," he pleaded. "You can't run off. Where will you go?"

He faced her close enough to feel electricity hum against his skin. Her eyes crackled with icy defiance as she refused to break the standoff. Davy stood next to her, his backpack clutched in one hand, his other fist clenched threateningly, poised to jump on Beck again if he had to.

"Get out of the way," she ordered, showing no signs of relenting. "We're leaving. I can't stay here. I have to protect this child." She swallowed hard and set her jaw.

"From the police?" Beck asked incredulously, wanting to understand.

"I don't know," she replied evenly. "But someone is after us, and they have guns. And they aren't stopping to give explanations or answer questions."

Her voice was quiet, but her eyes flashed a warning. Her breathing was fast and ragged. Her gaze, hard and challenging, never faltered. The tension was palpable, a black silence that chilled when she spoke again.

"Dammit, Beck, if you don't move your arm, I swear to God I'll break it."

He stood in dumb silence wondering if she could actually do that, though the fire flashing in her eyes and the steel in her voice told him she was going to try. She was looking frantically around the room no doubt searching for a weapon.

Davy dropped his backpack, reached up, and snagged his hands over Beck's outstretched arm. Bracing his feet, he pulled with all his might.

Beck didn't budge, his mind torn by indecision. He knew that if he let her go, she'd vanish from his life again. The police, or whoever was after her, would eventually find her anyway, and the consequences could be dire, maybe unspeakable. He couldn't let that happen. He blew out a big breath, and his muscles relaxed.

"Okay," he said, dropping his arm. "I'll take you someplace safe."

Allie's shoulders drooped, and her frozen expression melted in relief. She squeezed her eyes shut but couldn't stop the tears from spilling out.

"Thank you," she whispered, laying a shaking hand against his chest in gratitude.

"We'll have to hurry," he said, turning away, suddenly taking control. "I expect the desk clerk already called the police. They're probably on their way now."

At once, the room was charged with nervous energy as Beck gathered his belongings and tossed them into his bag. In less than four minutes, they were in his Hummer with the engine running. Red and blue pulsing lights announced the arrival of a patrol car braking to a stop outside the motel office under the sign that said REGISTRATION just as Beck rolled out the back entrance of the parking lot, turned right onto Montezuma Avenue, and headed east toward state highway 160. It was nearly midnight.

He kept his eyes on the rearview mirror as he sped out of town. There was little traffic, and it didn't look like anyone was following them. Just to be sure, a few miles past the entrance to Mesa Verde National Park, he turned off the highway and cut through San Juan National Forest, following a network of unmarked, hard-packed dirt fire roads.

No one spoke. Davy sat in the back. In the mirror, Beck caught glimpses of the boy's bright eyes watching him, alert, suspicious. Allie huddled in the front seat staring at the side mirror, wary, watchful. She was wired, uptight, barely held together by fragile nerves.

The forest was so thick in places moonlight couldn't penetrate the treetops, but he was familiar with the byways of the wilderness, so drove with a steady hand toward Wild Horse Mesa. The

Hummer's headlights bounced up and down as Beck negotiated the uneven dirt track. A deer, poised to run but curious at the sight of human intruders, stood at the side of the road, his ears twitching as they passed.

Beck barely noticed. He was thinking. He was thinking her story sounded like bullshit. It didn't wash, something was missing. What she said she'd done was completely outrageous. It would have been in the news. He would have read about it in the newspaper. There would have been an Amber Alert. It was the kind of story CNN would be all over. Yet, he couldn't recall seeing a single news report about a missing boy from Michigan Child Protective Services during the time she said she'd been on the run. The struggle to make sense of it sent his brain into overdrive.

He flicked another glance in the rearview mirror. His gaze lingered on Davy, and his mind snagged on a bizarre possibility. Maybe it was the boy. Maybe whoever it is, is after him, not her. Or maybe someone is after both of them, but it isn't Child Protective Services or the FBI, who would most certainly be called in for a kidnapping. And they wouldn't shoot up a motel room knowing a child was inside.

Clearly, there was something Allie wasn't telling him.

CHAPTER SIX

Sammy Oberski sprawled on a beach chair next to an octagonal-shaped pool in the heart of Key West's upscale ocean-front resort district one short block from the hubbub of Duval Street and the throngs at Sloppy Joe's Bar. He was holding a glass the size of a small bowl, sipping what was left of a strawberry daiquiri. And he was worrying. About sex, and about money. Or rather, the lack of the former and the impending lack of the latter. He was certain the sex deprivation would be resolved by sunset. It was the acquisition of money that presented more of a challenge, but by no means an insurmountable one. Sex and money came to him, often from unexpected sources.

Banana Key Resort, beside whose pool he lounged, was made up of a four-story white stucco low-rise, and six tropical bungalows tucked into and almost hidden from view in the lush palms and greenery surrounding the resort. Sammy had opted for a bungalow. Though the nightly rate was pricey, it offered the privacy he required and had a full kitchen in which he could cook and take meals, thereby avoiding the exorbitant restaurant menu prices. Plus, the waiters there expected big tips.

"Hello."

He opened his eyes and looked up to see a blonde with tight buns and big breasts standing over him, shielding her eyes from the sun with her hand. A white bikini almost covered her, and a large stone in her ring sparkled.

"Hello yourself," he replied, flashing a high-wattage smile.

"Is anyone using this?" She let her pool bag slither off her shoulder and drop to the padded lounge chair beside him. Her teeth were very white, her lips full. She was wearing expensive looking European sunglasses.

"No. Help yourself," he answered, holding her glance a second longer than necessary, before resuming his reverie, feigning disinterest. Beautiful women, especially older ones like her, were intrigued when men played a little hard to get.

Sammy had been in Key West a week, but might have to move on soon. For one thing, it was well into June and already the heat was becoming too intense to enjoy. For another, he didn't know how much longer he'd be able to use Allie's credit card. Surely, she'd discovered it missing by now.

He smiled, thinking about her. They'd met in Key West, at some off-the-beaten-track dive on the edge of town. Her husband, a cop, had recently died, and she'd rejected Sammy's advances at first. But after a margarita, a couple of tequila sunrises, and some heartfelt conversation during a stroll on the beach, they discovered they shared an aversion to loneliness.

After she left, he drove to Michigan and showed up unexpectedly at her door. He was needy. She was needy. So she agreed to let him stay until he found a job and got back on his feet. When he left, it wasn't because he necessarily wanted to. Allie was cute and sexy, full of backtalk and flirt, had a good job, and was smart. That was the problem. She was too smart, not like the bimbo babes he usually hooked up with. He moved out before she threw him out.

He was sorry about the television set and the credit card, but he planned to pay her back. He'd taken the TV down to Detroit, where he bartered it in Greektown for identification credentials that matched the name on the credit card. He'd used the card all the way down I-75, presenting it at the best resorts, staying only a night or two, all the while prepared to flee if the desk manager looked skeptical or questioned the card or ID during check in.

"My name is Mandy Matthews."

Sammy rolled his head to the side and watched the blonde rub suntan oil onto her skin, moving her hand up and down her luscious arms, smiling big, definitely coming on to him. Her lips were full and inviting. In the morning sun he could see some stretched skin around her nose and mouth, the result of expensive and quite good cosmetic surgery, and the boobs were almost certainly plastic underneath, but he didn't care. She smelled terrific. She smelled like money.

"I'm Al Hudson," Sammy said, giving her a lazy appraisal, propping himself on an elbow, leaning into her. "Did you just get here? I haven't seen you around the pool. And I would certainly have noticed you," he added, admiring her. He hoped he wasn't leering. Women, especially older ones, didn't like to be leered at.

But apparently she was flattered, because her smile was solid gold. "Yes. But I'm only staying until Friday." She glided oil on her long legs, taking extra time on her thighs, then hiked her shoulder in a lazy one-sided shrug. "You know how it is. Taking a break from the rat race. I'm vice president of an electronics firm in Chicago. My life is pretty intense."

It was at that moment Sammy decided to use Allie's credit card one more time.

"Maybe I can help there," he replied, warming to her seduction. "May I take you to dinner tonight? Afterwards we can watch the sunset from Mallory Dock. It's guaranteed relaxation."

Later, Sammy didn't hear the key in the lock, so he was surprised when the door of his bungalow flew open and banged against the wall, causing Mandy to roll off him with a yelp, effectively ruining his orgasm. The resort manager, a mustachioed

Cuban holding a master key, stepped aside to admit two men wearing suits. One of them was pointing a gun and shouting hands up, the other was holding a badge and yelling don't move. Sammy, pressed against the headboard, his hands hovering uncertainly somewhere around shoulder height, stared at them.

The two grim-faced men looked at Mandy cowering on the floor beside the bed with the sheet covering her nakedness, then at each other.

Then they glowered at Sammy.

"Where's Allie Hudson?" the man holding the badge demanded.

CHAPTER SEVEN

When daylight filled the bedroom window, Allie surfaced from sleep, and the minute she opened her eyes, the previous days flooded back to her. She lay there, carried headlong by the torrent of memories to this place, this room, this bed in a secluded cabin on the back acreage of Wild Horse Mesa Ranch.

While on the run, her only thought had been to reach safety, to escape unknown pursuers and an unspecified danger. It was her instincts that told her to flee. Now, safe, at least for the moment, she tried to put the pieces together, allowing her mind to turn over and examine the ones that didn't seem to fit. Like the phone call from Davy's mother.

Allie knew there were people who were out to get her. The nature of her work didn't endear her to many of the people she worked with. Parents did not like having their children taken away. Families did not like being torn apart. Often a parent or other family member ended up in jail for offenses against the child. Sometimes seething anger turned into a violent outburst of rage against The System of which Allie was a part.

And she couldn't discount the fallout from Paul's cop buddies after she testified against them. Their attempts at payback been ongoing and relentless.

How did that connect to the warning from Marie? Marie's ped up in the back of her mind. *Take Davy and run.* fe.

have known something, must have known Allie

was being set up for something. Street people were full of information, street gossip surprisingly close to reality. When Paul worked undercover, it was amazing the things he found out from the most unlikely sources, a result of the strange symbiotic relationship that sometimes developed between street hustlers and street cops. Spend enough time in the 'hood, he'd say, and anything going down on either side of the law became common knowledge.

Still, Allie didn't see how Davy fit into the equation. She didn't think whoever was out to get her would intentionally harm Davy.

But what would happen to him if I weren't in the picture? If I were in jail, or dead?

Marie was far from a model mother, but she loved her son and wanted what was best for him. Maybe she figured Allie was Davy's best—maybe his only—chance at a decent life. Maybe she knew Allie would find a way to keep him away from the drugs and crime that were a way of life in his parents' world.

It was a small measure of insight that didn't answer any of the questions swirling in Allie's mind. It didn't tell her who broke into her house and searched her office, who attacked her in her living room, who chased her car.

Warmth from the sun flowed into the room, and she stared at the familiar low-beamed ceiling. She was in what used to be an old miner's cabin between Crazy Woman Creek and Stage Mesa, but was now a compact rustic structure of wood and stone, its lower level spilling down a gentle slope. She permitted herself a smile remembering the times she and Beck had sneaked out here to be alone when they were teenagers. Since then, Beck had turned it into a combination research facility and living quarters, a place he could live and work undisturbed away from the main house at the front of the property. He'd posted before-and-after pictures on his web site when he finished the remode

The cabin was quiet. She slipped out of bed and padded barefoot down the hall, still wearing Beck's tee shirt and pajama bottoms. Beck's bedroom door was closed. The door to the room where she had put Davy to bed was open, but he wasn't there, and her heart pumped a soft downbeat of apprehension at the sight of his empty bed.

At that moment, a screen door squeaked open and clattered shut in another part of the house, and she hurried downstairs toward the sound, passing file cabinets, computers, and camera equipment set up on worktables in the spacious living room. A spectacular mountain view filled a wall of windows.

She entered the kitchen and through the screen door saw Davy standing outside on the pitch-roofed porch looking into the distance. His face was puffy with sleep. Beck's tee shirt hung limply on his thin shoulders, the sleeves falling below his elbows.

Davy looked up at her and smiled tentatively when she joined him on the porch. All during their cross-country flight, he'd been cooperative, doing what was asked of him with few questions, though she knew he was confused and at times terrified. Now she touched his shoulder, making a gentle connection.

"How are you doing today, kiddo?"

"Okay." He shivered slightly in the morning chill. Sunlight touched the far mountains, making their snow-covered peaks sparkle like sugar. Closer in and to the left, Wild Horse Mesa abruptly thrust itself into the clear blue sky, its rock strewn sides falling off sharply. At its base stood a small band of horses.

"Where are we?" Davy asked.

"In Colorado."

"Is this Beck's house?"

"Yes."

High on the mesa, things were greening up with the promise of summer. She could taste the earthy air.

"Are we going to stay here?" A hopeful light went on behind his eyes.

"Only for a little while."

Davy nodded, unprotesting, resigned to the inevitability of life's disappointments. He was used to them.

"Look at those horses," he said, stoically changing the subject. "Aren't they cool?"

"Seriously cool," she agreed. There were six of them, four bay, one roan, and one white, standing at the edge of a watering hole far enough away to be unaware they were being observed by humans. "They're beautiful."

"Are they Beck's horses?" Davy asked.

"No. They're mustangs. They don't belong to anyone. But Beck helps take care of them."

As they watched, the white horse waded into the water and lowered its head to drink. Slowly, the others followed and did the same.

"Can I ride one?"

"No, not those. They're wild horses. Beck is studying them." Davy's shoulders drooped slightly, and she added quickly, "But he has some gentled horses in the barn over there. Where is Beck?"

"I don't know. I didn't see him when I woke up."

"Have you had breakfast?"

"No, but I'm hungry."

"Come on in. Let's see what we can find in the kitchen."

Suddenly the white horse raised its head and looked toward them, ears pricking back and forth. When tires crunched gravel at the side of the house, the horses ran off throwing up a cloud of dust.

A truck door slammed, there were footsteps, and Allie hurriedly nudged Davy inside where they took a wary stance in the kitchen, on guard, prepared to run. Boots sounded on the wooden back porch steps, and she pulled Davy close to her, crossing her arms protectively over his chest.

In a moment, a man appeared at the screen door. He was tall, his body lean and muscular over the bones, his face furrowed with weather-beaten grooves. Grey hair hung to the collar of his plaid shirt. A cigarette was clamped between his lips. He opened the door and stepped in, then stopped in bewildered surprise when he saw them there.

"Oh, excuse me, ma'am." He stepped back outside, took the cigarette out of his mouth, crushed it on the ground, and came back in. " 'Scuse me," he said again. "I know ladies don't like smoke in the house these days."

"We're waiting for Beck," she said, pressing her back into the edge of the counter next to the dishwasher.

"Oh, I just passed him on the road. He'll be here shortly. I'm Jobby Bones. I help out around here, do the barn and yard work, fix things that need fixin'. I'm here most days, 'cept Sunday. Saturday night's the only night I get to stay out late, so I like to sleep in on Sunday."

He stood for an uncomfortable moment, then spoke again.

"Well, best be gettin' to work. Chores don't do themselves." He thumped down the porch steps and headed for the barn, his gait a little stiff legged as if from an old injury.

Just then Beck appeared from around the corner of the house. He stopped to greet and exchange a few words with the ranch hand before entering the cabin carrying half a dozen plastic Wal-Mart bags.

"Good morning," he said with a smile, putting the bulging shopping bags on the kitchen table. "Did you make coffee? Coffee fixings are in the cupboard next to the sink. Sorry I didn't make it before I left, but I knew you didn't have anything to wear. I was hoping to get back before you woke up."

He opened a bag, peered in, then handed it to Davy. "Here

79

Davy. This is for you. Jeans and tee shirts. There's new underwear there, too. Hope you like briefs, my man." He dashed his brows in an expression of mock gravity that didn't hide the twinkle in his eye. "Or do you prefer boxers?" His voice was serious, but a little grin tugged his lips.

The bashful smile that appeared on Davy's face told Allie the suspicious reserve he had displayed toward Beck the night before might be disintegrating a little. The child lowered his eyes and answered shyly. "Briefs are okay."

Beck turned to Allie, his eyes speculative, taking in her hips and thighs.

"I wasn't sure, but I guessed you were the same size you always were." He opened another bag and took out a pair of denim shorts, low cut, metal buttons at the fly. "Size four?" He held the shorts up to his waist. They looked as small as a postage stamp against his bulk. Next he took out a red rib-knit tank top and held it up to his chest over the shorts, making an outfit.

"This goes together, right?" he asked, seeking her approval. When she nodded, he set them aside to pair another shirt and shorts against his body. "How about this? Does it look all right? Do you like it?"

She opened her mouth to answer, but her heart was squeezed so tight she could not draw breath to speak. Reliable Beck, steadfast and nurturing, taking them under his wing, seeing to it they had what they needed. Going out of his way to please her. This is why she had fallen in love with him, why she loved him still. She nodded again, wanting to nuzzle into him.

Beck handed her the other bags. "I bought jeans for you, too, just a few things to tide you over. You can buy more later. There's shampoo and soap and toothbrushes in there, too, and, uh, other personal things I thought you might need." He shrugged. "You probably don't shop at Wal-Mart, but it's the only place open at this hour." He grinned.

"Thank you," she whispered, the words catching in her throat. "I'll pay you back."

Beck shook his head. "No need." His eyes, a hint of blue in their depths, steadied on hers, and he looked like he was debating with himself about saying more.

Davy's excited voice broke into the moment.

"Can I ride one of those horses out there?" Davy's love of animals seemed to be overtaking his distrust of Beck.

"No, not those. They're wild. But you can help me take care of them. After breakfast, I'm going out to check the water in the stock tanks and you can come with me."

"What are stock tanks?"

"Big metal basins that catch rain water so the horses can drink. It hasn't rained in a while, so the water might be low. If it is, I'll have to haul some out there. Do you want to come along and help?"

Davy nodded eagerly, but Allie objected. "No. I don't think that's a good idea. I want him here with me."

"He'll be fine," Beck said, palms out, shoulders in a shrug. "You come, too."

"No," she said firmly and took Davy's hand, pulling him to her. "Someone might see us. Besides Davy has to take a bath, and I have to—"

"Have to what?" Beck interrupted, looking at her, his eyes direct and searching.

Make plans, she thought. Figure out what to do next. Decide where to go.

"Oh, please, Allie. I want to. Can I?" Davy's upturned face had defeat written all over it even as he pleaded with her.

Gently she turned him to face her and laid her hand against his cheek. "It's not safe," she said. "There might be someone out there."

In a surprising display of willfulness, he squirmed away from her touch. "But Beck will be with us," he protested, throwing up his hands in childish exasperation, annoyed she didn't see the logic in that.

She looked helplessly at Beck, wanting him to back her up, but the squint lines around his eyes deepened and his lips twitched in a faint smile. As always, his presence dominated the room, his persona one of confidence and strength. He was standing legs apart, hands on hips, forearms bare. His years in Special Forces had bulked muscles that, she was certain, had squeezed the life out of bad men with little effort. Davy had obviously figured that out.

"Look, I have to go anyway, and I don't want to leave you here alone. You and Davy."

"Well . . ." She tried to summon up a countering protest but couldn't. "All right," she said, relenting. She turned to Davy. "But take a bath first."

Instantly, his face lit with glee. "Okay." He took off at a run but turned within a few strides. "Can I take a shower instead? There's a shower in Beck's bathroom. I peeked."

"Davy, it's not nice to—"

Beck's hearty laughter filled the room, interrupting her scold. "Never mind," he said. "It's all right." He nodded at Davy. "Yes, you can use my shower, but hurry. Breakfast will be ready in ten minutes."

After breakfast, all three piled into an old green pickup thick with dust and dried mud that was parked behind the barn. Beck stuck binoculars and a camera behind the driver's seat and slipped a spiral notebook and ballpoint pen above the sun visor. Allie propped her sandaled feet against a cooler that held bottled water, soft drinks, sandwiches, and trail mix. Davy, wearing new sneakers, new jeans, and a new Denver Broncos tee shirt, was belted in between Allie and Beck. A bit of color had returned to his cheeks, diminishing the grey smudges under his eyes.

Filled with misgivings about venturing out into the open, Allie scanned the distances like an animal scouting for approaching danger. Beck noticed and reached across Davy to give her hand a squeeze. There was something enormously significant in the gesture. You're safe here, it said.

He turned the key, and the pickup roared to life with a lot more enthusiasm than Allie would have guessed given its age and appearance. Switching into four-wheel drive, he bounded across a cattle guard and followed a narrow dirt trail back a mile. It opened up onto moderately sloping grasslands punctuated by piñon, juniper, and Douglas fir with clumps of mountain sage and serviceberry. Nature had been heavy-handed with aspens here, too. Come fall, they would be transformed by cold nights and sunny days into a golden counterpoint set against the snow-covered peaks of the San Juan Mountains.

The truck bumped along, cutting through low scrub. Whatever faint tire tracks may have preceded theirs had long since been obliterated by the hoofprints of wild wandering horses. Davy craned his neck, looking around, diligently searching the rock outcroppings and plateaus for the horse herd. Every now and then Beck stopped the truck and got out to walk down an embankment or up a slope, taking Davy with him to check water levels in the catch basins, before moving on.

At midmorning, while crossing a sandy wash, they found the ground pocked with the hoofprints of the wild herd. Farther on, fresh stud piles confirmed the presence of the horses nearby. Beck steered onto an overlook and pulled the parking brake. Davy scampered up a boulder heap to see if he could spot the horses, while Beck and Allie sat on the ground in the shade of an old spruce.

They'd not seen another person all morning, but that did

nothing to diminish Allie's wariness. She couldn't relax. Days of frenetic flight had instilled in her a finely tuned awareness of her surroundings. All her senses were magnified. Every movement caught her eye, the tiniest sound turned her head. Nothing escaped notice. Now, as her eyes swept the distance watching for the slightest movement, she felt Beck watching her.

"What?" she said, without looking at him.

"I was just wondering how you made it all this way. No car. No money. A child in tow. How did you manage?"

"It was a nightmare," she said. One she hoped someday would fade, but brought back to life now as she described it to him.

"I had enough cash on me to get us from Michigan to Omaha. I didn't want to use my credit card and leave a trail of receipts. My last forty dollars went for a motel room. We needed to sleep in a real bed instead of cramped in the car."

What happened next spun out in her mind as if it were happening again. One minute she was staring at the flimsy motel room door and the next Davy was shaking her awake. "Allie, Allie. Wake up. Someone's out there." Her eyes flew open and she sat up in bed uncertainly, watching the door, expecting it to open. Suddenly a great weight was thrust against it from the outside. Someone was trying to break it down. Wood cracked, but the lock held.

"Davy! Move!" The last word was like the crack of a whip, startling them into action. Frantic, they scrambled out the bathroom window and into the deep shadows of a wooded area behind the motel, down an embankment, and through a field; when they were certain no one had followed them, they hid in a farmer's barn. She'd left her suitcase, her purse, and her car keys behind, but Davy had somehow managed to grab his backpack. In the grey light that preceded dawn, they sneaked out of the barn and hiked down the highway to a used car lot, where they found a car, unlocked, keys in the ignition.

"It ran out of gas in North Platte," she went on. "I couldn't buy any, so we thumbed a ride to Denver. After that, we stayed in shelters, group homes, places where a woman alone with a child wouldn't be questioned or turned away. One of the women staying at a shelter had a car, so she drove us to a diner on the interstate." She heaved a breath, held it, let it go. "I told a trucker I was running away from a husband who beat me. He dropped us off in Cortez."

Beck was looking at her intently, the tracery of fine lines at the corners of his eyes showing again. Fleetingly, she wondered when they'd been etched there.

"What are you going to do now?" he asked.

There was no rebuke in the words, no judgment, just heartfelt concern, but the question had grown thin from frequent repetition in her own mind. She shook her head, a hollow feeling beginning inside her.

"I don't know," she said, and meant it.

Silence descended between them and in the long empty moment, he seemed to be forming his next words with great care.

"You have to take Davy back," he prodded gently, his voice a near whisper.

Anxiety fluttered in her stomach, and she threw up her hands as if to deflect the words. "Beck, look. I can't. It's not that simple. It's more complicated than you realize."

"That much I already figured out," he said. "Tell me the parts I don't know."

He was watching her, waiting for what she wasn't saying, what she didn't want to tell him. His expression was coaxing and commanding. It was a look she had always let persuade secrets out of her in the past, but giving in to it this time might not be the best thing. Telling Beck too much could be dangerous. His inclination would be to fix it immediately, to confront it head on, resolve it, then dust off his hands and move on, leaving it all nice and tidy behind. This time she wasn't so sure that was possible. This time she might be painting a target on his chest. The thought caused her to question the wisdom of her compulsion to seek him out. But where else could she have gone?

Rankled at the dilemma she'd put them both into, she tried not to let it show in her voice.

"Can we talk about something else, please?"

He took a breath, let it out, and the moment passed. "Okay," he said, backing off. "Then tell me about your life. You already seem to know all about mine." He smiled, then she smiled, knowing he was referring to what she'd told him about his web site, and good-naturedly forgiving her for it.

Struggling to find the straightest line through the turmoil that was her life, Allie told him the gist of it, stepping lightly around the more ignoble parts, skipping the worst of the stupid mistakes and self-inflicted messes she'd made along the way. There'd been more than a few. Most of all she avoided what she knew he most wanted to know—why she had left so suddenly all those years ago. That was something she wouldn't talk about.

"When I first became a child advocate," she said, bringing him up to date, "I wasn't sure I could handle the emotional distress of it. Working with abused and neglected children, runaways and throwaways—it's unbelievable what people do to their kids. But I made a conscious decision to live my life doing something that would positively affect people on a daily basis."

She paused and shook her head. "I've taken children from families to keep them safe and argued in court to let other kids stay home. I've had doors slammed in my face and been yelled at in the courtroom, but I always did whatever I felt was best for the child."

When she finished talking, his eyes were gentle and contemplative. Moonstone eyes, the color of transparent clouds through which a trace of blue sky shows. He was searching her face, his expression fixed in a question. After a long moment, he asked it.

"Are you married?"

Caught off guard, she recovered quickly. She knew he'd eventually ask and had been deciding how much to tell him about that part of her life. A great deal of it was entangled in what had sent her on the run. She weighed the idea of lying, drew breath for it, then let it slip away.

"I was married," she admitted cautiously. "For two years." She paused. "He died." She said it with deliberate finality, hoping Beck would drop it and not ask any more questions. Her marriage to Paul was just one in a long line of improvident life choices.

"I'm sorry," Beck said. "That must have been devastating for you."

She nodded. "Yes, it was," she answered blandly, then added, "but not for the reasons you think."

He raised an eyebrow in question, inviting her to go on. Haltingly, she did.

"His name was Paul Robbins," she replied, looking off, thinking back. "But after two years of marriage, it turned out I didn't really know him at all." She paused to reflect. "He was a cop," she went on. "A dirty cop. I turned him in."

Beck stared, a look of complete surprise on his face. "What happened? How did you know?"

"I didn't, not for a long time. Then one night he and his partner made a huge drug bust downtown. Under questioning, the drug dealer admitted everything, including having seventy-five thousand dollars in drug money in a suitcase in his car. Problem is, when the car was impounded, only sixty-three thousand was turned in and reported to the property room."

Taken aback, Beck frowned and blew a low whistle on a

breath of air. "Whoa," he said. "That's bad."

"Paul told me he'd taken it. I guess he thought I'd be relieved to have some of Aunt Helen's medical bills taken off our shoulders. We'd taken her in when she got sick," she explained, "just before she died." She looked off into the distance, as if the memories of those days were coming to life on a stage out there. "I couldn't believe he did it. I couldn't live with it, either. I told him if he didn't turn himself in, I would. He didn't, so I did.

"There was an internal investigation. Felony theft under cover of authority was only one of the charges, and there were others, too. But it didn't go very far. Cops tend to turn a blind eye to some of the laws broken by their brethren—domestic violence, brutality, theft."

Beck's lips were forming a question when Davy suddenly stood up and waved at them, calling out in a loud whisper.

"Hey, you guys! Come here." He was pointing to a sharp-crested ridge about a quarter-mile away. "I see them. Horses. Look." Beck grabbed the binoculars and took long strides up the slope to Davy's overlook. Allie followed and peered out across the grassy basin, squinting against the sun.

At first, they appeared as moving specks against the rocky backdrop, but took shape as they descended a steep path and drew nearer. The horses were making their way down to a broad valley at the bottom of a hogback. Beck squinted into the binoculars, following their progress.

"They look healthy," he murmured. "No ribs showing. No obvious injuries." He knelt and handed the binoculars to Davy, showed him how to adjust the focus.

Davy looked through the lenses, beside himself with excitement. "They have babies," he exclaimed.

The three of them stood silently watching the horses as they grazed near the river, the foals standing beside their mothers on spindly overly long legs. Suddenly the wind changed, and one of the mares raised her head, looked around, leery, sniffing the air. After a while she snorted, whinnied, then cantered off, leading the others away.

When the horses were out of sight, Beck stood and checked his watch. "Let's head back," he said. "I have some reports to write and phone calls to make."

In the truck, Davy talked endlessly about the horses as if nothing else in the world mattered. As if he hadn't just been dragged headlong across five states pursued by an unknown foe for reasons he couldn't begin to understand. Allie was marveling at the resilience of children, Davy's in particular, when he surprised her further.

"I wish we could stay here," he said, sliding a pitiful sideways look at her. "With Beck, I mean."

Fatigue sagged his features, and it wasn't just from lack of a good night's sleep. He was deep-down tired. Tired of running, tired of the unknown, tired of wondering where he'd lay his head come nightfall. He was just plain tired at his core and, frankly, so was she. Davy let Allie draw him to her in a hug, then rested his head against her. She smoothed his hair and sighed, holding on to the hug.

Beck looked at her over Davy's head, and she knew he was waiting for her to say something to that. When she didn't, he turned the key and shifted into gear.

The road wound down out of the canyon and banked along an overlook of rolling grassland. Before crossing over onto the ranch property, he made a turn in a wide part of the road and braked.

"Come on," he said to Allie.

Davy started to unbuckle his seatbelt, but Beck stopped him. "Wait here. We won't be out of your sight. I just want to show Allie something." He handed Davy the binoculars. "See if you can spot any more of the herd."

Beck took her hand and led her to the edge of an aspen grove. When he stopped, she followed his gaze to the gleaming white bark of an aspen and tugged a shaky breath.

"Remember this?" he asked.

Rough black ridges on the silky bark formed the shape of a heart. Inside the heart, carved in the genteel script she had favored in her teens were the words, "Allie loves Beck." It hurt to look at it, and she turned her head away, but Beck put his hand on the side of her face and tenderly turned it back. He eased into her until their bodies were just touching.

"Why did you leave me?" His voice was a raspy whisper, full of pain. His lips brushed her ear. She could feel his breath on her temple. He was too close. She didn't want him that close.

"I had to," she whispered. She pulled away and started back down the path, but he caught her up in his arms and made her look at him.

"Stay now."

"I can't."

"Just for a little while."

"It's not possible."

"It's not fair to Davy if you don't," he said, and she fell silent at the truth of it.

"No one will find you here," he said. "You'll be safe," he repeated. "Use my strength until you have your own back. Then if you need me to, I'll help you do whatever you think is best for the boy."

And that, of course, was what she wanted more than anything. Davy was no longer merely a case file, someone else's child she had vowed to protect. He was a child she loved as if he were her own.

Now was not the time to act impulsively. Now was the time to stop and think, to try and find the connections between the seemingly random events that had sent her on the run. It was time to lay low, let her trail grow cold. Because the dreadful and undeniable fact was, if she didn't figure out the past, she had no real future.

"Okay," she said, after a long moment of thought. "But only if you promise to let me decide when it's time to leave."

A look of sadness drifted past his eyes, here and gone in a split second, but he said, "I promise."

The weather was changing. Clouds stood on the mountains readying themselves for an afternoon shower by the time they got back to the cabin.

"Davy," Allie said when Beck parked the truck in its place behind the barn. "Have you unpacked?"

The boy took a moment to answer, his expression guarded. "No."

"Well, why don't you take your things out of your backpack and put them in that little chest of drawers I saw in your room?"

His wide grin took up half his face. "We're staying?"

"Yes. We're staying. But just for a while," she cautioned, not wanting to set his hopes too high.

Davy threw his thin arms around her waist and squeezed.

"Stop, stop," she said, laughing. "I can't breathe."

Davy bounded up the back porch steps and through the screen door, but stopped suddenly and took two steps back, bumping into Allie as she came in behind.

Standing in the kitchen was a woman whose toenails were painted the same color as the toenails of the tiny dog she was holding in her arm. Smooth and polished as a river stone, the woman's face needed no makeup; its classic bone structure and natural contours were sufficient for beauty. Her clothes were superbly tailored to fit, and obviously expensive. Allie could tell Manolo Blahnik shoes a mile away.

"Hello, Monica," Allie said into the silence that hung heavy in the room.

CHAPTER EIGHT

At the sight of Allie standing in the doorway between kitchen and porch, the woman's flawlessly outlined and perfectly painted lips pressed into a tight line. Her scrutiny was long, hard, and deliberate.

"Well," Beck's sister drawled after a very long moment. "If it isn't Allie Hudson. Back again." She turned her cool gaze, taking in all of Davy, his muddy sneakers, dirt-smudged shirt, grass-stained jeans, before turning imperious eyes back to Allie's face. "In trouble. As usual."

Instantly, Allie's thoughts flowed backwards in time, recapturing memories of Monica Williams from the old days as an impeccably dressed member of the most beautiful crowd, sailing through life haughtily passing judgment on her world and all its inhabitants. From the expression on her face, she didn't appear to have changed much. The silky dog she was holding began to bark, that irksome high-pitched yip of tiny dogs, but Monica silenced it with a quick kiss on top of its snout.

Beck came up the porch steps and through the door, brushing past Allie and Davy to greet his sister. Monica tilted her head up slightly to receive his brotherly peck on the cheek.

"Hi," he said. "When did you get back? I didn't expect you for another three weeks. The housekeeper hasn't been up to the house yet." With a nod he indicated the main house at the front of the property where apparently Monica resided.

Monica's graceful hand gently stroked the dog. Its tiny pink

92

tongue flicked out and licked her fingers. "The heat was insufferable, so I came home early. I called yesterday and left a message on your answering machine telling you when I'd be arriving."

"I was in Cortez giving a talk," he said. "I haven't had a chance to check my messages yet."

Monica's eyes slid back to Allie, as if Allie were to blame for that.

"You remember Allie . . ." Beck said, as if suddenly remembering his manners.

Monica nodded, a regal up-and-down motion of her head with no change in expression. "Oh, yes, I remember Allie," she said. How-could-I-forget? her tone implied.

"And this is Davy."

Monica regarded him with equal disfavor.

Allie pasted on a smile as Davy pressed closer to her, obviously intimidated by Monica's rigid composure, but his eyes were on the dog, who was looking back at him with interest.

An icy silence ensued, and Beck interrupted it. "How's mother?"

"Tiresome, but healthy," Monica replied, then added, "You'd know if you ever bothered to go down to Florida to visit her. She sends her love."

"Yes, I've been trying to get away. I'll go soon, I promise."

Monica studied Allie a moment, a long appraising gaze. "What brings you back to Wild Horse Mesa?" There was more accusation than curiosity in the question.

Beck answered before Allie could.

"Allie and Davy will be staying here for a while," he said without explanation.

Monica's shoulders stiffened, and something sharp flashed in her eyes. "Oh, but I . . ." she stammered. "I don't know if there's room at the house for a child . . ."

"No," Beck interrupted, clarifying his meaning. "They are staying here. With me. In the cabin."

Monica's eyebrows shot up and her lips formed a surprised, but soundless, "Oh," after which she promptly left the room, and then the cabin, her high heels click-tapping over the planked wooden floor, out the front door, and down the steps. A car started, then tires spit gravel as she steered a bronze-colored Lexus up the ranch road back to the main house.

"Maybe staying here is not such a good idea after all," Allie said, watching the car disappear through the trees, the sound of the engine fading.

Beck waved a dismissive hand. "You know how she is. All bark and no bite."

"I hope the same can be said for the dog," Allie put in dryly.

Beck laughed lightly. "I guess I'd better check my messages, though." He headed for his cluttered work space in the living room. Allie followed, and Davy tagged along.

"Doesn't she like kids?" Davy asked.

"She doesn't have any," Beck replied, "so she's not used to them. But don't worry about her, she's all right. You won't see her much, anyway. She stays up at the house most of the time. She writes mystery books."

Beck stood before his disarrayed worktable, hands on hips, and puffed his cheeks. It was piled high with assorted paperwork, bank statements, and unopened mail. The light on his answering machine blinked furiously. He sat down at one of the computers and tapped the keyboard, clicking into his e-mail.

"You could use some help," Allie said, looking around. Notebooks were awry on the floor and piled on the tops of the file cabinets. Colored sticky-notes, reminders of phone calls and deadlines, framed the computer screens. File folders plump with photographs spilled their contents. Large-format cameras and adapter lenses were shoved haphazardly on a shelf, unprotected, out of their cases.

"Why don't you let me take up the slack? I'm good at filing and organizing, writing letters, that sort of thing. Let me work for my keep. And Davy's. I owe you."

"You don't owe me," Beck replied absently, going through his e-mail messages. "In fact, I'll pay you to keep me organized. I was thinking about hiring someone anyway. I'll show you how I store photos. I do have a system . . . of sorts. Can you type? I'm always late with my reports to the BLM. Sometimes weeks go by before I even get a chance to transcribe my field notes."

"I can type," she said, "as long as you value accuracy over speed."

"I do. Thanks." He took his fingers off the keyboard and turned to look at her. "And don't let Monica get to you. She didn't mean those things she said after my dad died."

Beck was instantly sorry he said that. Allie looked as if he'd punched her in the gut, and he kicked himself for being so insensitive. "I'm sorry. I just meant . . . so much time has gone by—"

"Not enough, apparently—"

"She's probably forgotten—"

"I doubt it."

The silence that followed swelled with tension until it became uncomfortable, and Davy, looking confused, sidled up protectively beside Allie. Leaning against her hip, he slipped his hand in hers.

His emotional radar was uncanny, thought Beck. The boy's bonding to Allie was so complete he could sense every nuance of her frame of mind. From now on, they'd have to temper their conversations in front of him. At seven years of age, he was old enough to put the wrong spin on adult conversations he didn't understand, and the child already had enough turmoil in his life.

Beck reached out and ruffled the boy's hair. "Hey."

"Hey," Davy returned uncertainly.

"I've got a little portable television set in my bedroom. How would you like to put it in your room? Then you can watch some kids' shows. Do you like that guy who wrestles alligators?"

Davy's face brightened a little, and he looked up at Allie seeking her permission.

She nodded and affectionately slid her hand down his cheek and under his chin, cupping it. "Come on. I'll move it for you now."

Beck watched them go. For years, memories of her had been in the forefront of his mind, lying down with him in bed at night, meeting him when he first woke, clinging to him through long, lonely days. Now she was here, along with a child and a whole new set of problems and unanswered questions. He wasn't convinced Davy wasn't her son; she'd hesitated before answering when he asked her. But he didn't want to make an issue of it, not now. Not yet. There were other things to worry about.

Including Jazzy.

He looked at the calendar on his desk, flipping through pages covering several weeks. Jazzy wouldn't be back from Wyoming until September. Grateful for the reprieve, relieved that was one decision he could postpone, he sat back and redirected his thoughts to his diary of field notes, studying them.

The horse herd had migrated in from the open range until they were sometimes visible from the cabin in the early hours of the morning. That provided excellent opportunities for taking pictures, which he needed for the *National Geographic* article he was writing, but it wasn't necessarily good for the herd. Being so close to human habitation presented a variety of dangers to the horses—the chance of domestic dog attacks, or of drinking contaminated water. Human interaction sometimes caused unintentional harm to the mustangs, though sometimes it was intentional, like kids chasing them through the backcountry on ATVs or taking pot shots at them with BB guns or rifles.

As a rule, wild horses were shy and avoided populated areas. Beck considered that they were being forced to the perimeter of their range by insufficient forage. He'd have to spend a couple of days out there checking the range condition and availability of sage and saltbrush, wheatgrass and Indian ricegrass. If plant growth was weak or dwarfed, the BLM soil conservation people would be called in. If the forage was thinning due to overgrazing or overpopulation of the herd, the BLM would round some up for the Wild Horse Adoption Program.

Again, Beck examined his calendar, trying to decide which days he'd be able to spend surveying the forage. He could do a new population count at the same time, see how many foals had been born that spring. Maybe he'd take Davy along. The kid would enjoy that.

From the noises in the kitchen, he could tell Allie was making a late lunch. She brought him a plate, which he gratefully accepted, then returned to his work.

After a while, his concentration flagging, he became aware of voices drifting in from the other room, Allie and Davy playing Monopoly at the kitchen table. Beck allowed himself some guiltless eavesdropping.

"Try to buy the orange and red properties," Davy was telling her, his voice taking on the self-importance that comes with being able to tell an adult something they didn't already know.

"I thought the green properties were the best," Allie replied.

"No. The houses for the green ones are too expensive. And hardly anybody ever lands on the green. The orange and red come right after the jail space. Lots of people get sent to jail, then they land on the orange and red. And the houses don't cost too much."

"Okay," she said.

"Try to buy all the railroads, too," he told her. "They get landed on the most. That's called laying track."

"Aren't you afraid I'll beat you now that you've told me all your secrets?"

"Oh, I haven't told you *all* my secrets."

Beck chuckled to himself. The kid was damn smart, no doubt about it. As dice rattled and the game continued, Beck couldn't help marveling at the longevity of the classic board game that, despite the appeal of modern video games, had occupied countless hours of several family generations.

As a child, Beck had participated in some heated Monopoly tournaments with both his father, who was intense and driven though it was only a game, and his grandfather, who often let the grandchildren win. His grandfather had told him a story about escape maps and compasses being hidden in Monopoly games and smuggled into POW camps inside Germany during World War II. Real money for the escapees was covertly mixed into the Monopoly game money packs, and the enemy captors, unaware of the bounty the games contained, ignored the prisoners' seeming addiction to the pastime.

Beck decided the next time he went to Wal-Mart, he'd pick up a new Monopoly game for Davy. The one he'd been carrying around was pretty beat up, pieces missing and all.

Movement in his peripheral vision, and a noise from outside drew his attention to the window. A La Plata County Sheriff's patrol car, silver grey with black and white trim, had rolled up the driveway and was gliding to a stop in front of the cabin moving as smoothly as a ship entering port.

He wasn't surprised to see it. He'd been expecting just such a visit, was only surprised it hadn't come sooner.

Allie heard the car pull up, too, and when she caught a glimpse out the front windows, stood up so abruptly her chair scraped backwards and banged against the refrigerator.

"Don't tell them we're here," she pleaded, reaching for Davy and pulling him to her. "Please!" Her voice was strained, her eyes wide, suddenly filled with fear again.

Beck made a palm-out calming motion with his hand. "Easy. Go upstairs, take Davy with you. Quietly. I'll go outside and talk to him."

Beck waited a moment, watching them until they were out of sight, then strode casually out onto the porch, letting the screen door bang softly behind him. The sheriff swung open the driver's side door, unfolded himself from behind the wheel, and strolled up the dirt path to the porch, his boots crunching on stones.

Beck smiled a greeting and stepped down from the porch to meet him.

"Afternoon, Grady. Haven't seen you since the chili cook-off up at Purgatory Mountain. April, wasn't it?"

"Well," Grady drawled, "we've been pretty busy. They had that Willie Nelson concert up there, then the bluegrass festival. Those big crowds tend to get rowdy if there's no county uniform presence."

Beck nodded in feigned commiseration. "Yeah, you guys have your work cut out for you, all right. What brings you all the way up here to the ranch?"

Grady hiked and shifted his heavy-duty belt, settling it more comfortably on his hips. He was six-one, maybe six-two, lean and hard with the muscled shoulders and paramilitary bearing characteristic of law enforcement officers in far-flung remote counties of the West.

"Just checking something out for the police chief up in Cortez. Someone called in a report of a drive-by shooting at a motel up there," Grady drawled. "Turns out it happened in a room registered in your name."

Beck lifted his brows, making a pretense of surprise. "Really? When did that happen?"

"Last night. Said they heard some yelling. Sounded like a child."

"Must have been after I left."

"You were there, then?"

"Yeah. I gave a talk at the cultural center. I was going to spend the night, but at the last minute I decided to come home."

"What time was that?"

Beck frowned and turned down the corners of his mouth, a thoughtful expression. "Oh . . . must have been around ten," he lied.

"Why so late? Why not wait until morning?"

"I was worried about the herd. Spring rains were light and I was worried the stock ponds were low. I'd been away a week. Came back last night so I could go out and check the water tanks first thing this morning."

The deputy held Beck's eyes, and his jaw moved and flexed considering this but not commenting on it.

"Anybody with you at the motel?"

"Nope. Just me."

"Anybody see you leave?"

Beck shrugged. "I don't know. Don't think so. I didn't see anyone around. There didn't appear to be many people checked in. Only a few cars in the lot."

Grady's gaze didn't waver. Neither did Beck's; even a minute shifting of his glance, the slightest tightening of his eye muscles would send a signal of deception that would be instantly noticed, if not remarked on by the sheriff.

"Well, if you remember seeing anyone or anything suspicious, call the Cortez PD, let them know."

"I'll do that," Beck replied, his tone implying he'd be ever so helpful.

Grady stood there a moment, thumbs hooked in his belt loops. He shifted his weight, then cocked his head in the direction of the main house. "Saw Monica's car up there when I went by. She back from Florida?"

"Yeah. The heat chased her away. Mother did, too, apparently."

Grady nodded, laughed affably, but still didn't make a move to leave. "How's Jazzy?" he asked, keeping the conversation going. "Still digging up dinosaur bones?"

"Yep. You know Jazzy. She keeps busy."

Grady smiled. "Don't know how you two are going to find time to get married, busy as you both are."

"Yeah, well." Beck hiked a noncommittal shrug. Jazzy and the wedding. A wedding that had been postponed three times already. Twice by him, the last time by her.

Grady stood there letting the moment play out, then clapped a hand on his leather holster, lifting and shifting twenty pounds of police patrol gear back into place around his waist.

"Well, it's late. I got to get on home."

He walked to the patrol car and shoehorned himself into it, started the engine and drove away giving Beck a two-fingered salute as he circled the clearing and disappeared around the curve leading to the dirt road.

Beck stood there, listening to the hum of the motor until it blended indistinctly into the late afternoon sounds of the woods and the wind coming down the San Juans. Not until then did he release a bottled-up breath.

Grady hadn't mentioned Allie. Apparently, no one had seen her come to his motel room or leave with him. Still, something wasn't right. She'd been missing with a child she said wasn't hers for over two weeks and not a word about it anywhere. No

Amber Alert, not a mention on the news channels, and nothing on the Internet news services he'd checked first thing that morning. It didn't make sense.

Yet, she insisted the police were after her. He had no doubt that was true, but why no Amber Alert? Her husband had been a cop, but he was dead now. Was that connected somehow?

Beck turned and went back inside the cabin to find Allie, her face drained of color, standing at the top of the stairs. Davy peered down at him from behind her back, his eyes round with curiosity.

"What did the sheriff say?" Allie asked. She was standing in a shaft of sunlight coming in from an upstairs window. It formed a halo around her head, making her hair glow.

Instead of answering, Beck spoke to Davy. "Would you please stay in your room for a while? I need to talk to Allie about something."

Davy blanched, his expression first wounded, then cautious. "About me? Did I do something wrong?"

"No. You didn't do anything wrong. You're not being punished. Allie and I have to talk."

"Go along," Allie told him. "You can watch TV. We'll finish our game later."

Obediently, Davy turned, walked down the hallway and into his room.

When Davy's door closed, Allie came slowly down the steps.

"What did the sheriff say?" she asked again. "What happened? What did he want?"

"Somebody reported the shooting last night."

"Oh, God." She closed her eyes, and took a quivering breath to still the leaping pulse beneath her ribs.

"Allie. We have to talk."

She nodded and opened her eyes, but otherwise didn't move.

"Who wants to hurt you?"

She let a short breath escape that sounded like a laugh.

"Who doesn't?" she replied bitterly. "Mothers who've had their children taken away, fathers who've lost custody, grandparents from hell who've been denied visitation. All because of me."

"And the police?"

She nodded again. "The police, too."

"Why? Tell me the rest."

With a resigned sigh, she walked into the kitchen, leaned her hip against the counter, pressed her fists against her eyes, then crossed her arms over her chest. A pained expression held Beck's face, and she lifted her chin and met it directly.

"Paul wasn't the only one involved in that scandal in the police department."

He waited, eyes on her. "Go on."

"There were dozens of others, and numerous violations ranging from reckless driving and destroying evidence to, well, much worse. A sergeant sexually assaulted a suspect with a flashlight, then lied about it. Another officer harassed his girlfriend's ex-husband with fraudulent parking tickets. A detective was accused of putting a knife under the testicles of a fellow officer as he stood at a urinal, a personal grudge. Others . . ." She stopped and looked at Beck, shrugged. "Need I go on with the gory details?"

"No. I can figure it out. What happened next?"

"Not much. Some of the officers and detectives who had the years on the force took early retirement. Some had friends in high influential places, so got little more than a reprimand, but kept their jobs. A sharp defense attorney got most of the others off, or plea-bargained suspended sentences for them. The county prosecutor wasn't too anxious to pursue it, anyway. It was messy. Embarrassing to the department. Only a few of them went to jail, but most didn't. It's the ones who didn't that I'm worried about."

"What do you mean?"

"I testified at the trial, and later began calling for public oversight on police corruption. I wrote the newspapers, went on radio and television talk shows, tried to start a citizen's action group to force the bad apples out. That made the remaining dirty cops real mad, even the ones who had gotten off. They watched me all the time, just waiting for me to step out of line, hoping to nail me with something. They did that parking ticket thing with me, too, and they made up stories and spread lies about me, but that was as far as it went. At least, as far as I knew then. I was damned careful not to do anything they could arrest me for."

Until now. The thought spiraled into her head before denial could rise up and deflect it. From the expression on Beck's face, she could tell the same thought occurred to him.

"That's who is after you now? Those cops?" he asked.

She nodded. "Or friends of theirs. Paul's partner, too. He was one of the ones who got off but lost his job. He's a private investigator now."

"Ah," Beck said, sagely, lifting his eyebrows, pursing his lips, putting it together. "And, of course, now you *have* done something they can arrest you for."

She nodded again. "Exactly. That, or they could easily get rid of me and make it look like an accident like they did with Paul."

"They killed him? His own people?"

"He was killed in a SWAT training accident. They were supposed to be using blanks. Someone had mistakenly loaded live ammunition. It happened right before the trial, just after Paul decided to tell the Internal Affairs investigators what he knew."

"So you don't think it was an accident." It wasn't a question.

"No, I don't. They were sending a message. And I got it, loud and clear."

Beck whistled under his breath, and rocked back on his heels. His face was pinched and somber. She'd told him more than she'd wanted to and hoped she hadn't made a mistake by doing so. She wondered what he was thinking.

"What did you say your husband's name was?"

"Paul Robbins. I went back to my maiden name after he died. But they know who I am. Even before I left with Davy, I think the wheels had been set in motion to frame me for something as payback."

"What makes you think so?"

She shrugged. "There were signs. And warnings." She told him about Marie's phone message and what she thought it meant.

"Ah," he said, thinking. "And if the frame was good enough, you'd have been held and arrested."

"And if it wasn't, I'd have been set up later. Or have an accident. Like Paul." She took a breath, pushed on. "That's why I can't go back. If something happens to me, what will happen to Davy?"

She searched Beck's face for doubt, uncertainty, but found none. He seemed to be studying a thought hidden behind his eyes, but he didn't argue with her, didn't tell her she was imagining things or overreacting. His look of understanding said he believed her, but having him confirm she was in danger made the fear more real.

He held out his arms and she, recalling moments from a vanished past, went to him, hugged him. She was relieved to know that after hearing her story, he still wanted her in his arms. She went up on tiptoe, touched her lips to his, then sought his eyes. They were deep and still, busy with thought. A tense silence gathered until he broke it.

"Don't worry, babe," he said, tightening his arms, resting his chin on top of her head, holding her close. "We'll work it out."

CHAPTER NINE

Iris Neto closed her eyes and took two deep breaths in an attempt to relieve the burning pain of stress in her chest. She tried to take another, but the gravity of the situation before her crushed the breath from her lungs as if the air had been forced out by a hard punch to her stomach. Never did she imagine she would be such a failure at her job.

When she accepted the position as director of county Child Protective Services, she'd done so with the expectation of becoming a guardian of little lost souls, a savior of mistreated children, saw herself salvaging the inevitable flotsam of wrecked families. Instead, she had lost three children in as many years. Yes, lost them.

Eighteen months ago, Tommy Mandino, just turned three, had been found dead along the side of a road even though CPS records showed the child was well and cared for. Eleven-year-old Carmen Rodriquez had been missing for two years before they found her last month, four states and over a thousand miles away from her Michigan foster home in the company of a child predator she'd met on the Internet.

And now a CASA had run off with a child and taken him God knows where. Iris opened her eyes and with a shudder of dread gazed at the file lying open on her desk, fat, dog-eared, crammed with papers. The name on the tab was Davy Lopez.

Her superiors didn't know Davy was missing. She herself only found out because the court clerk had called looking for the final disposition report confirming the child had been returned to his parents as ordered by Judge Berriman. Because the agency was so short-handed, what with Tiffany Day leaving so abruptly and all, Iris had taken it upon herself to personally follow up with an on-site home visit. When Davy's father answered the door, after she'd knocked and knocked for what seemed like twenty minutes at least, she was stunned. She recalled exactly the heavy sinking feeling in the pit of her stomach when he told her he hadn't seen his son in months.

She hadn't told anyone at the county, nor at the court— everything was still in turmoil over there after the sudden death of Judge Emery—nor had she reported it to the authorities. Instead, she had called a private detective, hoping he would be able to find Davy and she could then quietly return him to his parents or place him back into the system.

And the CASA, well, Allie Hudson would be dealt with accordingly.

The success of Iris's cover-up plan was a long shot born of faint hope, but she'd had no choice. She couldn't risk the public embarrassment of another missing child. Fallout from the Tommy and Carmen messes had been volatile and ongoing. The subsequent scandal and shake-up at CPS had been daily chronicled by an investigative reporter from the *Detroit News,* a reporter who was still sniffing around. That Iris had kept her job in the aftermath was mostly a function of the agency being grievously understaffed, but also because anyone qualified to take her job would rather have hot needles stuck in their eyes than live with the strain of it. No one would take the job.

This time she would not be so fortunate. This time, she'd be out on her ass. Because besides the indisputably dreadful fact that a child had gone missing, there was something else.

An upcoming audit.

A previous audit of CPS records by federal and state authorities had identified a serious accountability problem—excessive expenditures at private placement facilities; failure to check the background of caregivers; incomplete, falsified or missing CPS case files. This new audit would discover more than financial discrepancies and missing files. This one would turn up expenditures for a private detective hidden in an unrelated line item of the departmental budget.

And another missing child.

Losing her job would be the least of it. She could be charged with a financial crime, and the agency would certainly lose some if not all of its federal funding. That eventuality would severely hamper the agency's work and cut their staff even more. Even if she went to jail, she didn't want to leave the agency in shambles, possibly dismantled, and its mostly good work discontinued.

She wrenched her mind away from those thoughts and looked at the man who had just taken a seat on the other side of her desk.

"Have you found them?" she asked without smile or preamble, a tremble in her voice.

"No," replied Mark Medora. "Not yet."

She sighed in frustration, listening as he brought her up to date on his investigation, thumbing through and reading from a spiral notebook on which notes had been jotted. All the while she fought rising panic.

"Mr. Medora, it's been over a month. You must find that child." Her voice was harsh from the tightness in her throat.

"We're doing the best we can, Miss Neto. We followed a lead to Florida, but it didn't pan out. We'll keep looking."

"Are you sure the CASA has the boy?"

"I can't prove it, but everything points that way. I'm not at liberty to reveal any details, but I'm familiar with Allie Hudson."

Iris noticed he straightened a little in his chair and a dark shadow passed behind his eyes. "You know her?" she asked.

"I knew her husband. I worked with him when I was with the police department. He was killed in a training accident."

He kept his voice matter of fact, but a frown and tight narrowing of his eyes suggested a darker meaning beyond his words. Iris didn't dwell on it, but asked instead, "What about Davy's parents?"

"We haven't located either of them, but we're still working on it. They don't exactly keep a schedule."

Iris sighed heavily, but said nothing.

"Allie didn't seem to have any friends, no one she confided in. She didn't socialize much on her off hours. Have you thought of any names? People she was friendly with here? Anyone she went to coffee with? Had lunch with?"

Iris shook her head. "No. She kept mostly to herself here, too. Especially after her law license was suspended. She and one of the family court judges sometimes went out to lunch together, but unfortunately Judge Emery was killed in a car accident." She thought for a moment. "Have you been to her house?"

Mark Medora nodded. "No sign of her. Neighbors haven't seen her, but they're not happy about the condition of her lawn. Needs mowing, weeds coming up. They rarely saw her except for a nod or a wave coming or going. She had a few boyfriends, but none of them stuck around long. She was a loner." The detective consulted his notes. "What about her last paycheck? Has it been cashed?"

"No. I checked with payroll this morning. Since she was an independent advocate, she wasn't on salary. She was paid by the case. I've turned her pending cases over to another advocate." Iris sighed heavily. "You've got to find that child." A huge pressure was building in her head. "I can't delay reporting it much longer. And my source of funds to pay you is not inexhaustible."

Mark Medora shrugged. "My partner and I are doing all we can."

"I have to remind you that it's imperative your investigation remain confidential. If the media gets wind of another child missing . . ." She let her words trail off, unable to face the thought of the potential consequences and give them substance.

They sat in silence until Iris's frustration got the best of her. "They've got to be out there somewhere," she said in a desperate whisper, waving her hand in the direction of a vague *out there.*

"Don't worry," he said. "I'll find them. I might have some other leads. There's nothing I want more than to find Allie Hudson." His eyes were unreadable, his mouth neutral, a shuttered expression. "And the child, of course," he added quickly, meeting Iris's gaze.

Then it came to her why he looked so familiar. She'd seen his picture in the paper, what was it, a year ago? Longer? It was during that scandal at the police department, corrupt cops taking payoffs, shaking down suspects, other things she couldn't remember. She wasn't sure he'd actually done any of it himself, but he'd been involved somehow.

After he left, with more haste than grace, Iris sat at her desk a long time wondering if Mark Medora had told her the truth about having other leads. Or if, as she feared, the trail had gone cold.

CHAPTER TEN

The seclusion of the Williams Ranch and the remoteness of the cabin made it almost possible for Allie to forget that just weeks before, she had been running for her life, and Davy's. The gut-wrenching fear she'd lived with while on the run now hummed as a sort of white noise, persistent and unrelenting, but in the background, hovering on the edge of consciousness. Hours would go by when she didn't think of it at all.

Gradually her priorities shifted. Her original intention to leave the ranch after a short stay grew less urgent. It might be safer to stay put, at least for a little while. Being in Beck's presence again was soothing to her. She could think more clearly.

The loner that Beck had become, and the nature of his work, didn't encourage visitors, human ones anyway, and life in the cabin existed in a comfortable solitude. Privacy was a valuable commodity in this southwest corner of Colorado, respected, honored, and steadfastly preserved by almost everyone who lived there, and quickly sought out by newcomers. Even Monica kept to herself, the thick curtain of evergreens and aspens filling the quarter mile between the main house and the cabin thoroughly blocking any view of one from the other.

Wearing Levis, sneakers, and a turtleneck against the morning chill, Allie made her way into the kitchen. She could tell by the dishes in the sink that Davy had already had his breakfast, and she peered out the back windows to see if he was out at the corral with the horses, or shadowing Jobby Bones as he went about his chores. When she didn't spot him right away, she poked her head out the screen door. Pale sunshine cast a buttery light over the outbuildings and fences, but the tip of the wind blowing over the remaining alpine snowpack high in the San Juans felt sharp on her cheek.

After a moment, Jobby Bones, favoring his bad leg, walked around the corner of the barn carrying a shovel, trailed by Davy carrying a bucket. They saw her and waved, and she, with quiet relief, smiled and waved back, then ducked inside the kitchen, closing the door on the nippy air.

She poured coffee, creamed and sugared it with a lavish hand, then carried her cup to the worktable. Beck had rearranged his work area to accommodate her as best he could in the limited space. He'd set up an extra computer for her to use, then moved the two worktables facing each other perpendicular to the front wall of the living room. A third computer installed on a console in the corner was a spare, used mostly for sorting and storing the hundreds of photos he shot to illustrate his articles on wildlife.

Beck, at his computer, work showing on the screen, was engrossed in building a spreadsheet for a report on the nutritional value of wild grasses. In his concentration, he didn't appear to notice her. She pulled a chair around and sat in it, then turned on her computer. While it booted up, she sneaked peeks at him, her eyes gliding over his face, all but caressing it.

"Where's Davy," he asked without looking up, and she realized she was staring and jerked her gaze away.

"Out back with Jobby." She sipped her coffee. "How long have you been up working?"

"A couple of hours. Davy already had breakfast."

"So I noticed," she said. "Thanks for fixing it."

"No problem."

After a while, he stopped typing, leaned back in his chair,

and stretched his arms, groaning noisily. "I'm going to town," he said at the end of a great huge yawn. "Do you want to come?"

She did. Some of the clothes he'd bought for Davy didn't fit, and she wanted to exchange them. She also wanted to get her hair done. She combed it back off her face with her fingers. The do-it-yourself bleach and hack job had served its purpose as a disguise, but now it was growing out dank and clumpy, and looked like moldy wheat growing on the ends of copper stalks.

But she said, "No, thanks. I think I'll skip it."

"Come on. You can't stay cooped up here every day. Durango has changed a lot since you left."

Since you left.

The words struck a discordant note, but thankfully, he didn't dwell on it.

"There's lots of shopping on Main Avenue now. There's even a mall and a Cineplex."

Tempted, she thought about it. "How big is the mall?"

"Well, small. There's a Penney's, a CD store, a place to buy, you know, bath stuff . . ." He named some stores.

She sat back in her chair. "Maybe next week." She ran her fingers through her hair again. "I'll make a hair appointment."

"Good idea. Ask Monica where to go. She knows all the best places."

Monica was the last person Allie would ask, but she didn't say so. It wasn't only the glacial reception she'd received that day she arrived. The few times their paths had crossed since, usually outdoors and at a distance, had left little doubt of Monica's iciness. But being snubbed by Monica was nothing new. Allie didn't have to reach very far back into memory to summon up visions of that elevated nose, those frosty sidelong glances. The disapproval had turned to contempt when their father, Jonathan Williams, died.

"I'll think about it," she said, and took a sip of coffee.

Beck busied himself getting ready to leave, saving his work on the computer, shuffling papers into some sort of order, self-consciously shoving a few paperclips around. Allie couldn't help noticing he was clearly stalling, and she wondered why.

"Would it be all right if I took Davy?" he asked, hesitantly, as if he already knew she'd object.

The familiar adrenalin-charged protectiveness kicked in automatically, and Allie stiffened. She opened her mouth to argue, but Beck jumped in.

"I won't let him out of my sight." The corners of his mouth turned up a quarter of an inch, and he raised his right hand, palm out. "I swear."

"But do you think that's a good idea?"

"Yes," he said. "I do. He hasn't been off the ranch since you got here."

"I know, but—"

"No buts. I want to get him some things. Toys, and things for him to do."

"He doesn't need anything. He's got plenty to do. He's got the horses, he's got books, I play Monopoly with him when-ever—"

"But I want to buy him something," he interrupted again. "Something special," he emphasized.

Their eyes met and she realized this was something he wanted to do for himself, too, not just for Davy, that the special something was important to him. He and Davy were on their way to forging an attachment, not a bond like father and son, but a closeness, like friends. Buddies. Beck enjoyed hanging out with Davy. And Davy, after his initial guardedness, was now crazy about Beck.

"Okay," she relented. "He can go."

That smile she adored lit his face, and he came to her, lifted her face with gentle hands, and kissed her lips lightly.

"Get him a haircut, would you?" she said, pretending to be miffed at giving in.

She made sure Davy changed clothes after his barn time and then walked out to the car with them. Davy, excited but trying to hide it from Allie, glanced back at her as he climbed into the front seat.

"Are you sure you'll be okay?" he asked in a most serious manner, as he buckled his seatbelt. "Do you want me to stay here with you?"

She smiled behind her hand. *Who's the grownup here?*

"No. You go ahead," she said. "I'll be fine." Then, when he still looked dubious, added, "Really. Now have fun."

After they drove away, Davy waving and grinning happily, Allie stood a minute, thinking about the familiar scene that had just played out, euphoria sinking in. It was almost like déjà vu. Only she was aware it hadn't really happened before except in her dreams.

She shook it off, returned to the computer, and, as she did each morning, checked the Internet news sites, concentrating on news outlets in Michigan. So far, no Amber Alerts had been issued, no mention of her, or of a boy named Davy Lopez. Nothing at all about CPS missing a child. On one hand, she was relieved, but on the other, it was disturbing.

Being a single woman with few friends to speak of, who spent most of her time at work or alone at home, her absence wouldn't necessarily be noted. Anyone who might have missed her would think she was spending the summer at her cottage up north, because that's what she'd told them she was going to do.

But how was it possible that no one at CPS realized Davy wasn't accounted for? Or did they know and, unlikely as it may seem, neglect to report it? Or worse, choose not to report it?

Sick at heart, she realized that was indeed possible. The inefficiency and mismanagement of child protective services in many jurisdictions around the country were notable, and her own was no exception.

She Googled her name and Davy's, and the usual links came up—old newspaper accounts about Paul's death, and her subsequent efforts to call attention to and derail local police corruption. Nothing to hint of what Marie had warned her about—*take Davy and run*—no clue to who had been in her house, who had attacked her, who had clung to the door of her Jeep, squeezing her face. She shuddered, remembering.

After an hour, just as she was about to give up and begin typing Beck's field notes, an article about identity theft caught her eye. Not the article itself, but a name that jumped out at her, and a picture. Mark Medora. Her husband's former partner on the police force, and ultimately, his partner in crime. The one who was allowed to resign instead of being arrested.

Quickly she skimmed the story, skipping over the statistics about the widespread crime of identity theft and how to protect against it, jumping down to a quote from Mark about a case he'd worked on. Then she saw another name. Sammy Oberski. Tracked down and arrested in Florida for using a stolen credit card.

Hers?

Of course, it was.

And just like that, something jarred, pieces of the puzzle snapping into place. Mark hadn't tracked Sammy Oberski to Florida. He'd tracked the credit card purchases.

Her heart speeded up and she drew in a breath, letting it slide out slowly as it became clear to her that Mark hadn't been looking for Sammy. He'd been looking for her. He hadn't expected to find a boozy playboy at the end of the trail. He'd expected to find Allie Hudson.

She took in another lungful of air and sat back in her chair, thinking. At least now she knew her original suspicions had been confirmed, but a whole new Pandora's box of questions had just opened. Like, how was Marie Lopez connected to Mark Medora?

Or maybe she wasn't.

And, if Mark had been off chasing a VISA paper trail, who had been chasing her?

"Come on, Allie," she muttered. "Think it out."

But no answers materialized.

Frustrated, she stopped her mind from spinning and closed out the news sites, found her place in Beck's field journal, then picked up where she'd left off the day before transcribing his notes, which were mostly chicken scratches and symbols.

But her mind wouldn't cooperate, wouldn't focus on the task. She lost her place, found it, lost it again. She made typos. Her thoughts kept drifting back to the night she returned from the cottage to find her house ransacked. Who had done that, what were they looking for? And what about her house now? Was the door locked? And what good did a lock do anyway? Someone had gotten in. Someone had been at the cottage, too. Who?

This game she was playing with herself of twenty-questions-that-have-no-answers was driving her crazy, and a waste of time. Again and again, she tried to lay it all out in her mind and work with the facts, but she had precious few of those.

The phone's abrupt ringing made her jump as though someone had lobbed a rock through the window next to the table, jangling her already frayed nerves, but she made no move to pick it up. With Beck's blessing, she let all his calls go to the answering machine, eliminating the chance of her voice being recognized by an unwelcome caller.

She shook her head to clear it, found her place again, and resumed typing, trying to ignore the incessant ringing. At last, the answering machine clicked on.

"Hi, sweetie, it's me."

Allie stopped typing.

The voice coming from the speaker, honeyed and moneyed and breathy and sexy, floated into the room. Like a heat-seeking missile, Allie's brain locked onto it.

"Oh, I'm sorry I missed you," the caller lamented, the voice smooth and syrupy. "I tried your cell, but there was no answer, so thought I might catch you at home. I'm in Cheyenne buying supplies while the crew does some backfilling at the dig site. We made some phenomenal finds! Can't wait to tell you about it."

Static grated, there were muffled voices in the background, then a sliding sound back and forth on the mouthpiece. "You won't be able to call me back, though, cell phones don't work out at the site, and I have to get back right away. But I miss you a lot. Really. Can't wait to see you. But . . . well, it might not be September. Look. I'll call you back and explain. Or I'll try to e-mail. Okay? Bye, baby. Love you. Mean it."

Allie stared at the red blinking message indicator, trying to invoke an image of the caller from the quality of the voice—someone blonde and delicate with superior posture that commanded attention when she entered a room. Someone whose words rolled off her tongue like silk off the bolt. Someone manicured and pedicured to within an inch of her life.

Allie looked at her own nails, then quickly closed her fingers into her palms to hide them from sight.

Apparently, Beck had forgotten to mention that love had come into his life in some spectacular fashion while she'd been bushwhacking her way through hers.

Not that she was owed any such explanations.

She closed her eyes and shook her head, then blinked rapidly a couple of times before she got hold of her emotions.

A soft noise fell behind her, a footstep, and she turned to see Beck's sister standing in the doorway leading in from the kitchen, looking more than usual wooden of face.

"That was Jazzy," Monica said, with a nod in the direction of the phone, grim satisfaction showing in her tight-lipped smile.

Allie swallowed hard and cleared her constricted throat so she could speak.

"Good morning. Beck isn't here. He went into town."

Monica stood stiffly, spine rigid, arms folded, her look measured and judgmental. "I know. I saw his car go by the house."

Allie offered a weak smile, uneasy at Monica's stony expression. "When he gets back, I'll tell him you want to speak to him."

"No," Monica replied. "It's you I want to speak to."

"Oh." Allie paused, immediately wary, her smile frozen in place. "What about?"

Monica moved out of the doorway and stopped in the middle of the room where she stood looking awkward but no less reproachful. Finally, through stiff lips, she said what was on her mind.

"It's none of my business, of course, but just how long do you intend to stay here?"

Allie's smile dissolved. "You're right," she said, turning, putting her hands deliberately on the keyboard. "It's none of your business."

Refusing to be dismissed, Monica stepped closer, forcing herself into Allie's line of sight. "Haven't you caused my brother enough trouble?"

Allie started to speak, to fling a rejoinder, but reined it in. In her old life, at her job, even in court, she'd never hesitated to tell anyone to go to hell if she felt they were out of line. She never suffered fools, and could give as good as she got from the worst of the assholes. But now she found herself on new ground that shook perilously under her feet. Here, she was a guest. No, not even that. An interloper. She inhaled sharply, swallowed the retort that rose to her throat, and held her tongue.

Seeing her advantage, Monica took another shot.

"We all knew you'd get yourself in trouble. It was inevitable."

Allie's heart thumped in her chest, suddenly afraid that Monica knew what had brought her to the ranch, that she knew about Davy. Allie waited.

"We just never dreamed you'd show up in Durango again. But here you are," Monica said, flapping her hand in a gesture that said, *ta dah, drum roll, please!* "An unwed mother dragging a child around."

Allie released a pent up breath, infinitely relieved to be branded an unwed mother instead of a child stealer. She said nothing while Monica went on.

"Beck has made a life for himself here." Her gaze, disappointed and reproachful, traveled around the room, taking in the bare-beamed ceiling, the wide-planked floor, the makeshift workspace. "Not the kind of life the family had wanted for him, especially not his father, but—" She shrugged, resigned. "It's what he's chosen.

"And he's become successful at it. He's made a name for himself as a photojournalist. He's well known as a wildlife researcher. And," she added acidly, her eyes drilling into Allie, "he has a future with a woman who loves him. A sensible, intelligent woman," she pointed out, no doubt elucidating Jazzy's attributes. "Who isn't always getting herself into trouble," she finished.

And expecting Beck to get her out of it, Allie added silently. Who doesn't slouch in her chair. Who chooses both her words and her battles with care. Who probably walks on water and leaps tall buildings in a single bound.

Monica was watching her like a cat watched a mouse. It was unnerving, and Allie's impulse was to demand that she get the

121

hell out of the house. Only it wasn't her house, it was Beck's house. And maybe Monica's name was on the deed, too. Allie bit back the words in her head and kept her mouth shut, letting the comeback die.

"He's getting married, you know. To Jazzy." Monica's eyes sparkled with malice.

Allie winced inwardly at a sharp pang of regret, and she struggled not to react, too stubborn to let Monica see how much her words had hurt. Her eyes burned, and she closed them, but immediately pictures formed in her mind—Beck kissing Jazzy, moving his hands on her body, stroking her hair, cupping her breasts and kissing them lightly like he'd kissed Allie's lips that morning.

With great effort, Allie banished the images and collected herself.

"I have no intention of spoiling anything for Beck," she said, trying to keep her voice steady, but still her constricted throat made the words sound weak and hollow. "I love Beck. I don't want to hurt him."

Monica frowned, her vision focused inward on thoughts only she was privy to. The air in the room grew so thick, Allie could feel the pressure on her skin. When Monica spoke again, there was wrenching sadness in her voice.

"Everyone loved our father. He and Beck were so close. Beck idolized him." Monica laughed softly, remembering. "Tried to emulate his father in every way, his walk, his manner of speech."

It was true. Jonathan Williams had been an enormous presence, admired and respected by everyone he came in contact with. Allie could still see them together, father and son. The way they leaned in a little bit when speaking to someone, the same crooked grin, charm and charisma personified. They even sat their horses the same way, comfortable in the saddle, body moving in rhythm with the horse, reins held just so.

Monica sighed heavily, her eyes moist with held-back tears. "It would have killed Daddy to know that Beck didn't follow in his footsteps and become a lawyer." Her gaze, overflowing with meaning, bored into Allie.

"If Daddy wasn't already dead, that is."

So there it was, what she'd really come to say. What had been on Monica's mind from the beginning was finally out in the open. Memories began prodding at Allie like sharp finger pokes.

Monica went on. "When they found him at the bottom of that pool, Beck wanted to die, too."

In one fleeting moment, the night Allie had spent years trying to forget came back to her, opening old scarred-over wounds. Her own pain was tolerable, but she could see that the agony she'd caused others was too awful to face. Beck's and Monica's. And their mother's, too. She swallowed hard.

"Look, Monica, I didn't—"

"You were with him."

"Yes, but—"

"You were the last one to see him alive."

"Yes, but I didn't know—"

"You should be in jail."

"The medical examiner said—"

"But we both know the truth, don't we?"

Their eyes locked, and Allie wondered not for the first time how much Monica really did know about that night.

"Your father died of a heart attack."

"Because you pushed him into the pool," Monica said.

The words were so weighty, so full of substance, Allie could almost see them coming out of Monica's mouth, one after the other like a freight train bearing down on her.

Because you pushed him into the pool.

The silence that followed fairly sizzled, until broken at last by the extreme slow-motion sound of a vehicle braking to a stop

123

out front, a car door slamming, and footsteps pounding the planked porch. When time began moving forward at normal speed again, the door flew open and Davy rushed in.

"Allie! Beck bought me a bike! Look, come see." Davy, his face beaming, his ears sticking out under hair freshly cut, came in the door followed by Beck, whose wide smile was instantly wiped away by the tension in the room.

He flicked a glance at Allie, then Monica. "What's wrong?"

Chin lifted, shoulders straight, Monica stalked out, the slam of the front door resounding like a cannon shot throughout the cabin.

Davy stared open-mouthed, his initial excitement all but deflated. "Is she mad at me?"

"No, of course she's not mad at you," said Allie, putting great effort into her smile. "She's just upset about something. Let's have a look at that new bike."

Davy, animated again, took her hand and pulled her outside.

"Come on. Beck let me pick out any color I wanted. I picked red. Do you like it?"

"I love it," she said, admiring the bike.

Beck came to stand beside her. "But you shouldn't have," she whispered.

"But I wanted to," he told her. "Come on, Davy, let's see you ride it."

But Davy was already astride, pedaling on the hard-packed dirt, circling in front of them. "Look, it's got fat tires. Beck said he'd take me trail riding sometime, didn't you, Beck?"

"Yep. I did, and we will. But not today. You can practice riding on the ranch roads, but don't go out of sight of the cabin. Okay? I have to talk to Allie about something."

Davy slowed and braked, his eyes becoming guarded again. "About me?"

"No, not about you. About grown-up stuff."

124

"About Monica? And her being mad all the time?"

"Hey, kid," Beck said, with a reassuring smile. "Don't worry about it. And don't go out of sight of the cabin," he reminded.

"Okay."

They watched Davy pedal away, then Beck took Allie's arm and led her inside where she dropped into a chair. She felt like the bones in her body had dissolved.

Beck faced her. "What happened?"

"I found something on the Internet," she said, knowing perfectly well he meant what happened with Monica, but she wasn't ready to talk about that with him.

Her redirection worked. "What did you find?" he asked.

She told him what she'd read about Mark Medora and Sammy Oberski.

"Sammy's an old boyfriend," she explained. "He took one of my credit cards. I forgot to call VISA to report it. Then, well, after that, I didn't have a chance to." Just one of the many things left unattended after she went on the run.

Beck thought a moment, realization dawning. "That detective thought he was trailing you."

She nodded.

"Would Sammy have any idea you might be here?"

"I don't see how."

"Well, if it wasn't that detective, who was it that was chasing you?" Beck's voice grew impatient. "Who followed you to Cortez?"

She shrugged. "I don't know," she replied mournfully.

"Goddammit, Allie, think. Who has a grudge against you? What do they want?"

"Well, goddammit, Beck, if I knew who it was and what they wanted, don't you think I'd have given it to them by now?" she snapped back.

He paused, calming himself, thinking about that. "Maybe it's

125

not you. Maybe it's Davy."

"What?"

"Maybe someone wants Davy." Then, "Does Monica know? Is that what she was mad about? Why she stormed out?"

"No. She doesn't know anything about it. At least, I don't think she does." Allie hesitated, then said, "She . . . she still blames me for what happened at the country club . . ."

"Oh," he said.

A profound pause followed, and if she hadn't been watching him so closely, she wouldn't have seen an infinitesimal shadow of doubt move behind his eyes, there in an instant and just as quickly gone.

"Look," she said into the silence. "It was a mistake coming here. Another bad decision on my part. I've disrupted your work. Your life." As she said it, she couldn't derail a sidelong glance in the direction of the answering machine. He caught it and followed her gaze, then hiked his brows in question, curiosity in his eyes.

"Someone called," she said. "You have a message."

"Who was it?"

When she didn't answer, he reached for the PLAY button and pressed it. Allie sat in glum silence while Jazzy's voice filled the room again.

When the message ended, Beck pressed his lips together, looked up at the ceiling and gave a cheerless little chuckle, then shook his head and heaved a sigh, but said nothing.

She watched his face. He was more handsome, more magnetic than she remembered. He'd borne the years well. The lines faintly etched around his eyes by the sun added to his attractiveness, and gave him a rugged, steely look.

"Do you love her?" Allie asked into the deepening void, and was immediately ashamed. "Never mind. Don't answer that."

"We, um . . ." He held her glance only for a moment before

126

he looked away in that awkward way men do when they're compelled to talk about something they don't want to talk about. After a bit more stalling, he spoke. "There was a time I thought I did."

His answer gave her heart a serious hitch and she tried not to grimace.

He was looking at her now, his expression guarded. "Did you love Paul?" he countered.

Good question, and one she'd asked herself at least a hundred times before she could answer it honestly even to herself. "No, I guess not."

"Then why did you marry him?"

"Love had nothing to do with it. It was just time." She sighed, then went on, feeling compelled to explain the complicated feelings she had about Paul. "I thought he was a good man. I respected his work. He treated me well . . ." And I didn't think I'd ever see you again, she thought but didn't say. "I wanted children. So did he. He loved kids." Then she shrugged. "It didn't happen."

He let that pass without comment.

Her gaze slid to his mouth, and she studied his lips awhile. "Monica said you were going to marry Jazzy." She stumbled a bit saying the name out loud.

A brief pause, a head shake. "We talked about it," he admitted, "but . . ." He shrugged and his words trailed off.

"But you are going to marry her. Eventually." She meant it to be a question, didn't want it to come out the way it did, like a foregone conclusion.

"She travels. She's a paleontologist." He said it as if it was some kind of an explanation for something, but she didn't know what.

Her eyes poured over him, demanding more than she had a right to know.

127

"I met her at one of my lectures. She'd read an article I wrote and came to see me."

Allie smiled sadly. Why not? He belonged on a *Hunks of the National Forests* calendar. He probably even had his own set of groupies, girls and women who showed up at all his lectures. She was pretty sure she couldn't write Jazzy off as merely one of them.

"We dated and spent time together, and people just sort of expected something to come of it. But she's busy with her work, and I'm busy with mine, and . . ." Again he lost words, but quickly found them. "And I don't want you to leave," he said with finality.

He reached out and put his hands on her shoulders, and gently pulled her out of her chair and up against him. His mouth came down on hers. He held her crushed against his body, her hands and arms pinned between them. His lips softened and he kissed her gently again and again, incredibly sweet kisses. The warmth of his kisses, the smell of his skin, the hardness of his body were intoxicating. Then his mouth became more urgent, she tasted his tongue with hers and his lips continued caressing her lips until she thought she would go mad, yet she wanted the madness to go on.

She wanted to sit on him and wrap her legs around him, and bury his face in her breasts, and feel nothing but the deepest physical part of her sated. When at last he lifted his head they were holding each other close, breathing each other's being, searching each other's eyes for confirmation. *Did you feel what I felt? Was it like before?*

Voices shouting from outside pulled them out of their embrace. Through the window, they saw Davy jump off his bike and let it fall to the ground.

"Allie!" The door burst open and he rushed in, eyes wide, cheeks flushed. He headed full tilt toward her, reaching out, and she opened her arms to him.

"What's the matter? What's wrong?"

Monica sailed in close behind, carrying Sadie the Schnauzer in her arms.

"You stay away from my dog," she demanded, glaring at Davy.

Allie pulled him closer, and he tightened his arms around her waist.

"I didn't do it. Honest. I wasn't stealing Sadie."

Monica began shouting again, but Beck interceded. "Hold it. What's going on?"

"Him!" Monica's voice rose in pitch as she glared at Davy and pointed an accusing finger in his face. "He let Sadie out while I was in the garage getting something out of my car."

"I did not! Honest, Allie, I didn't."

"Don't you ever touch her again," Monica yelled. "Do you hear me?"

"Monica, they can hear you in New Mexico," Beck said evenly, holding up his hand to stem the tide. "Calm down. Stop shouting." He turned to Davy. "It's okay, Davy. Take a breath."

Seething, Monica pressed stubborn lips in a tight line. Davy hung on to Allie and gulped back tears.

"Now," Beck said. "One at a time. What happened?" He looked at his sister, letting her go first.

"I came out of the garage and saw the back door open and Davy holding Sadie. He was taking her."

"Is that true?" Allie asked Davy, looking down at him.

"No," he said, in a quivery voice. "I mean, yes, but I wasn't taking her and I didn't let her out. She was already out. The door was open a little, and she must have squeezed through. I saw her running down the driveway toward the road, and when I called her, she came right to me. I picked her up and was petting her." He glanced at Beck before he continued. "I was going to put her back in the house. That's when she saw me and yelled."

Monica said nothing, but stood her ground, the expression on her smooth, unlined face was obstinate.

"Is Sadie hurt?" Beck asked her.

Monica took a moment to give the dog a quick going over. "No," she relented. "She seems fine."

He turned to Davy. "How about you? Are you all right?"

Davy nodded slowly.

"Then no harm done." Beck looked at his sister. "Right? No harm done?"

Her reply was curt and sullen. "Not this time, anyway," she conceded. "I trust there won't be a next time."

After Monica left, the cabin itself seemed to breathe a sigh of relief.

Tentatively, Davy asked, "Can I go outside and ride my bike?"

"Yes, you can," Allie answered, running her hand over his head, smoothing the cowlick that despite the new haircut sprouted up in back. "But don't go up to the main house, and don't bother Monica."

"I won't," Davy replied in all seriousness, eyes wide, meaning it. "I promise."

"Later, if everybody's in the mood after dinner," Beck said, "I'll challenge you both to a game of Monopoly before bedtime."

"Deal," said Allie with enthusiasm.

Davy nodded excitedly. "Cool," he said, reaching up to smack hands with Beck in a huge high-five.

Okay, time to reevaluate, Allie decided that night before falling asleep. Like magic, the decision put the steel back in her spine. Fear and self-doubt died in her chest like a fever that had run its course.

It had been an emotionally draining day, but also a noteworthy one whose greatest significance was not the appearance on the scene of Jazzy whatever-her-name-was, but rather what the Internet had revealed. Namely, that Mark Medora, apparently still bent on revenge, had followed a false trail to Florida, and, she assumed, there reached a dead end.

That, along with the absence of any missing child alerts—though why CPS hadn't notified the FBI was a puzzle—signified there was a good chance her trail had gone cold. Taken together, that probably meant they were safe where they were.

For the moment, anyway.

Lots of people came to tiny mountain towns or other remote pockets of the West to chill out, space out, or hide out. And that was fairly easy to do here given the local population's proclivity for minding their own business. It didn't mean there wasn't still danger, but hopefully whatever and whoever it was had been left behind in Cortez.

Regular meals, plenty of sleep, and time to reflect had rejuvenated her both physically and mentally. No longer operating in panic mode, she was able to think more clearly.

Never before had she run away from trouble; some would say she sought it out. It was true that in her youth Beck pulled her out of jams when she got stuck, but she later learned to deal with her own messes.

But that was when she was alone. She'd only run this time because she had a child in her care.

Now it was time to stop running and figure out who was doing the chasing. That's what made it so dangerous—the not knowing.

At least now she knew who it wasn't. It wasn't a rogue cop bent on revenge, and it wasn't the FBI with handcuffs in her size. Not yet.

The Four Corners was the kind of place you could pretend parts of your life had never existed. It was a place to start over, begin anew, carve out a new identity. And it was time she did that.

If she laid low and remained vigilant, no one would find her in Durango. No one knew she grew up here. After she left, she'd avoided mentioning it. The safe haven of the ranch would allow her to expend her energies searching for answers instead of jumping at shadows. To be sure, there were obstacles to staying put. Monica was one, but Allie was sure she could handle that. As for the other, she'd have to learn to deal with Jazzy, which was going to take real courage. The courage to love Beck all the while knowing she might end up having to give him up to Jazzy. He said he'd loved Jazzy once. That love could bloom again.

Allie stared at the moon shadows making shapes on the ceiling. Maybe she'd been a damn fool to come here, and maybe she was a damn fool to stay, but there were worse things than being a damn fool. Dead was one. Failing to protect a child was another.

For Davy's sake, she had to create some semblance of normalcy until she had the answers she needed to put everything back on track.

Later, she dreamed about Davy's new bike. It was red and shiny and had fat tires, and Davy rode around on it for hours, which was a very strange thing because, in the dream, the bike was connected to a chain attached to the front porch.

CHAPTER ELEVEN

The rooftop patio of the High Country Brewhaus and Bar overlooked a busy intersection and was perfect for people watching, which was exactly why Millie Worthey chose it. She just hadn't expected it to be quite so busy.

In fact, she hadn't expected Durango to be what it was, either. Never having been there, or anywhere out west, she'd imagined small town Colorado to be a quiet two-lane highway bypass populated by sun-bronzed farmers, rugged cowboys, and shoot-that-varmint locals. What she'd found was an upscale ski town bursting at the seams with high-net-worth interlopers, and the inevitable growth and development that followed.

That wasn't to say there were no cowboys. She'd seen some sitting on barstools at Scootin' Boots, their butts encased in skintight Wranglers, their stomachs hard as boards under big belt buckles, or walking the main drag with their dusty full-length trail coats billowing out behind. But those cowboys were all hat and no cattle, with attitude to spare, whose sweat-stained hats were custom made and cost large sums, whose age-creased boots were handcrafted of imported leathers and skins.

Almost everyone else wore whatever, faded and worn, some torn, tee shirts and jeans and cutoffs, but a close second look revealed designer labels stitched into the seams of nearly every garment. This underfunded look everyone seemed to be trying for was further given the lie by the number of expensive SUVs on the streets and at the curbs, and by the amount of daytime money spent at saloons like the one Millie was sitting in.

When she'd first arrived in Durango, she immediately took steps to tone down her personal style, which she saw right away would be considered flamboyant by local standards. Off came the heavy makeup she favored even in the daytime, opting instead for a lightly powdered natural look. Except for the false eyelashes, she kept those. Next, the big hair was combed out and tied back in a ponytail. The last thing she wanted was to be noticed. The success of her assignment depended on her fading into the background.

Which actually came quite easy to Millie. By necessity and by design, she'd become adept at blending into the circumstances of life as they altered course. Flexibility had become a personal strength. In her past, littered with the remnants of hopeless poverty, bitterly poor judgment, and the struggle to survive, she'd waited tables, stripped in a gentlemen's club, talked dirty as a phone sex operator, and once or twice run some weed into Canada. While still in her twenties, she'd decided to try prostitution, but was arrested her very first night. That particular indignity propelled her into the military where she learned hand-to-hand combat, and mastered the intricacies of computer technology, skills she later taught at martial arts studios and junior colleges in and around Detroit.

When she met Reverend Jackson Worthey, it was these last two proficiencies he found particularly irresistible in her and useful to him, but she had other qualities he valued. For one thing, she never inquired about the nature of his non-church business activities. For another, she was available to him at all times and catered to his every whim, in bed or out, at the Church of Spiritual Light compound. For all those reasons, he was inspired to marry her twenty-eight days after laying eyes on her in the front row of his sanctuary, where she'd come determined to turn over another new leaf. Going to church had worked better than she'd expected, and quicker, too.

Being the wife of a preacher was a huge step up for Millie, and as such, she tried, though not always successfully, to conduct herself with dignity and restraint, curtailing her tendency to act impulsively and quenching her penchant for sudden rage. In the process, she had learned a valuable lesson. She had learned that patience was often rewarded.

And now, appropriately dressed down, Millie was in Durango at the request of her husband, patiently waiting.

From where she sat at her rooftop table she could see the intersection of Eighth and Main on her right and, to her left, the entrances to a couple of art galleries and a newly built three-story office condominium. Directly across the way, running perpendicular into the street, what used to be an alley was now a picturesque tumbled-brick walkway leading to a fashionable boutique, a couple of outdoor cafés, and a hair salon. Rumor had it that sooner or later everyone passed within eyesight of the High Country Brewhaus and Bar, so that's where Millie spent most of her time looking for Allie Hudson.

So far, Allie had proved elusive. The men sent by Reverend Worthey to search Allie's house and cottage in Michigan had made a mess of it, found nothing, and, in the end, one of them had landed in the emergency room needing stitches. Later, when they caught up to her and lost her in Omaha all in the same night, Reverend Worthey had summoned them back to Michigan and called on Millie's expertise.

Millie went directly to the one source she was sure would provide the most and best information. Allie's home computer.

A check of the hard-drive history revealed hundreds of hits on one particular web site, which gave her the name of Beck Williams, and ultimately led her to the Cortez Cultural Center. Her instincts had been right on. Millie had already been there when Allie arrived with the kid, both of them looking like something the cat dragged in.

Reverend Worthey—everyone called him that, even her—had been most unhappy about her blasting into the motel room the way she did, but she'd only been trying to scare them, flush them out so that in the confusion she could grab the boy and be gone. Unfortunately, it hadn't worked out that way, and then she'd lost them when they disappeared off the highway. She had a license number, though.

Next day, through persistence and subterfuge—by pretending to be an insurance investigator—she had persuaded the young Navajo girl at the registration desk to pull a guest card and slide it across the counter so Millie could peek at the address. Regrettably, it showed a post office box instead of a physical address, but the line asking for a license plate number was filled in, and it matched the number she'd made note of, the one belonging to Beck Williams.

After a few days spent crisscrossing county roads in her rental car, Millie gave up looking for the Wild Horse Mesa Ranch. She didn't stop to ask any of the neighboring ranchers for directions, either. These folks probably looked after each other, and strangers asking questions would set off all kinds of alarms. Instead of risking that, she hung out in Durango waiting to spot Allie and the kid.

Millie tipped her glass, finishing its contents, and was getting ready to order another when her gaze snagged on a blonde wearing sunglasses emerging from the glorified alleyway across the street and below. The woman stopped at the curb and looked in both directions as if deciding which way to go.

Millie regarded the woman somberly. The hair was wrong, and she was too thin, but the height was about right and the heart-shaped face looked familiar. Still, she couldn't be sure. Quickly, Millie threw some money on the table and, ignoring the two half-shot old-timers sitting at the end of the bar trying to catch her attention, headed down the stairs to take a closer look.

Allie walked out of Back Alley Hair Design, which she thought a rather inelegant name for such a fashionable hair salon, feeling thinner and taller, the way she always felt after getting her hair done. It had been cut and colored by a gorgeous young thing with a tiny gold stud in her tongue and an emerald chip stuck high on the side of her nose, wearing a cropped tee shirt, no bra, and low-rise jeans. Very low-rise. Allie had gotten an up close and personal look at the gold ring that pierced her navel. When she spotted it, she cringed away, feeling a sharp poke in her own belly.

Deciding it was best to stay as unrecognizable as possible, Allie had opted for close-cropped and champagne colored, a look unlike the fiery flowing auburn that had defined her in the past. Besides evading whoever it was looking for her, she wanted to avoid any old acquaintances she might encounter on the street.

Beck had let her drive the Hummer into town—she hadn't yet figured out what to do about a driver's license—and since he'd insisted on paying her to work for him, she had a little money in her purse. She stood at the curb trying to decide if she should have lunch, go shopping, or head directly back to the ranch.

Squinting, she glanced up at the High Country Brewhaus and Bar, then looked at her watch. Mentally she checked off items on her errand list. She'd already stopped at Wal-Mart to return some of the clothes Beck had bought for Davy, replacing them with the proper size, and while there purchased a new Monopoly game for Davy's birthday and some makeup for herself. She'd picked up inkjet refills at Office Depot for Beck's printers, used his Blockbuster card to rent some movies for

Davy, and stopped for coffee beans at Grinders Coffee Company.

Beck had taken Davy out to shoot pictures and to count foals for his spring census report to the BLM. They weren't expected to return until dinner time, but if she hurried, she could take a quick walk through town and peek in some of the new shops.

Ignoring the beginnings of hunger pangs, she turned left, then right on Main, and began walking, sneaking sideways peeks at her image in the windows of the storefronts as she went by. She'd made a good choice. Blonde suited her. She'd always hated being stereotyped as tempestuous and fiery and any number of other insulting nicknames attached to redheads, even if some of them were a little bit true about her. But no one would recognize her now. She almost didn't recognize herself.

She hardly recognized the town, either. In her absence, Durango's old mining town ambience had been overlaid with a veneer of Ralph Lauren trendiness. Starbuck's had taken up residence near the movie theater, and so far she'd counted four Internet cafes. New furniture stores and art galleries had sprung up, and there was a French bakery on the corner of Ninth. The number of real estate offices seemed to have doubled, and so had the prices of the available properties pictured in the windows.

Wooden benches lined the fronts of ski shops and upscale boutiques, some of them occupied by suntanned, bandannaed young men with big shaggy dogs on leashes. She pretended not to see them, avoiding eye contact, uncomfortable if she thought anyone was taking particular notice of her, until she realized they weren't recognizing her, they were admiring her. She relaxed, slowed her breathing and her gait.

A bulletin board in the window of a store she'd never seen before called High Country Traders—Supplies for the Counterculture—caught her eye. Index cards and scraps of paper were tacked up advertising rooms and apartments for rent, requests for rides to Jackson Hole or Taos, used books and furniture for sale, pleas for the return of lost dogs and cats, and invitations to join yoga classes. Curious, she entered the shop.

The woman sitting on a stool behind the counter by the door had peach-colored skin and vanilla hair falling straight over her back and shoulders. She didn't have a teaspoon of fat on her, and Allie would have bet money the woman would say she didn't eat anything with a face. She was dressed in the fashion of sixties hippies in a loose flowing dress, draped about her shoulders with scarves and beads. Allie wouldn't have been surprised to learn that the woman had woven the cloth on her own loom and dyed it with the juice of roots and berries grown behind the store. She was braceleted up to the elbow with silver that jangled when she moved. However, she wasn't moving very much; she was watching a story on CNN about the environmental dangers of oil drilling in Alaska.

The store smelled of sandalwood or patchouli, Allie wasn't sure which—she never could tell them apart. Racks made from pipe were hung with garments reminiscent of the counterculture era, dresses and long skirts made from hemp and other natural fibers, flowy, gauzy tops in earth colors, some with gypsy ruffles. Allie dragged hangers along the pipe racks, and after some deliberation, she selected several styles and headed for a fitting room. She decided on a dress in a shade of amethyst, a color she never would have chosen as a redhead, and picked out a pair of dangly earrings. As she was paying for her purchases, she felt a sudden drop in the pit of her stomach when her eye caught the news item scrolling across the bottom of the television screen below the talking head.

The body found in the Detroit River has been identified as 28-year-old Michigan woman Marie Lopez. Authorities are following several leads and seeking the whereabouts of the woman's husband as a person of interest.

A bubble of nausea rose to Allie's throat, and she held her breath to contain it, her eyes frozen on the television screen.

"Receipt?"

"What?"

"Here's your change. Do you want your receipt in the bag?" The skinny clerk was looking at Allie quizzically, holding out some coins in her translucent fingers.

"Oh. Yes." Allie grabbed her purchase and her change, and hurried out the door.

Millie, seated on the barstool closest to the window at Scootin' Boots almost choked when she saw the blonde run out the door of that hippie shop across the street. The sunglasses were off now, and Millie's heart quickened at the sight of the familiar face. Millie set her bottle down hard, snatched a ten off the stack of bills on the bar, leaving the ones, and hurried out to the sidewalk.

Crowds on the sidewalk had grown, and Millie darted between pedestrians in her mad dash, keeping her eye on the woman, who was also dodging pedestrians on the opposite side of the street. The woman stopped at the crosswalk at Seventh and when she turned to look for oncoming cars, Millie got a good look. It was Allie Hudson. The boy wasn't with her, but Millie had no doubt he was somewhere close by.

At the public parking lot behind the movie theater, Millie saw Allie get into a black Hummer. Millie made a note of the license number and grinned. It was Beck Williams' SUV.

Millie's rental car was still parked at the High Country Brewhaus and Bar, so she had to run back two blocks to get it. Luckily, Allie got caught at the light near Albertson's supermarket, allowing Millie to catch up two cars behind and then follow the Hummer along the state highway through thickly wooded mountains whose tops disappeared into weather, the slopes beginning to drop into shadow.

CHAPTER TWELVE

Beck, riding a big strawberry roan, and Davy, on a small gentle mare, threaded their way up a rock-strewn ravine, past fir trees and a deadfall. They stopped and scanned the northern rangeland.

Davy pointed. "There," he said. "I see some."

Beck lifted binoculars to his eyes, then handed them to Davy. "How many foals do you see?"

Davy looked, adjusted the focus, and studied the band. "Two. No, three."

Beck nodded. "What color?"

"It looks like two brown and one sort of spotted. White and light brown."

"Good." Beck made a note in his field book, closed it, and returned it to his saddlebag.

Davy handed the binoculars back and stared wistfully at the horses in the distance. "I wish . . ."

"What?"

"I wish I could have a foal, take it back to the ranch with us," Davy said.

"They're pretty young. You wouldn't want to take it away from its band would you? A band is like its family."

"With a mother and father?"

"Well, yes. Every band has a lead mare and a dominant stallion. That's sort of like a mother and a father. The lead mare makes sure all the other horses get water and food, and that the babies are taken care of. The dominant male is like the daddy horse. He protects everyone in the family. That's why we can't get too close, especially now that there are foals. He might get mad if he thinks we're threatening them."

Davy studied the horses. "Is that him in front?"

"No, that's the lead mare. See? She's taking them to that water hole."

"Where's the daddy?"

"He follows along behind, ready to fight off attacks from coyotes or mountain lions. Or sometimes dogs."

"Or people?"

"Sometimes people."

Davy thought a minute. "Well, I wouldn't hurt them, and I don't think Sadie would, either."

Beck chuckled lightly at his mention of Monica's dog. "No, but they might hurt Sadie. She's an inside dog, not an outside dog."

They'd been out most of the morning while Allie went into town. She'd let her guard down enough that he'd gotten her to agree to get out of the house, gladly letting her drive the Hummer even though she didn't have a driver's license, because it finally gave him the opportunity to be alone with Davy. Helping with the horse census was only one of the reasons he'd brought Davy out in the field with him this day. The other reason was to pump him for information, see if he could fill in the blanks.

Because none of it fit. No Amber Alerts issued by authorities, no mention at all of a missing child, and it had been weeks. Then the police trailing Allie's credit card purchases to a dead end. So what or who did that leave on her trail? He needed to know what was going on, and hoped Davy could add something that would give him a clue.

They made their way across arroyos and along switchback deer trails that zigzagged up to the ridgeline. Beck let Davy go ahead of him so he could keep his eye on the boy along the difficult terrain. Davy had progressed quickly in the riding lessons under Jobby Bones' tutelage, and now sat solid in the saddle, confidently guiding the mare along the trail.

"How are you holding up?" Beck asked. "Do you want to stop and rest? Or if you're up to it, we can ride to the top of the mesa and have lunch. There's lots of sage and saltbrush, and the horses like to graze on it."

"I want to go to the top."

"Okay."

They guided their horses up a gently undulating path. At the top, they rode slowly along an animal trail looking for signs of the herd. The faded ghost of a road forked out through clumps of brittlebush, sun-dried grass and weeds, then disappeared on the other side of a streambed. In the shade of an overhanging ridge, they dismounted and stretched their legs.

Davy found an old horse skull in the brush, and he picked it up and turned it in his hands. Frail and brittle, bleached white from the sun, a run of sand spilled out when he turned it over. He looked up at Beck. A light sprinkle of freckles peppered his nose and checks, and there was a question in his blue eyes.

Beck took a stab at an explanation. "Sometimes the horses don't make it." He didn't know how much Davy knew about death, wasn't sure he wanted to be the one to explain it now, but he went ahead.

"It's a hard life out here for them," he said. "They share the land with predators, coyotes, mountain lions. Bears. And only the strongest can live through the winters. There's not as much food then, and it gets pretty cold."

"Too bad you don't have room for them all in your barn." Davy replaced the horse skull and rubbed his hands together, dusting off the sand.

Beck opened his saddlebags and took out their lunch,

wrapped sandwiches and bottled water, and they sat on the ground to eat.

Davy took a big bite of his sandwich, chased it with a swallow of water, then wiped his mouth with the sleeve of his shirt. "This is just like the cowboys did it in the Old West, isn't it?"

"Uh huh," Beck answered.

Davy took another bite and chewed thoughtfully. "How many foals have we counted so far?"

"Seventeen. That's quite a lot. The herd is getting pretty big. Might have to have an adoption this fall."

Davy dropped his hands to his lap, still holding the half sandwich, and looked at Beck. "An adoption? For horses? Horses get adopted? I thought only kids got adopted."

"No, horses, too." Beck chewed and swallowed. "They get rounded up, then people adopt them and take them home to care for them."

Davy stared at him. "You mean anybody can do that?"

"Just about. Ranchers, farmers, anybody who promises to gentle it and take care of it can adopt one."

Davy thought about this. "Does it cost a lot of money?"

"Not much. There's a small adoption fee. Maybe a hundred and fifty dollars or so."

Davy ate silently, thinking this over. "Is a hundred and fifty dollars more than a truckload?"

Beck looked at him. "A truckload of what? Money?" He laughed, trying to remember what a truckload of money looked like to a seven-year-old. "No. I wouldn't say so. Why?"

Davy shook his head. "No reason. I just wondered," he said, silence settling in. Then, "If I adopted one, could I keep it at your ranch after Allie and I leave? That way I could come and visit it sometimes."

"You're leaving? Where are you going?"

Davy shook his head. "I don't know for sure, but Allie says

145

we can't stay here."

"Don't you like it here?"

"Oh, yeah. I like it here. A lot. But Allie says we have to leave."

"What do you think about that?"

Davy shrugged. "I dunno."

"Doesn't Allie like it here?"

Davy shrugged again. "She didn't say, but I think she does. It's just that . . ."

"What?"

"Someone's after us."

"How do you know that?"

"They chased us in a car."

"Do you know who it is?"

Davy shook his head.

"Davy, do you want to talk about what happened when you left Michigan?"

Davy was silent.

"Allie doesn't want me to."

"But Allie asked me to help. I can't help unless I know the whole story."

Beck let a longish silence go by, then gradually led Davy back through the questions that had been bothering him.

"What happened when you got back to Allie's house, after you left the cottage?"

"I'm not sure. Allie went in first, because I was sleeping in the car, but then she ran out and we left right away. She told me later that my mother told her to take me away and take care of me."

"Do you know who was there? At the house?"

Davy shook his head. "Allie was real scared, though. Some men chased us, but it was dark so we couldn't see their faces. She said she thought they had a gun. She had a gun, too."

"How many men were there?"

"Two, I think. One jumped on her car and put his hand on her face, and squeezed. Like this." He demonstrated, pressing the fingertips of one hand into his cheeks, squishing his lips into a vertical fishface.

"What did she do?"

Instead of answering, Davy cast his eyes down, and looked away.

"What did she do, Davy?" Beck prodded.

"She drove real fast. And she bit his finger. She tried to put her fingernails in his eyes, but he fell off." He paused a moment, his expression pinched. "Then somebody else chased us in a car. I was real scared. So was Allie. We hid in the parking lot under the mall. She thought they weren't chasing us anymore, so she drove back to her lake house, but when we got there, somebody was there, too."

Almost without emotion, Davy related their cross-country journey. Beck listened without interrupting or asking questions, trying to pick up any nuance that might throw light on the identity of their pursuers. But there was nothing new in Davy's version of what happened; it only confirmed what Allie had already told him.

When Davy finished, he asked, "Do you think they followed us here?"

"No. I don't. And I don't want you to worry about it."

"Why?"

"Because that's my job."

Davy thought about that a moment, then nodded. "Well, anyway, Allie said we can't stay here. So when I get the money, can I adopt one of those horses and keep him here?"

"Sure," Beck said. "Sure you can."

Purple clouds stacked up, and the smell of rain was on the breeze. The light was fading, the afternoon drawing on, too late to take any more pictures.

"Let's head on back. Allie should be home from town by now. I think she went to get her hair and her nails done."

"Why? She's already pretty."

"Yes," said Beck. "She's beautiful."

"You like her, huh?"

"Yeah. I like her."

"Me, too. Before we go back, can I pick some wildflowers for her?"

"Sure, she'd love that."

"I'll pick some for Monica, too. Maybe that will make her happy."

Beck waited while Davy, taking his time and making his selections carefully, picked wildflowers. That kid is something, thought Beck, adaptable and nearly fearless. Even Monica didn't intimidate him, and she could curl the toes of just about any man she met, and probably had. But Davy seemed determined to win her over. Of course, it might be because he wanted access to Sadie. So he was smart, too, thought Beck, amused.

Davy gathered a bouquet bigger than he could manage, so Beck tucked some of the flowers into his saddlebags, blooms protruding, and they cantered off.

They crested the top of a steep rise and entered a shallow basin, surprising a small band of horses. The horses startled and galloped away, all except the stallion who tossed his head and snorted and took a defensive stance.

Beck and Davy quickly reined in, drawing up their horses. Beck reached out to take hold of the bridle of Davy's mare. The mustang snorted a few times and pawed the dirt, then stood his ground, curious about the newcomers, but ready to defend. The band had stopped a few hundred yards away and turned to watch, gathering close together.

"Hold still," Beck told Davy, his voice barely above a whisper.

Davy froze, but couldn't take his eyes off the animal. Fascinated, his eyes shining, he stared at the stallion who stared back at him.

"Don't move," Beck warned.

If Davy panicked, made a fast move, there was no telling what the mustang would do. Their natural instinct was to run from humans, but they were sometimes surly and unpredictable. Beck had seen them protect themselves and the band by thrusting out hammer-like hooves that drove with the power of a pneumatic sledge.

Beck's horse blew out a snuffle and shifted his weight, causing the saddle to creak lightly, but otherwise stood in place. After a few tense moments, the mustang, big and black with a battle scar on his hind quarters, advanced, nostrils flaring, sniffing at Davy's horse. The mare sniffed back, stretching her neck until their noses almost touched. Suddenly the mustang whinnied, then wheeled and galloped toward the band that turned as one and galloped away down the slope, throwing up a swirling cloud of dust.

Awestruck, Davy gazed after them. "Wow," he said, drawing out the word.

"Yeah," said Beck, letting out a sigh of relief, marveling at the boy's composure in a situation that could easily have had a disastrous outcome. "Wow."

CHAPTER THIRTEEN

No pressure.

That's what Beck had promised Allie. And time. Time to rest, time to clear her head, time to get grounded before taking the next step, whatever that was. But he was going to break that promise tonight. He had to. There were too many questions demanding answers.

Outside, storm clouds hovered low, taking the evening light from the sky. Beck could hear the murmur of Allie's voice drifting downstairs from Davy's room as she read him a bedtime story, her inflection rising and falling in the telling as the story called for. It was an age-old time of bonding usually reserved for mother and son, and Allie went to great lengths to honor the nightly ritual. He waited patiently for her to finish the story and come back downstairs so he could talk to her.

She'd been watching at the kitchen window when he and Davy returned from taking the foal census, and had waited there while they stabled the horses and put away the tack and gear. When they entered the house, she'd squared her shoulders and juiced up her smile, but Beck could tell there was a lot of effort behind it. Something had happened. She was hiding something. He laughed to himself. So what else was new?

With Allie, he'd never been surprised by the unexpected, but her showing up with Davy the way she had, on the run and scared senseless, well, that was something he could never have imagined.

He didn't want her to leave again, and he wanted to be jubilant about her reappearance, but he couldn't get past all the loose ends. At that, his mind jumped to Jazzy, because she was undoubtedly one of them.

The timing of her phone call couldn't have been worse. He'd tried to explain Jazzy to Allie, and done a piss-poor job of it because he hadn't been able to come right out and say he wasn't sure how Jazzy fit into his life, and hadn't been sure even before Allie's return.

For years, he'd waited to hear from Allie. After he'd worked through the pain of losing both her and his father at the same time, he'd had full intentions of keeping his heart and emotions open for her return. That didn't mean there hadn't been other women. There had, but now when he tried to think of the name or face of just one, the only one who came to mind was Jazzy.

His relationship with Jazzy, though sexually satisfying, had been mellow and emotionally undemanding. Her work as a paleontologist consumed her, taking a lot of her time. She had many friends, mostly people she worked with, and when they got together, all they talked about was their work and the excavation projects that sometimes took them to the other side of the world. He'd respected Jazzy's dedication to her career and admired her passion for her work. Maybe, he thought now, that had been her appeal. Maybe her unavailability was what had attracted him, because it left room in his heart and his life for Allie.

He knew he'd have to decide what to do about Jazzy, but forced the thought back where it belonged. First things first. He needed answers and not just to all the new questions that had accompanied Allie's reappearance with Davy, but to some old ones, too.

Upstairs, storytime over, Davy was fighting sleep, retelling Allie about his day, speaking with childish animation. Beck pictured her up there sitting on the edge of his bed, listening intently, her eyes on Davy's as if what the child had to say was the most important thing in her life.

Allie, like most of the women he knew, was hardwired to nurture. Some doted on their children. Some, like Monica, lavished affection on a pet. But with Allie there was an instinctive, almost primal disregard for consequences or social conventions when it came to protecting kids, this one especially.

Her grim determination reminded him of a day in India when he saw a troop of furious monkeys bring traffic to a standstill after a baby monkey was hit by a car on a busy street. At least a hundred of the animals came running from all directions and encircled the injured infant as it lay listless on the road, its hind legs crushed. Chattering and screeching, some of the monkeys blocked off traffic, preventing Beck and the others from driving through the intersection for more than half an hour, as the monkeys tried to care for the baby primate by massaging its legs. Eventually, the animals left the scene, with one of the young females carrying the injured infant to safety. Allie was acting out of that same kind of single-minded instinct. Only she didn't have a hundred monkeys to help her. She was trying to do it alone.

The storm that had been threatening all day finally unleashed its fury. Rain hit the windows like a fire hose and tap-crashed on the metal overhangs of the front and back porches. He got up, stacked wood and kindling in the fireplace, and held a match to it. He stood watching the flames, but turned when Allie came in the room. She'd been preoccupied and distracted through dinner, and now her face was tight, her eyes shadowed with worry. He held his hand out to her, and when she took it, he drew her down beside him on the sofa. He loved her hair cut short and longed to nuzzle her ear. He wanted to bury his face in her breasts and taste her. All of her.

But she sat stiffly, her muscles tense.

"What is it?" he asked. "What's wrong?"

"Something's happened."

"What? Tell me."

"Davy's mother has been murdered."

Beck stared at her, momentarily speechless as he tried unsuccessfully to fit this new piece of information into what he already knew. "How do you know?"

"I heard it on the news this afternoon when I was in town. The police pulled her body out of the Detroit River." Her voice was even, but her eyes held a mixture of sorrow and fear.

He kept his face impassive, not wanting her to know the shock of unease that had flared within him. "Do they know who did it? And why?"

Allie shook her head. "There were no details, except they're looking for Davy's father. But I don't think he did it. He's a junkie, not a killer. It was someone else."

Beck was unable to respond for a moment as new uncertainties circled in his brain. "How does her murder fit into . . ." he gestured vaguely, helplessly, "into the rest of it?"

"I think it's connected to her phone call warning me to take Davy." She thought a moment. "But what does it have to do with the police, or Mark Medora?"

"Hell if I know," Beck said. Then, after a moment of thought added, "I'm not so sure it has anything to do with it. The police don't go around killing innocent people and throwing them in the river."

The rain was coming down harder now, and the wind blew a swath of it horizontally across the window. Thumping came from outside, the porch chair bouncing along the wooden decking, then down the steps pushed along by the sudden gust. Three jagged bolts of lightning hit the ground at once.

Allie sat, her face pensive, a decision being debated behind

153

her eyes. "I've got to tell Davy about his mother."

"Not yet," Beck said.

She started to argue, but he raised a finger stopping her. "Hear me out."

Frowning, she waited for him to go on.

"I think we need to wait until we have more information. What are you going to say? Your mother was murdered and thrown in the river? No. We need to know more. Whoever killed her might be planning the same for you. Or . . ." He paused to make sure she was listening.

She raised her eyebrows, signaling him to complete his thought.

"Or for Davy."

He let that sink in before going on. "We can't defend against adversaries who are hidden and faceless. We have to try to figure out who it is and what's going on."

In the end, she agreed to hold off telling Davy, but sat dejected, shoulders slumped, looking as frustrated as he felt.

He took both her hands in his. "Look. Let's go over everything again, from beginning to end, just the way it happened. Don't leave anything out. Maybe something will come to you that wasn't there before."

"Okay," she said, and taking a deep breath, began again, Beck interrupting to ask for clarification on points that didn't seem important before, but might be significant now. When she finished, a disappointed silence descended between them. Nothing new had surfaced, and nothing fit. There were still too many pieces missing.

Slowly, a memory whispered around the edges of Beck's mind as he recalled his conversation with Davy that afternoon about a truckload of money. He told Allie about it.

"This afternoon out on the mesa, Davy asked me how much it would cost to adopt one of the mustangs. He said he wanted to adopt one when he got the money. He didn't say *some* money. He said *the* money, like he already had some, or was going to get some. What did he mean by that?"

Allie shrugged and shook her head. "I don't know. His parents were dirt poor. They had nothing. I have no idea what he could have been talking about."

They fell into silence again, their thoughts turned inward. He reached for her, pulling her close, wrapping both arms around her. She tucked her feet up on the cushion and nestled into him, and they sat that way a long time, not speaking. Her body was warm against his, but soon the fire died and a chill penetrated the room.

He yawned, and then she yawned. "I'm worn out," she said raising sleepy eyes to his. "I can't think about this anymore. I'm going to bed."

He could not move his eyes from her face, her neck, her bare arms. He wanted to touch his finger to her earrings, jiggle them and make the shiny surfaces dance. They must be new. He didn't remember seeing her wear them before.

There were moments like now when the unsettling thoughts of the past stampeded through his mind devouring everything in its path. He needed to talk about that past, about why she had left, but now was not the time to drag those old skeletons from the closet. They had far more immediate concerns.

He stroked his hand up and down her arm. "Okay," he said, unwilling to let her go but knowing he had to. "See you in the morning."

She stood. "Good night."

He watched her walk up the steps, hating it that he needed her so much. He waited until he heard her door close, then he rose, stirred the glowing embers in the fireplace, turned out the lamp, and went upstairs to bed.

He dropped off in a few minutes, but woke instantly when

Allie's hand touched his mattress at the foot of his bed. He opened his eyes to see her standing there, looking lost and adrift, yearning in her eyes.

"Can I sleep in your bed?" she asked him.

He could almost feel the animal attraction vibrating between them. He had a sense of hovering on some sharp brink with a strong force pushing him from behind.

He lifted the covers and she crawled into the warm cave and lay down, her back to him, spooning into the curve of his body. He splayed his hand across her belly, gently pulling her closer against the ache in his groin.

Driven by a longing he couldn't control, he kissed the tender skin behind her ear, feeling her pulse against his lips, and without a word, she turned, slid her leg over his then pulled her nightgown above her knees and hiked herself over his hips, straddling him. He was hard instantly. She leaned down and kissed him on the mouth. He cupped her breasts, and she reached down and held him in her hand and lifted her hips slightly, widening her knees.

She put her face next to his, and he felt her eyelash brush his cheek as she closed her eyes, heard her quick intake of breath as he entered her, felt the warm exhale of her breath on his ear. He had the stomach dropping sensation that the two of them were falling through space together. He kissed her, tasted her, smelled her. He was awash in her essence, so full of her. She held him tighter, then tighter still, and made a sound of pure pleasure, her body moving against him, and Beck was sure in that moment that no evil could ever touch their lives.

At daybreak, they lay in silence, their arms around each other, their cheeks touching, their lips occasionally brushing like a whisper. He watched the numbers on the digital clock and concentrated on the smell of her skin, the smell of him on her skin, the smell of her on his hands.

Now she was here, but it was not like old times. He couldn't decide if everything had changed or if nothing had changed. They hadn't bothered to discuss the past, or what had gone wrong and how they could prevent it in the future. Who knew if they had a future?

She opened her eyes. Her hair stuck up in back from sleeping on it wrong.

"My arm is asleep," he said.

"Oh," she said, lifting her head. "Just a minute." She climbed on top of him and stretched out, pressing her breasts and hips against his body. "Is this better?" she asked.

"Not quite," he answered as he slid his knees between hers, spreading her legs and pulling her toward him, entering her again.

"This is better," he said.

CHAPTER FOURTEEN

Beck spent the next morning scouring Internet news sites for details of Marie's death, but found little. Wildfires in California had already knocked the story off the web sites and front pages. Even the Michigan news sources had dropped it. Murder of the underclass from poverty-stricken neighborhoods held little residual news value. Still, Allie made a point to monitor Davy's television watching just in case, urging him to read or watch movies instead.

Beck took Allie to his bed that night and the next and the next, even as he became increasingly torn about what the future held for them. He didn't like things the way they were now—she, guarded, with one foot out the door; he, fearing she would leave at any moment. That constant lurking dread about the future and the past overshadowed and plagued the present.

It was beginning to seem like a normal state of being, this feeling of always being caught off guard, always worried that some new and horrible problem was just around the corner. He didn't want to live without her, but he couldn't live a life of uncertainty with her, a life full of doubts and maybes and what-ifs.

The lingering scent of the pizza they'd had for dinner was still detectable as Beck finished walking through the house, checking windows and locking doors, going through the motions as he did every night. But the familiar end-of-day routine did nothing to relieve his increasing torment. In a bedroom across the hall from his, just yards from his bed, and sometimes in his bed, was the woman of his heart, but a woman of mystery, closed and secretive. A woman he might wake up to find had gone away in the night. A firestorm of emotion grew within him.

He hadn't thought he'd survive her leaving the first time. His father's death had devastated the family, tearing them apart, and by the time he'd surfaced from his grief, she was gone. Blind with misery and longing, all he'd wanted was to kiss her, hold her, make love to her. He was convinced her return would instantly erase the years of empty nights and lonely days.

But the circumstances of her return were so distressing, they had poisoned any joy he might feel at having her back. Even so, he couldn't bear the thought of losing her again.

He'd tried calling Jazzy, leaving messages on her cell phone and at her base camp at the Holiday Inn in Cheyenne. He was a little relieved that she had not yet returned his calls, because he wasn't exactly sure what he was going to say to her, or how he was going to say it. He'd been practicing the words in his mind, going over and over how to begin.

Jazzy, I have something to tell you. No, too blunt. There's this woman I used to know . . . No, that's not right, either. Look Jazzy, would you mind if we called off the wedding? Permanently? That might work, but was dishonest and underhanded and made him feel like a louse.

The moon lay on the ridge of the mesa, past full now, but still large and heavy with gathered light. Through the windows, he could see the dim shapes of the barn and outbuildings, the outline of the corral fence.

Overhead, he heard Allie's bare footsteps pad down the hallway toward the head of the staircase, stop, then descend. When she entered the living room where he was sitting in the dark, his heart lurched at the sight of her. He opened his arm, and she lowered herself next to him, tucking into him, laying her head on his shoulder. He pulled the throw from the back of the sofa and wrapped it around them both, tucking in the edges.

His hand moved to her breast and he stroked it, enjoying its plump fullness, the way her nipple hardened under his fingers, the feeling sending heat to a spot low down in his stomach. He nuzzled her hair, letting strands of it feather his lips. He inhaled the sage and wild ginger fragrance of her shampoo.

"What are you doing up?" he whispered.

"I couldn't sleep, either," she said. "I was thinking about Davy's birthday next week. I'm as excited as he is."

"Jobby is reconditioning his old saddle to give to him as a birthday gift. He works on it in his spare time."

"Really? Oh, Davy will love that." Then she had a thought. "Did you ask Monica if she wanted to come over for birthday cake?"

"I asked her. She didn't say no."

"But she didn't say yes."

Beck shook his head. "No. Did you know Davy's been sneaking over there to play with the dog?"

"Mm hmm. But I haven't scolded him for it or let on that I know." Suddenly she looked up at him. "Why? Is Monica mad?"

"She didn't say."

He let the conversation fall away, enjoying the feeling of having her close while he debated how to broach the subject he most wanted to talk about. He'd been building up to it for the last several nights, and now, taking a chance his timing was right, took her hand, pressed her palm to his lips and left it there while he spoke.

"Allie, honey? Can I ask you something?"

Allie forced herself to stay still and not react. She knew what he wanted to talk about; the ghostly presence that had been hovering over them since the day she arrived. He was going to ask her about the night his father died. She'd hoped she would never have to tell him, and now frantically searched her mind for something to say, but the silence held until he spoke up again.

"After you left, I tried to find you, but your aunt wouldn't tell me where you went."

"Please don't blame her. She didn't know. Not then. Later, I made her promise not to tell."

"But why? You said you loved me."

"I did, and I love you now. It's just . . ."

"What? It's just what?"

In the silence Allie heard a night bird call. An answering call came from somewhere in the distance. Beck was waiting for his answer.

"Your family," she began, feebly. "The police, everyone thought I had something to do with your father's death. Your sister still blames me for what happened that night."

"What did happen?" His blue-grey stare was insistent, his tone urgent, demanding an answer. She was finding it hard to resist.

"Beck, please. I'm asking you to trust me. There's no point bringing that all up again, rehashing everything. You already know what happened."

"I know what the police report said. That he tried to take your engagement ring off your finger." Beck straightened, holding her away a little, forcing her to look directly into his face. The fringed throw slid off and fell to the floor. His eyes grew hard as he looked at her, probing for the lie hidden in the unspoken words. A shadow of doubt crossed his face so fleetingly she almost missed it. But it was there, and unease flickered in the depths of her heart.

"But there's more, isn't there?" he persisted.

"I . . . we weren't . . . he . . ." She broke off, her shaky sigh swallowing her words.

"He what?"

"You know he didn't approve of us," she said, then amended it. "Of me. Okay? Of me. It was okay when we were kids and hung around together, but he didn't want you to marry me."

A coal of anger was forming in his eyes, and she saw him struggle to smother it. "Tell me the truth, Allie," he commanded softly. "I want to spend the rest of my life with you, but there's no chance for us to be together if you don't tell me. I've got to know everything just the way it happened." She sensed a rending sorrow beneath the surface of his calm rise up and grip his heart.

A wind blew down from the mesa, and tree branches waving across the yard lights made shadows that washed back and forth on the wall. Her gaze trailed away to look at them over his shoulder, but he put a finger to her chin and turned her face back to him, forcing her to look at him. His eyes bored into her. Dread tightened her chest as she gathered the courage to tell him something it would surely kill him to know.

He dropped his hand and they stared at each other across the lengthy silence as she struggled with the decision to tell him or not.

"Tell me."

Suddenly she felt vulnerable, dangerously exposed, and picked up a sofa pillow and wrapped her arms around it. As she began to talk, the events spun out of the past in a whirlwind of memory, and it felt as if they were happening again.

It had been the night of Beck's farewell party at the country club. He was leaving for college in a few days and had asked her to come with him instead of waiting until after graduation to get married. He'd gone to get the car. They were going to elope that night. She was waiting for him by the pool.

Jonathan Williams, black hair shot with silver precisely where it ought to be, blue-grey eyes bold and determined, though watery now from the booze, was drunk as usual as he staggered down the steps toward the pool where she was waiting for Beck.

She'd been greatly in awe of Beck's father, as everyone had been in those days, but she hated being near him when he was drinking. Nevertheless, out of politeness, she offered a pleasant greeting.

"Hello, Jonathan."

He held a glass in his hand and sipped from it, his eyes on her, a half smile on his lips. "Hello."

He approached unsteadily and flopped down next to her on the white wrought iron bench.

"I'm waiting for Beck," she said, eyeing him closely, easing away from the uncomfortable touch of his thigh against hers.

He set his glass on the patio table, reached out and took her hand, gently at first, in what she thought was a fatherly gesture. But suddenly his hand tightened on hers, squeezing her fingers, as he tried to take the engagement ring off her finger. She pulled her hand away and put it behind her back.

"You can't marry my son." He said it as if it were a foregone conclusion, as if anyone who thought otherwise was an idiot.

Surprised, her heart took a leap. "Why not? I love him and he loves me."

Jonathan's eyes, Beck's eyes in his father's face, reflected the pool lights and looked like icy blue fire. "It's not you he loves," he sneered. "It's what you do for him. What you give him."

"Please don't talk to me that way, Mr. Williams," she said, any pretense of civility gone now.

"I know what you two do when you sneak out to the cabin."

"That's none of your—"

"Is it money you want?" he interrupted. "I'll give you money. How much do you want? I'll write you a check tonight if you never see my son again."

Leaping up, she faced him angrily, forcing herself to remain calm. "It's not like that. You don't understand."

There was a cold creepy edge to his smile. "Oh, I understand perfectly. Your kind is only too happy to lift your skirt and spread your legs for someone like Beck, someone with money and breeding." He dragged his gaze over her, looking like he had a bad taste in his mouth. "Get him to marry you, and you won't have to end up waiting tables in a gin mill like your aunt."

Angrily, Allie spun around to leave, but he sprang up out of his seat, lunging forward, grabbing her arm. She winced as his hand pinched the soft flesh on the inside of her forearm just above her wrist.

"He's not going to marry a tramp like you. Wild. Always running around, getting in trouble. You're only good for one thing." Before she could react, he bent her arm behind her back and put his other hand between her legs, squeezing hard, his fingers digging in, hurting her.

She struggled and twisted around, pushing at his hand trying to escape his painful grip. "Stop! Stop it!"

Quickly, he flung his other arm around her waist, pulling her against him, thrusting his hips against hers and seeking her mouth with his. She turned her head away, and took a breath to cry out, but his mouth covered hers making it hard for her to breathe. The feeling of his tongue moving inside her mouth was the most disgusting sensation she had ever experienced, and she nearly gagged.

She pounded at him with her fists, but he pushed her back against a rock pillar, still grinding his hips into her pelvis. The rough surface of the stones scraped her skin, their sharp corners cutting into the small of her back. She cried out in pain and tried to call for help, but he quickly locked his hand over her mouth, muffling the sound.

"Stop fighting me." His lips were touching her ear, and he spoke in a whiskey burdened voice. "You give it so easily to everyone else, I want some of it, too. You like Beck's cock? Well, you'll love mine."

With that, he pressed his full weight on her, holding her in place, trying to unzip his pants, while she flailed her arms and pounded him with her fists. In her struggle to get away, her elbow smacked into his ear, and he threw his head back and grunted in pain. Furious now, he threw her down onto a cushioned chaise lounge, falling on top of her, forcing his knee between her thighs, spreading her legs. His boozy eyes glittered like shards of glass, terrifying her.

In the distance, she could hear rock music coming from the band in the clubhouse. Loud voices and shrieks of laughter rolled through the garden and down the terraces to where she was living an unbelievable nightmare.

"Help me," she pleaded. "Somebody, please help me." But nobody came because nobody heard.

Heart pounding, she tried to fight him off, squirming under him, kicking her legs, turning her face away from his foul breath. He smelled of liquor, his whiskers scratched the tender skin of her chin and cheeks and neck. He was so much stronger than she was, and when she began to tire, her attempts to fight him off grew weaker. He loomed over her, leering like a madman.

Breathing hard, muscles sore and aching, she stopped fighting and lay back weakly, spent. Apparently thinking he had the advantage, he shifted his weight slightly to unzip his pants, and she took that moment to drive her knee into him, aiming for his groin. But she wasn't quick enough. He felt it coming and arched his back dodging away.

"Nice try," he said with a bitter laugh.

With one last burst of energy that matched the intensity of her fury, she pushed with all her strength and managed to shove him off. He hit the pool deck tiles with a thud. She leapt up, her unsteady knees barely supporting her, and took off at a run.

Despite his drunkenness, Jonathan recovered quickly and caught up with her at the deep end of the pool. He was frenzied now, slapping at her, reaching for her with his big hands as she backed away, bumping into pool furniture, knocking it over in her frantic attempt to evade him.

She was in her stocking feet, having lost her shoes in the struggle, and could feel the dampness at the edge of the pool. Frantically, her eyes darted around the pool enclosure seeking a way out, a way to safety. She focused on a spot over his shoulder, looking toward the broad staircase leading to the upper terraces outside the clubhouse. A silhouette, a figure moving into the shadows, or maybe it was the wind tossing weeping juniper branches about. She opened her mouth to call for help.

Jonathan, his face fearsome, lunged, hooking his fingers in the top of her dress, tearing the fabric away to the waist as he lost his balance and plunged drunkenly into the pool.

Recalled to the present by Beck's harsh little bark of a laugh, Allie's voice dissolved into a thready whisper. Anguish stormed in her chest, but gathering her courage, the words strangling in her throat, she went on, trying to explain the unexplainable.

"I knew he was a good swimmer, like you, so I ran home, expecting you to come for me. It was later that night I found out he had a heart attack and drowned. When the doorbell rang, I thought it was you. But it was the police. They told me."

She was rambling now, filling the empty space with words, trying to ward off the doubt and hurt and denial building in Beck's eyes as he stared at her, trying to buttress the waves of repudiation rolling off him, smothering her. She hurried on, the words rushing out of her mouth as if they'd been building up under pressure.

"I called your house, but they wouldn't let me talk to you.

They—the lawyers or whoever answered the phone—told me you didn't want to speak to me. Finally, Monica came on the line and told me to stop calling and harassing the family or she'd have me arrested, that they might arrest me anyway. She said you didn't want to see me again. She said the scandal would ruin my life. I thought it was better if I left. I didn't want to ruin your life, too."

In the telling, Beck's energy had seemed to diminish, and he slumped against the back of the sofa. Astonishment seemed to have knocked the air from his lungs, and he gaped, speechless. His blazing eyes bore down on Allie. She knew what that look meant. It meant he didn't believe her.

"What are you telling me?" he asked, his voice so harsh it was unrecognizable. "That my father assaulted you? Tried to rape you?"

Her heart ached as she tried to negotiate the emotional minefield she'd opened the gates to.

"He was drunk, he didn't know what he was doing," she said, trying to ease, to soothe, to take some of his torment into her own chest. But, of course, that was impossible.

Strangely, Beck laughed, the sound incredulous, hostile, and bitter all at the same time. His look was beyond angry. It was venomous.

"My father wouldn't do that," he said.

She felt the clench in the pit of her stomach that is learned in childhood when blame is forthcoming and punishment inevitable.

"My father would not treat a woman like that. He was an honorable man, a gentleman, respected by everyone. He loved my mother, was devoted to his family. Yes, maybe he drank too much sometimes, but he would never do that to you or anyone." His eyes glittered with raw hurt.

Beck stood, his arms hanging helplessly at his side, his hands curling into fists, looking like they wanted to strike out, to smash, to destroy. His dark gaze touched on her face, his scrutiny was long and hard. He looked as though he were trying to get something straight in his mind. At last he spoke the words she was sure had never before made their way beyond nagging doubts in his mind.

"You're lying."

The moon slid behind a cloud, and the weight of the silence blanketed them as heavily as did the darkness. The accusation lingered in the air between them until his cell phone rang, shattering the moment. He picked it up from the coffee table and flipped it open.

"Hello," he said dully. After a brief moment, his eyes flicked to Allie, then quickly away.

"Hi, Jazzy." His voice broke and he cleared his throat, then paused and narrowed his eyes as if sorting alternatives, making a decision. "I'm glad you called. I've been trying to reach you."

Without a further glance at Allie, he moved away, and slowly walked upstairs.

"When are you coming back?" she heard him ask just before he closed his bedroom door, hard, causing something to crumble inside her chest.

In the days that followed, Beck, unfailingly polite, but aloof, found reasons to be away from the house. When he was at the cabin, he buried himself in work, his back to her, maintaining a precise silence while he pored over photographs he planned to use in his *National Geographic* article, composing and recomposing each one on his computer. She watched him when he wasn't looking, hoping for a warm glance, a forgiving smile. She was disappointed when she didn't get one, but relieved she didn't get a *fuck you* glare, either.

She was tied up in knots on the inside, the same ones she

had picked at off and on in therapy through the years with only a little success. She'd taken a risk and told the truth. Though the result was just what she'd feared, in some spot beyond her consciousness she knew it had been the right thing to do.

Once or twice she tried to talk to him, tried to soften the truth about what happened that night, but what happened with his father was her reality, not his. There was nothing in his world that would convince him that the father he adored and had spent his youth trying to emulate was capable of such a thing.

She was putting a bowl of cereal on the table in front of Davy when Beck turned off the computer, gathered his camera equipment, carefully fitting lenses into a leather case, hitched the strap over his shoulder, and headed for the back door. Fearing a further attempt to smooth things over would net another rejection but unable to help herself, she reached out and put her hand on his arm as he went by, stopping him.

"Beck?"

When he turned, his eyes fell short of connecting with hers. His look was mildly curious but otherwise remote.

"I can't change the past and you don't want to forgive me for it, so where does that leave us?"

He drew away and continued for the door. "Let's just get through this, okay? Then we'll see what's left."

By this she knew he meant a multitude of things, her and Davy and the birthday party tomorrow and the trouble she'd brought upon his house. She stared at his back as he went down the steps, taking his car keys from his pocket. In a minute, she heard the sound of an engine fading into the distance, Beck driving away for the day.

She straightened her shoulders and took a deep breath, then hurriedly rinsed dishes and loaded them into the dishwasher while Davy finished breakfast. He didn't say anything, but his eyes followed her busyness with curiosity.

He scooped up a spoonful of cereal, put it into his mouth, and chewed slowly, watching her.

She noticed. "Are you ready to help me bake your birthday cake for your party tomorrow?" Allie asked, falsely cheery.

Davy nodded. "Uh huh."

They both knew that Davy's help was limited to licking the spoon and the batter bowl.

Allie opened the pantry and stood with her hands on her hips, studying the stocked shelves. "Do you want chocolate, white, or spice?"

"White," he replied. "With chocolate frosting. And sprinkles."

"Okay," she said.

She set the cake mix box on the counter, then took out an electric hand mixer and bowls, measuring cups, spoons, spatulas.

Davy finished his cereal then dutifully took his bowl and spoon to the sink and rinsed them out before putting them in the dishwasher. He hiked himself onto a stool at the breakfast bar and watched Allie's preparations.

She was breaking eggs into a bowl when he asked, "Are you mad at Beck?"

She looked at him quickly, and then away. "No," she said.

"Is he mad at you?"

She nodded. "Yes, I think he is," she said after a pause. "He's very mad at me."

"What about?"

"Oh, something that happened a long time ago."

"What?" Davy pressed.

"He found out something disappointing about someone he loved and was very close to, and it hurt his heart. He's having a hard time believing it."

"Was it about you?"

"No," she answered, but wondered silently if it was as much

about her as his father. "Maybe."

"Well, he won't be mad at you for long."

"I hope not." She stirred the ingredients into a large bowl, then picked up the hand mixer.

"He won't," Davy insisted. "Because he really loves you." He had to raise his voice to be heard over the whirr of the beaters.

She turned off the mixer and set it on the counter, then used the spatula to scrape the sides of the bowl.

"How do you know? Did he tell you?"

"I'm not a baby, you know," he said, childishly offended. "I can tell."

Quickly, she turned her face away so he couldn't see her sad smile. After that, they fell into a comfortable silence as she poured cake batter into round pans. When she was finished, she handed him the bowl and spoon. She opened the oven and carefully put the cake pans on the middle baking shelf.

"Allie?"

"Hmmm?"

"Have you talked to my mother lately?"

Allie hadn't expected this, but without missing a beat, she closed the oven door and began wiping the kitchen counter.

"No, I haven't. Why do you ask?"

He shook his head. "No reason. I just wondered." He was licking his finger.

She folded the cloth, draped it over the faucet, then dried her hands on a dish towel. It was time to tell him about his mother. She had wanted to wait until after tomorrow, after his birthday, but since he'd brought her up, she felt it would be dishonest not to tell him now.

She let the silence linger until he looked up at her again. He had cake batter smeared on his chin, and she tore a paper towel off the roll and gently wiped it off.

"Davy, I have to talk to you about something."

171

A soft knock sounded at the screen door, and Allie turned to see a woman standing there, peering through the screen, smiling in at them. She was on the plump side, with a frizzy bleached blonde ponytail, and hard living on her face. False eyelashes looked like spiders under her eyebrows.

"Can I help you?" Allie asked, moving to the door, instinctively reaching for the handle to check the lock.

"Hello. I'm sorry to disturb you. I'm a guidance counselor from the elementary school in Durango. I'm taking a census for the upcoming school year." She lilted up the end of the sentence in a quasi question, the way some people speak to very young children.

"The school board wants to get an idea how many new students we can expect this year, so I'm going door to door." The woman laughed lightly, the sound pleasant and friendly. Nonthreatening. "So many new families are moving in, we might have to build a new school soon." She laughed again, good-naturedly.

Allie relaxed, but only slightly, and returned the smile, then opened the door to step out, but before she could, the woman pulled it wide, entered the kitchen, and peered around the interior of the cabin.

Still smiling, she turned to Davy. "Hello, young man. What's your name and how old are you?"

Davy, completely disarmed by this soft-spoken, overly friendly woman, told her his name, and added, "I'll be eight tomorrow."

The woman's smile widened, and she extended her hand. "How do you do, Davy? I'm happy to meet you."

Uncomfortable with what she felt was inappropriate familiarity from a stranger, Allie spoke up, reaching for Davy and drawing him close.

"Well, I'm sorry to say Davy won't be attending school here. We're just visiting. We're leaving in a few days." Davy looked up at her, but said nothing. "Going back to California," Allie lied.

At that, Davy shot her a look, his face puckering with silent inquiry. Hoping to forestall the question she knew was forthcoming, and not wanting to discuss it in front of a stranger, Allie opened the screen door and stepped out onto the porch before he could ask it. She held the door open expectantly, inviting Davy and the woman to follow, and they did. The woman kept her smile going, but Allie wondered at the sincerity behind it. It was the smile of a cold-calling salesman.

"Even so, I need information about all the children in the district. It's an administrative policy." The woman took a notebook and pen from her bag. "A statistical thing required by the state." She gave Allie a look that said she was only doing her job. "You know how it is."

Allie let the woman ask questions, but kept her answers vague and misleading, and strangely, the woman didn't seem to mind. Though her pen was poised over her notepad the entire time, she took only a few notes. Instead, her eyes darted around, lingering on the cabin, the yard, the corrals, as if studying the surroundings, getting the lay of the land.

When the questioning began to run out of steam, Allie turned up the corners of her lips in a faint smile.

"If you'll pardon me," she said stiffly, reaching for the door. "I have a cake in the oven I have to check on. Thank you for stopping by. I wish I could have been more help." Taking Davy firmly by the shoulder, she ushered him inside, and closed and locked the door.

Allie hurried to look out the front windows and saw a car she didn't recognize parked outside. She wondered why she hadn't heard it drive in. Maybe it had arrived while she had the mixer going in the cake batter.

She ducked back when the woman came around the side of the house, opened the car door and got in. As the car took a slow wide circle around the clearing and drove through the trees toward the county road, Allie noticed the yellow and black sticker on the license plate identifying it as a rental car. That, and the false eyelashes struck a discordant note, but seeing no hint of menace in it, Allie shrugged it off and went to check on the cake.

CHAPTER FIFTEEN

Jason Bright propped his ample butt against the fender of his Jeep Wrangler, lowered his binoculars, and congratulated himself on his phenomenal instincts. His friends and fellow reporters at the *Detroit News* would say it was dumb luck—and call him a braggart to boot—but he knew different. Besides having spot-on instincts, Jason had a knack for taking a rumor and jabbing and poking and whittling away at it until he reached its core. That's where the truth was hidden.

This intuitiveness had rooted out crime and corruption at all levels of government, and built his reputation as a trusted investigative reporter, a position he'd turned down promotions to management to keep, preferring as he did the adrenaline high of chasing these kinds of elusive stories. He pursued nearly all his news tips with a whirlwind intensity that had allowed him to break more stories, earn more awards, and achieve more recognition than any other reporter in the city of Detroit.

Along the way, he had acquired a large stable of contacts—okay, informants—some lowborn, some high, all of whom had his personal cell phone number and fed him rumors, sometimes in exchange for favors. The favors were mostly nothing that would even remotely be considered a bribe or misconstrued as paying for a story, heaven forbid—just a few dollars tucked into the grimy fingers of a panhandler with good hearing and eyesight who'd been in the right place at the right time, or four Red Wings box seat tickets slipped into the breast pocket of someone in the mayor's office.

Yes, Jason loved rumors, the juicier the better. He'd built a career on juicy rumors.

Last year, when he'd broken the story about those missing kids at Child Protective Services—one child found beaten to death in a ditch, another on the run with a child molester—he'd done so because he had unrelentingly followed an unbelievable, unthinkable really, rumor to its source. The resulting stories on the malfeasance at CPS had been front page news for weeks, and had turned the city, the county, and the state upside down. The result was that some heads rolled, the governor screamed bloody murder, lawsuits were filed, and the CPS director promised to clean up the agency.

But experience had taught Jason something else about rumors. They were like snakes. Where there's one, there's usually another. So with that in mind, he'd continued to dog the offices and waiting rooms of CPS and family court, strolling the hallways, sitting in the back row of courtrooms until, sure enough, a couple of months ago, right after that judge was killed in a car accident, he'd heard from one of the social workers that another child had gone missing and so had one of the advocates.

After that, information dried up in a hurry, though a few names had been mentioned. So Jason tucked away what information he had and waited for more.

But he didn't let any grass grow under his feet. While he waited for more on the missing kid and the advocate, he turned his attention to another rumor, this one about suspicious activities at the Church of Spiritual Light.

Gossip had been circulating for years that there was more to Reverend Jackson Worthey's organization than praising the Lord. There'd been insinuations of a variety of financial inconsistencies, money laundering even. And word on the street was that much worse was going on, but so far nothing the police could catch him at.

So Jason had kept an eye and ear out, tracking the Wortheys' activities. When he heard that Millie, who usually stayed close to home, had suddenly left town headed for Durango, a ski town in Colorado, Jason suspected the Reverend was up to something in that church complex of his. When, after a couple of weeks, Millie didn't return, he figured something was up elsewhere, so he packed a bag and headed west himself.

When he finally caught up to Millie, he was disappointed to find she spent most of her time sitting in bars. He had no idea she'd eventually lead him to this cabin on the edge of a piney national forest where the truth was hidden inside another rumor, namely Allie Hudson.

He knew her instantly. He was one of the first reporters to interview her after her husband was killed, and she began making waves all over town about police corruption. He also knew her law license had been suspended and she was now an advocate in family court.

What is Allie doing here, he wondered. And how in hell is she connected to Millie Worthey? He raised the binoculars again.

Millie and Allie were standing on the back porch of the cabin, talking, but he was too far away to hear what they were saying. A little boy stood between them, looking up, turning his head from one to the other as they spoke. Allie lifted her hand and absentmindedly stroked her fingers through his hair, then pulled him to her in an affectionate hug. Suddenly, Allie hurried the boy inside, and Millie left.

Amazing, Jason thought, lowering his binoculars and congratulating himself. Here in the mountains of southwest Colorado, under a blue blaze of sky, he'd scored a double header.

CHAPTER SIXTEEN

Outside, the sky was darkening, a tangerine blush rimming the far mountains all that was left of a fiery sunset. A coyote whooped and moaned on the mesa, challenging the moon to hurry up and show its face.

Inside the cabin, the kitchen was decorated with balloons and streamers that swayed with the breeze coming through the screen door. A paper banner hanging from the ceiling beams spelled out, "Happy Birthday Davy."

Allie set the birthday cake, white with chocolate frosting and sprinkles exactly as ordered, on the table, and Beck dimmed the lights. As the final words of the birthday song drifted away, eight little candle flames dancing on the cake cast flickering shadows over the faces around the table. Allie, Beck, Davy, and Jobby Bones.

"Make a wish," said Jobby, looking almost as excited as Davy. "Make it a good one." When he smiled, his kindly face resembled crinkled brown paper, which only added to his rugged handsomeness.

"Okay." Davy's eyes were twinkling, his color high.

There were lots of gifts, Allie and Beck had splurged indulgently. Allie knew Davy had never received so many presents or owned so many toys, and the boy's excitement was palpable.

Davy concentrated hard, eyes squeezed shut, forehead

pinched. At last, his eyes flew open and a grin broke across his face.

"Okay, I've got it. I wish—"

"Wait," Jobby held up his hand, palm out, stopping him. "You're not supposed to tell."

Allie frowned, wishing Jobby hadn't done that. She was curious to know what Davy would wish for, wondered what was on his mind.

"Oh, right. I forgot." Davy repeated his wish silently to himself, then took in a great gulp of air and blew. All eight candles extinguished to enthusiastic applause.

Davy smiled. "That means my wish will come true." He flicked a look at Allie, then quickly away, and she wondered what part of his wish involved her.

"Time for presents," said Beck. He got up and brought a stack of wrapped packages to the seat of honor at the head of the table where the birthday boy sat. Allie was cutting the cake and passing around plates that said "Happy Birthday."

"Wait," Jobby Bones said again. "Can I give my present first?" He jumped up. "I wasn't able to wrap this with paper, so I'm just going to bring it in." He stepped out onto the back porch, and came in carrying a saddle decorated with a big red bow.

Davy's jaw dropped. "Is that for me?"

"Yep."

Davy slid out of his chair and approached the saddle reverently. He reached out his hand, stopping short of actually touching it.

"Go ahead," said Jobby. "It's yours."

"It's beautiful," Allie said. She could smell saddle soap and leather conditioner.

"It belonged to my daddy," Jobby said. "He gave it to me on *my* eighth birthday. I thought Davy might like to have it. He's doing good on his riding lessons—pretty soon he'll be wantin' a horse of his own." He ran his hand over the oiled leather. "I cleaned it up and fixed it, and it's good as new."

"Thank you." Davy was beyond words, his eyes glittering with delight.

Allie skimmed her fingers over the floral tooling that covered nearly every square inch of the leather. Silver buckles and hardware gleamed, as did the engraved silver horn cap. Highly polished copper stirrups seemed to glow with an inner light. The back of the cantle was edged with silver beneath which initials were embossed into the leather.

"Whose initials are these?" she asked. "It looks like a B and a J." She looked up at Jobby, questioning.

"Yes, m'am. They're mine," Jobby replied. "My name's really Bobby Jones, but when I was little, my grandmother—she had thirteen other grandchildren in the house—always got her tongue mixed up when she called us. I ended up being called Jobby Bones. It stuck."

Beck was taken by surprise. "You never told me that."

Jobby shrugged. "You never asked me."

"Sorry, Jobby," Beck said, a sheepish grin conceding his lapse. "I've never known you by any other name and it never occurred to me to ask."

Allie wanted to be encouraged by that light-hearted exchange, mild though it was. But as soon as Beck's half-smile vanished, his face closed up again and he retreated to that private place within where he'd been spending all his time.

"Can I ride on it tomorrow when I have my lesson?" Davy broke in excitedly.

"Sure can. I'll take it out to the barn and it will be ready for your lesson in the morning." Beck held the back door open for Jobby to go through with the saddle; a coyote yipped up on the mesa. An answer sounded in the near distance, and Jobby peered warily into the darkness.

"I better check on the horses in the barn," he said to Beck. "I saw coyote tracks by the corral fence last night."

Beck nodded. "Let me know if you find anything."

After Jobby left with the saddle, Beck carried the other presents to the table. He took two off the stack and set them in front of Davy. They weren't, Allie noticed, wrapped in the usual discount store wrapping paper, but rather the heavy, lush-to-the-touch gift wrap sold at high-end boutiques.

"Monica sent these over," said Beck.

Davy smiled, a rascally lopsided grin. "She must have liked the flowers I gave her, huh?" he said to Beck, and proceeded to rip off the paper with the same disregard he used for the less pricey version.

"Oh, boy. Look, Allie," he said, holding up a remote controlled truck for her inspection. The other package contained toy night vision spy goggles with lime green lenses and a purple Velcro headband, which Davy promptly put on. Mini-flashlights flanked the lenses.

"How do I look?" he asked.

"You look like an insect from an alien planet," Allie told him.

A frenzy of present opening resulted in a variety of books and games and movies, as well as a Mind Blowing Science Kit, a picture book with stunning photographs of horses, and from Beck, a Spiderman flashlight and a new backpack.

"It's time you got a new one, don't you think?" he asked.

Davy nodded. "Thanks."

"Here's the last one," Allie said, handing him a flat box. "It's time for a new one of this, too."

"What is it?"

"You'll see."

Opening it on his lap, Davy stripped the paper away to reveal a brand new, cellophane wrapped, never-before-been-played Monopoly game. His features seemed to melt on his face as he paled, and red blotches bloomed on his stark white cheeks. Suddenly, Davy pushed back from the table and sprang from his chair. Disregarding the Monopoly game as it fell to the floor, he ran for the stairs.

"Davy?" Allie started after him, reaching for his arm, but he checked her with his elbow. She stared after him, then turned to Beck. "What's wrong with him?"

"I don't know," he answered. "Let's just give him a minute."

A dark uneasiness settled over Allie as she listened to Davy in his room opening and closing dresser drawers, pulling things from shelves, letting them fall to the floor. Rapid-fire pounding on the steps announced he was on his way back down. He stormed into the kitchen.

"Where's my other Monopoly game?" he demanded. "The old one." His lips were pressed grimly together and he pinned his glare on Allie.

"Well, I threw it out," she said, taken aback at his reaction.

"Did my mother say you could?" A brittle light flickered in his eyes.

For a brief second her mind went blank as she tried to make a connection between Marie and the Monopoly game.

"Your mother?" She traded puzzled looks with Beck. "Well, no . . ."

The tears Davy had been holding back broke loose and poured down his cheeks. His face crumbled miserably.

"Bring it back," he said, his voice ragged and pathetic.

"What?"

"Bring it back!" he wailed.

"Davy." She reached out for him again, but he backed away. His face had a childish pissed-off look she wasn't used to seeing, and she dropped her hands to her sides.

"I want the other one back," he said stubbornly, his face fierce with childish determination.

"But, why? I thought you'd like a new one. Look. It has a brand new board, new cards, new playing pieces," Allie pointed out stupidly, trying to pacify him.

"NO! I want the old one!" He took in a lungful of air, struggling to control his breathing.

"Okay, Davy," Beck said quietly. "Don't cry." He'd been watching Davy intently, his expression serious and thoughtful. "If Jobby hasn't hauled the trash to the landfill, I'll get it back."

His words were meant to soothe, but Davy, inconsolable, threw himself in a kitchen chair, put his arms on the table, dropped his head into them and sobbed pitifully.

Allie touched Davy's shaking shoulders, then pulled the reluctant boy out of his chair and into her arms, holding him while he cried mournfully. When his wrenching sobs subsided into snuffles, Beck picked up a napkin from the table and wiped the child's face and nose.

Davy hiccoughed and stared at the floor, refusing to look at either one of them. Beck reached out and slowly spun Davy around, lifting his chin with gentle fingers, forcing Davy to make eye contact.

"Tell me, Davy. What's in that game that's so important?"

Davy sniffed and began shuffling from one foot to the other, looking from side to side, avoiding Beck's penetrating gaze. His eyes focused briefly on Allie before retreating to the safety of the floor. He opened his mouth as if he were about to speak, then closed it and said nothing. Tears streaked his face and he involuntarily sucked in a breath.

"Davy?" Allie coaxed gently. "It's okay. You can say it. No matter what you tell us, no matter how bad you think it is, I'm sure we'll be able to fix it."

Then two words tumbled out, yanking more tears with them.

"My key," he said, his voice barely above a whisper.

She hadn't expected that. "What key?"

"In the game."

"The key you use as a playing piece? That key?"

Davy nodded, and looked up at her, his expression bleak.

At that, Beck heaved a sigh and chuckled, squeezing Davy in a quick hug. "Well, that's no problem," he said, holding on to the hug. "I can get you another key. That's easy."

Davy shook his head. "No. I need that one."

"Why that one?"

From the look on Davy's face, Allie was afraid he was going to shut down again and refuse to talk, but after a moment, he transferred his gaze to the ceiling and seemed to be building up his courage.

At last he spoke, the words wrenching reluctantly from his throat, his breath still coming in jagged gasps. "My mother gave it to me."

Allie met Beck's surprised expression with one of her own.

"Davy," Beck prodded gently. "Was that key special in some way? I mean besides the fact your mother gave it to you."

Slowly Davy nodded again, then lowered his eyes to the floor and kept them there.

"Tell me what was special about it. What did your mother say when she gave it to you?"

Davy released a shaky sigh. "She called it my future."

"Your future? What did she mean by that?"

Davy shrugged and lowered his eyes again. "I dunno."

"Davy. Look at me." Allie smoothed his hair off his damp forehead.

He raised his head, his expression anxious. "But I promised not to tell," he whined, his face crumbling as he began to cry again.

"No, no. It's all right. Don't cry." She hugged him to her and rocked gently. "It's important to keep promises. Really, it is. But sometimes things change, and the person you made the promise to wouldn't mind if you broke it."

Davy narrowed his eyes and looked at her uncertainly. "Why?" He sniffed and Beck handed him another napkin.

"Well, sometimes the reason you were asked to keep the promise has changed. Maybe it's not so important to keep it secret anymore."

He blew his nose in the napkin. "Do you think it's not important anymore?"

"It may still be important, but maybe it's more important that you tell us. I don't think your mother will mind this time." Allie cringed after she said that, remembering she hadn't yet told Davy his mother was dead. Now she feared she'd made things worse by not telling him right away.

Davy stood in front of her, hands limp at his sides. He appeared to be considering Allie's words, trying to decide whether or not she was right. Finally he spoke up, but reluctantly.

"She said to hide the key and not tell anyone I had it. She said it was the key to my future, and that she'd come for me and then we'd have a truckload of money."

Stunned, Allie's heart seized up in her chest, but she hid her shock from the boy.

Beck moved forward to the edge of his seat, reaching for Davy.

"Is that what you were thinking about the other day when you asked if adopting a horse would cost more than a truckload of money?"

Davy moved his head slowly up and down, and his chin puckered and trembled. He looked at Beck through watery eyes. "Can you get my game out of the trash?" he asked mournfully.

"I'll do my best."

Beck stood and headed for the back door, but Allie could tell by the look on his face there was faint hope of ever seeing that old Monopoly game again.

Davy saw it, too, and his shoulders drooped woefully. Watery eyes, red and puffy from crying, followed Beck out the door.

A hollow unsettled feeling swelled behind Allie's breastbone. She dared not tell Davy about his mother now, not now, not in the state he was in, and she wondered if there would ever be a good time to tell him.

Take Davy and run.

She realized now that Marie's warning had been about a key and a truckload of money. Somebody else's key and somebody else's money. Allie doubted the key or the money had belonged to Marie, and now she was dead, and somebody wanted what belonged to them.

Allie glanced out the window, saw Beck standing under the yard light outside the barn talking to Jobby. Jobby was gesturing and pointing toward the mesa. Beck, feet spread, thumbs hooked in the back pockets of his Levi's, looked off in that direction.

"Do you want to finish your piece of cake?" she asked Davy, unsurprised when he shook his head no. His face was drawn, his eyelids drooped. He was emotionally worn out.

"Okay, then," she said. "I'll help you get ready for bed."

"No," he said, not looking at her. "I can do it myself." He started up the stairs, then stopped halfway and turned to face her.

"Thank you for the birthday cake and stuff."

He said it politely with an absence of anger, but he couldn't hide his sadness and disappointment. He turned and continued up the stairs, the sound of his footsteps receding overhead to his room. His bedroom door closed softly.

Allie was still standing in the middle of the room when Beck came in carrying a rifle. He put it on a rack over the door, then knelt before the fireplace and began stacking kindling.

Noticing the tension in the muscles of his face and neck, she withheld comment on the rifle. He spent a moment or two on the fire before speaking.

"Jobby didn't get to the landfill this afternoon. The trash bags are still in his truck. He's going through them now."

Relieved, and grateful that Jobby would do such a thing, Allie sighed, and slumped into a chair. She put her fingertips to her forehead and temples, massaging gently, and closed her eyes. She was so tired. The last of her energy was draining away along with any hope of normalcy ever reasserting itself.

When the flames caught, Beck sat down on the sofa and stretched out his long legs, feet propped on the coffee table.

"Well, now we know what they want," he said after a long moment of staring into the fireplace. "Whoever they are. They want that key."

She nodded. "Yes."

"Look. I don't want to alarm you, but Jobby told me he saw tire tracks out back about a quarter of a mile. On a rise at the west end of the mesa. He came across them when he ran the coyotes off. Someone's been driving around out there."

She lowered her hands and stared at him, letting the words wash over her. "Who was it?"

Beck shook his head. "I don't know. But the tire tracks don't match any of the ranch trucks. There are footprints, too, like someone parked up there, and walked back and forth along the ridge." He hesitated. "You can see the cabin from up there. It's a direct line of sight to the back yard and the porch."

Allie stiffened. "Is that why you brought the rifle in?"

He held out a staying hand, a gesture that said hold on now, relax, but his effort to calm her failed miserably.

"I'm sure it's nothing to worry about. It's federal land out there, open to the public. Except . . ."

"Except what? You're thinking something."

187

"I'm thinking it's nothing to worry about," he dodged, "but Jobby's laid out a bedroll in the bunkroom in the barn, and he'll stay over a few nights. To be around, just in case."

If that was meant to reassure her, it, too, failed. Allie looked at the rifle over the door. Beck intercepted her glance.

"Davy won't be able to reach it up there, and it has a trigger lock anyway. I'll show you how it works."

"Okay." She paused in thought. "Maybe you should talk to Monica," she suggested.

"I will, first thing in the morning. Ask her if she's seen any strangers on the access road, but Jobby said he didn't think whoever it was used the access road. He thinks they came in from the fire road on the other side of the river and crossed BLM land to the mesa. It's all public land until you get to the westernmost fence that borders the ranch. The gate's never locked."

Allie thought of the woman from the school who visited yesterday. Allie hadn't heard her drive in, hadn't a clue she was there until she knocked on the door. The illusion of the ranch providing privacy and safety was quickly eroding.

"Where's Davy?" Beck asked.

"Upstairs getting ready for bed. He didn't want me to help."

"Is he all right?"

She gave her head a quick shake. "I don't think so," she said, even though she'd heard his sobs subsiding. "I'll check on him in a few minutes, tell him Jobby's looking for his game."

"What do you suppose that key is for?"

Allie released a sharp breath. "I wish I knew. I can't believe he's been hiding it all this time without telling me."

"Do you know if the police found Davy's father?" Beck asked, switching focus.

"No, they're still looking for him, and no one's been arrested for Marie's murder."

The mention of Marie brought a piercing reminder, and their gazes met.

"No," Allie said, answering Beck's question before he could ask it. "I haven't told him about his mother, yet. I don't know how."

"It won't be easy," he said.

"No, it won't," she whispered.

Jobby came in from the kitchen. His denim jacket was smudged with grime, and he was stuffing work gloves into his pocket. He handed Beck the battered Monopoly game.

"The top came off and everything fell out, but I think I found the key. Is this it?" He held it up for them to look at.

Allie got up and took it in her hand. She studied it, turning it over and over.

"Yes. That's what he used as his playing piece. Every time. He never let anyone else use it."

"Let me see." Beck extended his hand and she gave it to him, then turned to Jobby.

"Thank you for finding it," she said. "And thanks for staying. I'll get you some extra blankets. Are you sure you wouldn't rather sleep in here? That sofa opens into a bed."

"No, ma'm, but thank you. I'll be fine in the bunkroom. Extra blankets would be nice, but I don't expect I'll be sleeping much. I don't like critters botherin' the horses, and I don't like two-legged critters sneakin' around, either."

Allie went upstairs to the linen closet, and as she walked past Davy's door with blankets, heard him crying softly in his sleep. Quietly she opened his door. The floor of his room was littered with the things he'd swept off shelves and out of drawers in his search for the old Monopoly game.

The child was laying crosswise on his bed, fully clothed, his pillow knocked to the floor. She stepped over the things on the floor, unfolded one of the blankets and covered him with it, then picked up the pillow and put it under his head.

Gently she stroked his cheek with her fingertips. He stirred, and his eyelids fluttered, but he didn't wake.

"Mommy," he murmured. His voice thick with sleep broke on a sob. "Mommy."

Her heart shattering into a million pieces, Allie closed the door, and wiped away sudden tears before taking the blankets downstairs to Jobby.

"Don't forget to lock the door," he said on his way out.

"I won't." She turned the deadbolt.

Beck had taken all the game pieces out of the box and laid them out on the coffee table, examining them one by one. Wearily, she sat down next to him.

"Find anything?" she asked.

"Nope." He dropped the pieces in the box, put the top back on, and picked up the key, studying it again.

"Any idea what this goes to?" he asked her.

"No. It never occurred to me to wonder why he used it, since most of the original pieces were missing anyway."

"I don't think it's a car key; it wouldn't fit an ignition. It looks more like a house key, don't you think? Or maybe it goes to a padlock of some kind." After a moment longer, he put it on the coffee table next to the game box. The expression on his face was solemn.

"What do you know about his mother's background? What was she into?"

"Besides prostitution? I don't really know."

Allie went over everything she could remember from the family assessment report in Davy's file. Without the file folder in front of her, details were hazy.

"Where does his father work?" Beck asked, interrupting her.

"He didn't work. Oh, wait. I remember now. Judge Berriman said something about Davy's father being a janitor at Church of

Spiritual Light. But I have my doubts. Marie brought most of what little money there was into that family."

"Hold on a sec. Go back. What did you say? Church of . . . what?"

"Church of Spiritual Light. It's a big church south of Port Huron, Michigan. I don't know a whole lot about it. The church owns land out in the country just outside Imlay City. I drive by it on my way up to the cottage. One day I noticed the name on a little sign on the gate at the entrance. You can't see much from the highway, but I think it must be quite a good-sized piece of property. There's a lake and some sort of log structures back in the trees. It's a children's camp, or retreat of some kind."

Beck's yawn garbled his next words. She wasn't sure if he was talking to himself or asking her a question.

"What?"

He rubbed his eyes with the heels of his hands. "Oh, I was just wondering if they had a web site. Tomorrow I'll see what I can find on the Internet."

They sat next to each other in front of the fire, not touching, not talking, each lost in their own thoughts.

"Beck?"

"What?"

"I'm sorry."

He heaved a heavy sigh, but continued to stare wordlessly at the flames.

"For everything," she pressed on, "for—"

"Shhh," he said, quieting her. He took her hand and squeezed it, then laced his fingers in hers.

"But I—" she tried again, desperate to restore even a tiny remnant of their previous connection.

"Not now," he said with finality. Then, softening his tone, he gave her hand another squeeze and added, "Later." He turned

191

to meet her gaze directly. "Okay?" he pleaded, his eyes tortured.

"Okay," she said, unsettled, but relenting.

She sat that way, her hand in his, enjoying the warmth of it, not wanting to end that temporary comfort. When her eyes began to drift shut, she let them.

Hours later, she woke with a start shivering in the predawn chill, the fire having died to a wisp of smoke and a heap of rubies. Beck was asleep, snoring lightly, head thrown back, mouth open. She slipped her hand out of his, slid the Indian blanket off the back of the sofa and covered him with it, and went upstairs headed for bed.

On her way she stopped at Davy's door, turned the handle quietly, and peeked in. The window curtains were pulled wide, the pale light from outside draining all color from the room, casting it in predawn shades of black and grey. It looked for all the world like a grainy Ansel Adams photograph.

She narrowed her tired eyes, focusing her gaze to penetrate the dimness. She could make out the shape of the clock on the dresser, the outline of the television set on a stand in the corner, and heaps of blankets and pillows on the bed. The room was still in disarray, but now the bedspread was crumpled on the floor where it had been hastily flung.

She was overcome with a kind of swooping vertigo as the moment of understanding unfolded with nightmarish slowness. Only the hammering of her own pulse filled her ears as she stared with disbelief at the empty bed. The feather pillow was there, bunched and shaped to the impression of Davy's head, but Davy was gone.

She stared at it for one long bewildering moment, then called for Beck, shattering the silence of the house.

He came bounding up the stairs two at a time, meeting her just as she started down. Her legs began to melt away, and he wrapped his hands around her upper arms, holding her erect.

"What? What happened?"

"Davy's gone!" she breathed.

"What do you mean gone? Where is he?" Beck let go of her and ran to Davy's bedroom. He burst inside and began flinging blankets off the bed. "Davy? Davy! Are you in here?"

He opened the closet door and with a swoop of his arm swept all the hangers and clothes to one side. He knelt to look under the bed, then stood slowly, his eyes suddenly leaping to the top of the dresser and locking on a piece of paper propped against the lamp. Allie could see handwriting on it, a child's painstakingly printed block letters.

Beck snatched it up, read it, then looked up with disbelief.

"He's run away. Gone to find his mother."

Allie closed her eyes and drew a deep breath, her hands clenching into fists. Her heartbeat was thundering in her chest, deafening her with the roar of blood in her veins. She wanted to cry. She wanted to scream out. She pressed her trembling fists against her eyes and fought for control.

"Maybe he's in your bed," offered Beck, igniting a spark of hope.

But he wasn't there and he wasn't in Beck's room, either.

"Go through the house," he ordered. "I'll look around outside. He's probably in the barn with Jobby."

Beck thundered down the steps, across the living room, through the kitchen and out the door. Dazed, unable to think clearly or move, she stood staring at Davy's bed, her chest painfully tight.

With great effort she forced herself to move through the house, calling for Davy, looking in closets, in the bathrooms, in dark corners, all the places she'd already looked.

She walked out on the back porch, gulping air. Beck was in the yard with a flashlight, its beam bouncing along the hard-packed dirt, darting over sagebrush, ricocheting off trees and undergrowth. A light came on in the bunkroom, then Jobby hurried outside carrying a high-powered battery-operated lantern, joining Beck in the search for Davy.

Allie leaned against the porch railing, air spilling from her lungs. She thought she felt a passing ground shudder, but realized it was her legs wavering. Her stomach heaved and she fought to keep from throwing up.

A million thoughts went through her mind, crushing her under their weight. Where was he right now? Was he hungry? Was he cold? Was he hurt? Then she remembered the howl of the coyotes, their tracks close to the house, and her thoughts launched off into another scenario, an unthinkable one.

Suddenly she was shaking so hard she had to sit down. She dropped to the top step, and doubled over, sobbing.

Beck trudged back across the yard and lowered himself beside her.

"He's not in the barn," Beck told her, but of course Allie already knew that, knew something terrible had happened to Davy, or would.

Beck gently put his arms around her drawing her in. She rested her head on his shoulder, curved her arms up his back, and closed her eyes. She fit against him perfectly, as if she belonged there.

"We have to call the police," he said.

Foreboding pressed down on her, squeezing the hope out of her heart. Thunder rumbled in the distance and she opened her eyes to see lightning bubbling in the clouds over the mesa.

"Call now," she whispered, defeated.

Inside, the kitchen wall phone rang, and they froze, clinging to each other.

CHAPTER SEVENTEEN

"Sadie. Be quiet. It's not morning yet."

The tiny dog braced all four legs on top of the quilt at the foot of Monica's bed, glared in the direction of the window on the driveway side, and made a sound low in her throat that, despite her best effort, would have frightened no one.

"Hush, Sadie. Go back to sleep."

Monica had already gotten out of bed twice to let the jittery dog outside where she did little more than sniff the air, whine fretfully, and prance around in a nervous doggie dance. Ordinarily, Sadie slept through the night, comfortably tucked under Monica's chin, but so far this night little had been achieved in the way of sleep for either of them. The dog would not settle down.

And now she was barking her head off.

"Hush."

Chill bumps rose on Monica's arm as she patted the top of the quilt, hoping to coax the dog back to the warmth under the covers, but Sadie paid her no mind. Instead, she began a series of excited little barks, the annoying yip-yip of diminutive dogs that was especially irritating when one was trying to sleep.

What is that dog barking about? Exasperated, Monica raised her head and peered at the lighted numerals on the clock radio. Sadie took that as a signal to jump off the bed and skitter to the kitchen where she took up a relentless barking at the back door.

"Okay, okay," said Monica, giving in. "I'm coming."

Rising through the fog of sleep, she threw back the covers and swung her legs over the side of the bed. She grabbed up her robe and slipped it on, then in the dim glow of the night light in the adjoining bathroom, searched futilely for her slippers.

When Sadie's barking became more insistent, Monica gave up on the slippers and plodded barefoot to the back door.

Just as a new mother can interpret the cries of her infant, Monica could tell Sadie's was not a bark of distress or danger. Strangely, it was more like the greeting she usually reserved for company which, of course, they rarely had, and never at this hour. Unlike other dogs of similar size and breed, Sadie wasn't given to pointless barking and carrying on. Nor was she one to challenge coyotes, raccoons, bears, or anything else on four legs that outranked her in size if not in intellect.

Just the same, Monica showed caution when she opened the door a tiny crack and peeked out. The fragile silver glow of an overcast sky illuminated the flat surfaces with a pale patina, but rendered the hollows and recesses deeper and darker. The thick curtain of trees on the far side of the driveway and along the backyard perimeter looked particularly menacing. She wasn't afraid of the dark; in truth, she had a curious fascination for the nighttime. But she also respected its secrets, and its impenetrable shadows.

After one last look around, she swung the door open, letting the dog dash through, and as she always did, stepped out to keep a watchful eye while the dog did her business. Only, much to Monica's annoyance, Sadie didn't do any business. Instead, she ran directly to the garden shed at the edge of the back tree line, sniffed at the shed door, then, wagging her tail and whimpering, looked back expectantly at Monica.

"Sadie, come back. Come here. Sadie!"

Ignored, Monica gritted her teeth and hobbled over the stones in her bare feet to retrieve the recalcitrant dog. That's when she noticed the shed door was ajar.

A tiny unease spiraled through her mind, and quickly she scooped up the dog and held it protectively to her chest. There was a faint stirring inside the shed, the sound of something bigger than a squirrel but smaller than a bear. Unwilling to investigate in the dark, she turned to scurry back to the house but stopped when she heard another sound. A cry followed by a low moan, unmistakably human.

Tightening her grip on the squirming dog, she turned back and hooked a finger over the top of the shed door, then slowly inched it open, the hinges creaking eerily. Peering inside through the half shadow, she saw a form huddled on the floor.

Monica gave a startled cry and took a step back. Her mind went blank as she tried to make sense of what she was seeing—a strangely familiar creature with a purple and green contraption covering one eye.

"Davy!"

He was hunched over, shoulders rounded, hugging his drawn up knees, and he was shivering. The bizarre looking goggles he was wearing were broken, one of the lenses missing, the other shattered. Carefully she removed it from his head and peered at his dirt smudged face.

"What happened to you?"

Tears clogged the boy's throat, making his words unintelligible, but it sounded like he said he fell off his bike.

Without trying to make sense of why he would be out on his bike at that hour, she looked him over, trying to assess how badly he was hurt and whether or not she could move him. Sadie wriggled out of her arms, and squirming and whining happily at the sight of the boy, jumped on him and began licking his chin.

"Sadie, don't." She moved the dog and spoke to the child. "Does Allie know where you are?"

Davy tried to answer, but his words were garbled. Gently, she moved her hand over his head feeling for bumps. He flinched when she found one, then she felt something warm and sticky on her fingers. He was bleeding.

"Come on, let's get you inside. Can you walk?"

He couldn't, so she wrapped her arms around him and picked him up. Her grip was awkward because of the goggles in her hand and the bulging backpack strapped to his shoulders, but she managed to make it across the yard, wincing and curling her toes as sharp stones dug into the tender bottoms of her feet. Sadie, like a worried mother hen, took stiff mincing steps beside her, obediently staying out from underfoot as Monica carried the boy up the steps and into the house.

Gingerly, she laid him on the sofa, pulled his backpack off one shoulder and tried to remove it completely, but he grasped it, refusing to let go. She took off his muddy shoes and covered him with a knitted sofa throw, then turned on a low light so she could take a closer look at him. His face was scratched and scraped with deeply embedded dirt. Fresh blood seeped from a gash on the side of his head.

"My head hurts," he said, whimpering pitifully, and raised his hand to touch it. When he felt the blood, his sobs rose toward hysteria.

"There, there," she said, unfamiliar with what you said to a child when he was hurt, but doing her best. "You're all right," she said, hoping he really was.

Sadie whined in sympathy and danced around in crazy circles before jumping on the sofa. She scooted on her belly until she could rest her head on his knee.

"Can I pet Sadie?" Davy asked.

"If you want to."

Monica knew that Davy sneaked away from the cabin now and then to hide in the trees, hoping for a glimpse of the dog.

She'd seen him there, and pretended not to notice. This of course emboldened the boy, but she always looked the other way and allowed them to play together. It had occurred to her quite suddenly one day that Sadie needed the boy's affection as much as Davy needed the dog's.

"Let's get you cleaned up. Stay here and don't move. I'll be right back."

Leaving him on the sofa, Monica quickly gathered clean washcloths and towels, put a bar of soap in a plastic washbasin, and ran warm water into it while she telephoned the cabin to alert Allie and Beck. When she returned to the living room, she found Sadie stretched out on Davy's chest staring at his face with a worried doggy expression.

Kneeling, she dipped a cloth in warm water, then soaped it up. As she wiped dirt from the cut on Davy's head and from his face, she began putting the pieces together, reconstructing the scenario. Sadie must have heard Davy go by on his bike, then again when he came back after he got hurt and collapsed in the shed. That's why Sadie had been so agitated. She knew Davy was out there.

As she tended to the boy, he closed his eyes and seemed to drift off. She remembered reading somewhere that you were not supposed to let people with head injuries go to sleep.

"Where's your bike?" she asked to keep him awake.

"On the road."

"The road . . . you mean on the highway?"

"Uh huh."

"Where were you going?"

His eyes fluttered open, and he looked at her. "To Michigan to find my mother."

That didn't make any sense, and Monica wondered if Davy was merely confused or if his fall had actually damaged his brain.

199

"Your mother isn't in Michigan," she reminded him gently. "She's right here at the ranch. In the cabin with Beck. She'll be here in a minute. I just called her."

"No," he said. "That's not my mother. That's Allie. Allie's only taking care of me."

Monica squeezed excess water from a clean soapy cloth, held her dripping hands over the washpan, and looked at Davy, momentarily bewildered.

"Well, if she's not your mother, who is she?"

"She's part of the court."

"What court?" Monica asked, stupefied.

"The court that takes care of kids."

Despite weariness from lack of sleep, Monica processed what Davy said. Slowly, realization dawned that Allie was some sort of advocate or officer of the court responsible for the welfare of children. Or at least this child.

But if that were the case, why hadn't she or Beck said something? Why had they led her to believe Allie had shown up on Beck's doorstep with an illegitimate child?

No . . . wait.

They hadn't led her to believe that. She'd assumed that on her own. But they'd allowed her to believe it. Not that she had given either one of them an opportunity to explain otherwise.

A car pulled up outside, Allie and Beck arriving. Car doors opened and slammed shut, and footsteps hurried up the path. Beck was the first one in, his face serious, his mouth tight, followed by Allie, looking haunted, her face shadowed and drawn with worry.

At the sight of Davy, her expression melted in relief, but she stiffened again when she saw the blood on the side of his head, the red stained washcloths, and pink tinged water in the basin.

"Oh, Davy," she cried, crossing the room to kneel at his side.

Davy put his arms around Allie's neck, buried his face, and

held on tight. "My head hurts," he sobbed into her shoulder.

Allie clenched her teeth and winced as if his pain were seeping into her own body.

"What happened?" Allie crooned sympathetically. When he didn't answer, she looked at Monica.

"He said he fell off his bike."

"His bike? Where was he going on his bike?"

Monica paused, waiting to see if Davy would offer up an explanation. When he didn't, she related in a soft, even tone what he'd told her.

"He said he was going to look for his mother."

Monica took note of Allie's sidelong glance as it collided with Beck's, a silent communication taking place, a very private one.

Interesting, she thought, but said nothing.

Finishing up, she dropped the washcloth into the soapy water and wiped her hands on a towel. "I think he needs to be seen by a doctor. It doesn't look too bad, but you never know with head trauma."

"You drive," Beck said to Allie as he lifted Davy, still clutching the backpack, from her arms. "We'll take him to emergency."

The early morning atmosphere of the hospital waiting room was subdued, and everyone spoke in hushed tones. Beck, worried sick but trying not to show it, sat next to Allie holding her hand. She was grateful for the comfort of it. Monica had come, too, following in her own car. She sat across the room, alternately leafing through a magazine and casting curious glances in their direction.

The rush of relief at finding Davy had left Allie light-headed, but by the time they arrived at the emergency room she'd recovered enough to have answers ready for the questions she knew were forthcoming. She made short work of the check-in procedure by telling the admitting clerk she was Davy's mother, a necessary lie she hoped would eliminate all kinds of red tape and delays. She'd heard of hospitals refusing to treat children without parental authorization.

When asked about primary care physicians and previous medical history, she improvised quickly and told them all medical records had been destroyed in a hurricane in Florida. The question of insurance was settled when Beck promised to pay before leaving the hospital.

The paperwork completed, an ER nurse had assured Allie and Beck that Davy would be fine, then she shooed them off to sit in the waiting room while doctors did their medical magic.

Allie directed a steady stream of questions at Monica, who went over everything again, patiently repeating what she'd already told them, filling in what details she could.

"I must admit the night vision goggles gave me a jolt, but Sadie knew right away it was Davy." She paused and shot Allie a look. "He's been coming over to visit."

"I'm sorry, Monica," Allie said quickly. "I asked him not to bother you or Sadie."

"Oh, that's all right," Monica said, her manner softening. "He's actually no bother, after all. They play together when I'm working in the garden. He really seems to love Sadie, the way he handles her, very gently. And it's clear Sadie loves him, so . . ." Her voice trailed off, and she shrugged. "I guess it's all right." She gathered herself to leave. "And speaking of Sadie, I'd better get back home. She'll be wanting her breakfast and her morning walk."

"Thank you for finding him and taking him in," Allie said, her voice cracking under the weight of pent-up emotions. "I can't tell you how grateful I am you went outside to look around."

Monica nodded. "I guess we have to thank Sadie. She's the

one who told me he was out there. And when Sadie talks, I listen."

Her eyes were temperate, their usual off-putting distance replaced by a genuineness Allie had not seen. A faint smile appeared briefly and was gone.

Monica stood, took her car keys out of her jacket pocket, and approached Beck. "Call me if there's any news," she said, leaning over to give him a quick hug.

She made a move to touch cheeks with Allie, but before she could, Allie stood and pulled Monica into a fierce hug, hoping to convey the depth of her gratitude. She expected Beck's sister to pull away, and when she didn't, said, "Thank you, Monica, for being here. For being there, for taking him in when he needed someone."

Monica returned the hug, and patted Allie's shoulder in a gesture of comfort, saying only, "He's a good little boy."

After she left, Allie dropped back in her chair, dejected. Beck put out a hand and smoothed the worry lines from Allie's forehead. "The doctor said he's going to be all right, okay? Stop worrying."

"I know," she said. "It's just . . . Everything," she finished dismally.

Fast determined footsteps sounded in the hallway, rubber soles squeaking on the polished floor. A nurse entered the waiting room carrying Davy's belongings. Short and grey-haired, rounded by middle age, she was the kind of nurse who looked like she'd been a nurse forever, the kind of nurse everybody wants caring for them when they're really sick.

"Are you Davy's mother?"

Anxiously, Allie straightened in her chair. "Yes."

The nurse, her face pleasant, her quicksilver movements competent and self-assured, approached Allie and held out Davy's backpack. "Here are his things. The doctor is just finishing up now. You can talk to him in a few minutes, and then take your son home."

Relieved, Allie thanked her, settled Davy's bulging backpack, the new one from Beck, on her lap and opened it. She removed a sweater, a change of clothes including underwear, the new flashlight he'd received for his birthday, and the now ruined night vision goggles. Her heart sank as she realized how many of his birthday presents had aided in his running away.

Sighing, she dug deeper, pulling out rocks of various sizes and colors, a pencil, a selection of treasured items he'd kept in a Navajo basket on top of his dresser. Apparently he hadn't planned on coming back any time soon. She unsnapped an outside pocket and took out a folded piece of paper. Curious, she unfolded it, stared at it a moment, and said, "Beck. Look at this."

His brows lifted quizzically, and he took the slip of paper from her hand. "What is it?"

"I found it in Davy's backpack. It's an address in Detroit. But it's not his handwriting. It was written by an adult."

"Is this his house? Where his parents lived?"

"No."

His eyes narrowed as something occurred to him. "Could this be where he was headed?"

"I don't know. He told Monica he was going to find his mother. I don't know what this place is."

Beck handed it back. "I'll run an Internet search on the address, see what comes up."

She hummed a note of agreement, folded the note again, and put it in her purse.

What a mess this all was; despite her good intentions, it had gotten worse, not better. She tried not to dwell on how much of it was entirely her fault, the result of panic and poor judgment. There was no getting around the fact that it was all her fault, one hundred percent of it. At least it was at the beginning. Since then, she recalculated to sixty percent her fault, forty percent the unknowns consuming her every waking moment.

The key, of course, changed everything.

There was no way she could take Davy back to Michigan now, not if danger awaited him there as she and Beck had come to suspect after what Davy had told them about the key. Marie's murder was a clear indication of what lengths the owner of the key was willing to go to get it back.

But the way they were living now was hell. Davy's entire life turned upside down, and now ripped to shreds over a secret he shared with his mother, a secret Allie had made him tell, then his running off to find his mother not knowing she was dead. Allie shuddered to think what might have happened if Monica hadn't found him in time.

And Beck. She looked at him sideways, sitting there glum faced, his faith in her irreparably damaged. They couldn't go on this way. Her head started spinning, and she forced her thinking to slow down so she could sort her choices, which she realized were few.

She could go back to Michigan alone, turn herself in, explain about Davy, hope CPS would believe her and keep Davy safe. But she knew she couldn't count on that.

An absurd and utterly selfish thought came into her head, a thought she had entertained more than once since arriving in Colorado. Maybe, just maybe, she and Davy could hide out somewhere, here or in New Mexico. She'd seen it on numerous true crime television shows, murderers and bank robbers who went on the run and lived a secret double life for many years. In the end they were only caught because the authorities had a plethora of scientific and technological resources available to help track them down. She'd never heard of anyone being found by the bad guys, except in a novel.

Before she could reach any resolution, her thoughts were stilled by the nurse returning to say Davy was ready to go home.

CHAPTER EIGHTEEN

Beck pulled the handbrake, switched off the ignition, and stepped out of the pickup. Peering at the vast landscape before him, he took his time studying the topography, gauging distances and elevations. Straight ahead near the horizon was an eons old volcanic neck, a black tower of rock that at some point in the dawn of time had filled the vent of an erupting volcano. To the right of it, but closer in and separated by many miles was a low point in the ridgeline, a broad flat saddle between steep, craggy peaks marked by a swath of landfall debris.

He took a photograph from his shirt pocket and held it up, comparing the images and contours in the background of the photo to the landscape laid out like a picture postcard before him. He adjusted his angle of focus and let his eyes follow the ridge line, then drop down a gentle slope to a boulder pile the size of a house. Beyond that, parallel drag marks curved away and disappeared, then reappeared farther on and drifted beside an empty streambed through clumps of brittle, sun-dried grass and weeds. What had looked in the photograph like faults in terrain softened by wind and rain were, in reality, tire tracks where there was no road.

The picture, a fast action shot of a lead mare at a gallop, the herd careening behind her, had been the subject of the photograph, but while composing and editing it on his computer, he'd noticed the odd markings in the blurred background. Now, viewing the setting without the camera confirmed his suspicions.

He took off his hat, wiped his brow with his sleeve, put it back on, and tilted the wide brim against the sun. Pocketing the snapshot, he reached into the cab of the truck, took a rifle from the rear rack, and started off on foot to take a closer look at the tire tracks and, most importantly, see where they led. He carried the gun against a chance encounter with a rattlesnake or a cougar, at least he hoped that's all he'd need it for.

The day was quiet and still, the air hot and dry with no sign of the summer monsoons to come. The rains were already two weeks late, and he'd had to haul extra water out for the herd. A tracery of narrow gullies zigzagged south across the desert floor toward New Mexico. Now dry, during the rainy season, they would be filled with raging torrents.

Here, on the elevated tableland, it was fairly easy going, his footsteps silent in the sand. Soon the land undulated and gently staircased down to a spot near the boulder pile, where the sandy ruts made by tire tracks disappeared. Beck followed them, crossing the shallowest part of a dry wash. Warily, he loped up the sandbank on the other side. At the top, he stopped cold, stunned.

Down below but still at quite a distance he had an eagle's eye view of the cabin and most of the outbuildings. The angle of the sun through the windows was just right, and he had a clear view of the kitchen, the living room, and the alcove where he'd set up the computers.

Allie was loading the dishwasher. Davy, home from the hospital a week and fully recuperated, stitches removed, was on the back porch playing with Sadie who had been left in his care while Monica attended a mystery writers' conference in Denver.

And directly below Beck, on a long narrow relatively level bench of land breaking the continuity of the slope in the shadow of a rocky overhang was a man looking through binoculars aimed at the cabin.

Beck, the sound of his boots muffled by the deep sand, took cover behind a thick growth of sagebrush next to the upward slope. He leveled his rifle atop a large rock.

"Hold it right there," he said.

Startled, the man froze and his shoulders hitched. He took the binoculars from his eyes, but held his position.

"Keep 'em up," Beck ordered, "and don't turn around. Set the binoculars on that flat rock over there. I'm armed, and if you are, you'd better tell me now."

Obediently, the man sidestepped to place the binoculars on a rocky ledge denuded by wind erosion, then lifted his arms again, his movement slow and deliberate.

"I'm not armed," he said over his shoulder, his voice shaky. "Honest."

"Let's just make sure of that, okay? Flatten your hands high up on that rock wall, and keep them there. Spread your legs, and don't turn around."

The man complied without hesitation, and Beck, muscles tight with anticipation, stepped into the open, aiming the rifle.

"Who are you and what are you doing here?"

"Name's Jason Bright. I'm a reporter with the *Detroit News*. My identification is in my wallet." He dipped his head toward his chest, indicating his wallet somewhere on his person. "Check it out. But don't shoot."

"Turn around. Do it slow."

The man, portly, red-faced and breathing hard from nervousness rather than exertion, did as Beck ordered. He was wearing leather street shoes unsuitable for the terrain. A rumpled ill-fitting suit coat hung open, and the extra flesh around his middle pushed outward, stretching his shirt at the buttons.

"My wallet's in my inside coat pocket."

"Take off your jacket and toss it over here toward me. Your shirt, too."

Jason shrugged out of his jacket and shirt, tossed them on the ground in Beck's direction.

"Now your pants."

At that, Jason balked. "What?"

But Beck insisted. "Do it. Throw them over here on top of the jacket. If I don't find any weapons, you can have your clothes back."

Jason grumbled, but stripped to underwear and socks. Beck picked up the clothes and checked all the pockets. Cell phone, roll of bills, some change, car keys. Finding no weapons, he took out the wallet, flipped it open, glanced at the man's driver's license, then studied the picture a brief second before holding it up and comparing it to Jason's face. A laminated employee pass tucked into a credit card slot confirmed Jason Bright's employment with the *Detroit News*.

Satisfied the man's face matched the credentials, Beck put Jason's wallet in the back pocket of his Levi's and relaxed his grip on the rifle.

"Why are you spying on my house? What are you looking for?"

"I'm looking for Millie Worthey."

"There's no one here by that name."

"She was here. I saw her at the door talking to Allie Hudson."

"How do you know Allie?" Beck asked, surprised. "Who are you?"

"I told you. I'm an investigative reporter. I'm working on a story about the Church of Spiritual Light."

Beck recognized the name. That's where Allie had said Davy's father worked.

"And what does that have to do with me, or Allie?"

"Maybe nothing. But maybe something."

"Don't be stupid, Mr. Bright. You're trespassing on my land, and for what it's worth, the sheriff is a friend of mine. In addition, you had to drive across restricted federal land to get here, and the feds don't take kindly to trespassing, either. Now talk."

"I'll be happy to tell you the whole story, Mr. Williams. Do you mind if I put my hands down?"

Beck considered this, then nodded. "Do it slow."

Jason lowered his arms, then dropped his gaze to his clothes where they lay on the ground. "May I put my clothes on?"

"Not yet. Start talking."

"Okay. Okay. I'll come right out with it, then," said Jason. "I'm not sure what Allie's connection is to Reverend Worthey and his Church of Spiritual Light, but it can't be good. Rumor has it that Church of Spiritual Light is a conduit for laundered money. Some say the money goes to Mexico for drugs. Others say it finances terrorist activities."

After a moment of shocked silence, Beck burst out laughing. "That's ridiculous. Allie has nothing to do with anything like that." Good God, he hoped not. "You're out of your mind," he said to Jason Bright.

Unruffled, Jason continued. "Word is some church documents are missing and the Reverend is pissed about it. He wants them back. At any cost."

Instantly, Beck thought of Davy's key, and he lowered the rifle.

"Okay," he said. "Put your clothes on and tell me the rest of it."

Allie was at the computer when she heard Beck come in through the kitchen. She hadn't expected him back so soon, and she turned her head, surprised, then jumped reflexively when she saw the strange man with him.

Before she could speak, Beck hurriedly introduced Jason Bright. "He knows about you and Davy."

Allie rose quickly, scowling at Beck. "Why did you tell him—"

211

"Don't blame him, Miss Hudson," Jason stopped her. "He didn't tell me. I was able to figure it out myself. But you have nothing to fear from me. I'm not here to make trouble for you or the boy."

Allie's startled gaze darted back to Beck. "What's going on? What's an investigative reporter from the *Detroit News* doing here?"

Beck put a steadying hand on her arm. "You'd better sit down. Jason has something to tell us."

Allie looked from one man to the other. "About what?" she asked warily.

"It very likely has something to do with Marie's warning," Beck answered. "And Davy's key. At least, it might help us fill in some of the missing pieces."

Cautious but curious, she let herself be led to the kitchen table.

For half an hour, Allie stared, speechless, at Jason Bright as he told them what his investigation had turned up about Reverend Jackson Worthey and the Church of Spiritual Light.

"So far, the feds haven't been able to prove anything. The church launders some sizeable amounts of drug money, usually through Mexico, but it isn't in the same league as the multinational operations. Worthey's not that big—but big enough, mind you—so he's been able to operate mostly under the radar, especially after the terrorist attack on the World Trade Center. That's when the Banking Secrecy Act came into effect, which blew the lid off the large money launderers by exposing their business dealings to the light of day."

"How?"

"Before the terrorist attack, most large scale money laundering operators used wire or electronic transfers to move funds around. And they were able to do it with relative ease, because they could remain pretty much anonymous and, also, it was easy to disguise the origin of the funds. Now, the Banking Secrecy Act requires financial institutions to keep records that contain identifying information—"

"You mean they didn't do that in the past?" Allie asked, incredulous.

Jason shook his head. "No. Unbelievable, isn't it? At least not like they do now. Under the new Banking Secrecy Act, banks now have to gather detailed information on all payment orders. Who sent it, who received it, and the identity of any intermediaries the funds come in contact with along the way.

"Anyway, since the inception of the new law, the Reverend has reverted back to the physical transmittal of funds. In other words, cash carried by trusted operatives—which is the most difficult to track because there's no paper trail."

"You mean cash in a suitcase?" Allie asked. "Packets of bills in wrappers? Like in the movies?"

Jason chuckled. "Well, sort of. One of Worthey's preferred methods is, literally," he lifted his shoulders and his eyebrows at the simplicity of it, "money in a truck. That's practically back to the Middle Ages where modern money laundering is concerned."

"But how does he get it across the border?"

Jason waggled his hand in a "this or that" motion. "Worthey has a way of spreading money around where it will do the most good when he wants something done."

"You mean bribery," Allie said.

"Exactly."

"But why would he take it all the way to Mexico? He's right across the river from Canada."

"Nuh uh," replied Jason. "Canadians are too scrupulous. As a rule, their border guards won't accept bribes. They don't need to. Canada's not awash in poverty. Mexico is, so crossing our southern border is easier and more profitable even considering all the extra gas, miles, and time."

"Well, I still don't see how Davy's father is involved. He was only a janitor at the church. What does Norberto Lopez have to do with any of this?" She looked at Beck. "And the warning from Marie."

"He's getting to that," Beck put in. "You'll see how it comes together."

"Okay, but hold on a sec. I want to check on Davy and make sure he isn't listening to any of this."

It didn't take her long to find him. She simply followed the sound of his voice to the front yard where he was playing with Sadie. He looked up when she came to the screen door.

"Can I go up to Monica's house for a minute?" he asked. "I forgot to bring Sadie's favorite squeaky toy. I left it on her back porch."

"No, I'd rather you didn't," she answered. "If Sadie can wait a few minutes, I'll go up there with you to get it for her."

Davy huffed and rolled his eyes. "You never let me do anything!" he grumbled petulantly. He plopped back down on the ground with the dog, muttering under his breath.

"Davy, I want to you promise me that you'll stay here."

He nodded, his jaw thrust forward.

"Promise?"

"I said I would, didn't I?" he replied over his shoulder without turning around, his voice whiny and impudent.

She swallowed the reprimand that jumped to her throat and stood watching him, saddened that he was no longer the good-natured, agreeable little boy he was before the fateful birthday party. Thankfully his head injury hadn't been serious, and he was on the mend physically, but he'd become sullen, given to pouting and sulking. He refused to talk to her about his failed attempt at running away, and he rarely met her eyes directly, his insolent gaze usually landing somewhere over her left shoulder.

The disconnect had created a painful chasm between them.

"He's fine," she said when she returned to the kitchen. "He can't hear us." Allie seated herself and studied Jason's face. She remembered being interviewed by him outside city hall the first time she'd gone to the mayor's office to demand an investigation into police corruption. It seemed a million years ago.

"So, go on about Davy's father. How do you know all this?" she asked him. "How do you come to have such information about the Church of Spiritual Light?"

"I have my sources," he said, "most of which I can't reveal or they would cease to be my sources. But I've had my eye on the Wortheys for over a year."

"Okay, go on."

"Well, the Reverend deals mostly in cash, but he only deposits small amounts of it in banks. He spends the majority of it on hard goods, on assets that hold their value. Like homes, cars, jewels. But being a minister, he can't live too lavishly or his parishioners will start asking questions. The feds suspect he forms legitimate companies to run the money through, or he invests in real estate. Not the best investment in Michigan these days, the economy is so bad. But because of that there aren't many buyers around, either, so no one asks a lot of questions."

Jason paused, interrupting himself to add a footnote. "By the way, did you know the church leases that land where the children's summer camp is located?"

"No, I didn't," said Allie.

"Yep. They lease it for an overblown monthly rental from a real estate investment company called Radiance Land Development. County records show Radiance Land Development is owned by the Church of Spiritual Light. In effect, the church owns the land it's paying to lease."

"Well, that in itself isn't illegal," offered Allie. "For a holding company to set up that sort of financial arrangement."

"No, maybe not, but the trails of money into and out of Radiance Land are so convoluted it would take a room full of accountants a year to figure it out. And maybe not even then."

"But how can he disguise his source of money?" Beck asked.

"Yes," Allie added. "It's a church, after all."

"His money comes from a variety of sources, and there are any number of ways for a church to disguise income," Jason assured them. "For instance, Church of Spiritual Light financial records show some very large donations from a charitable organization in Mexico called Mexican Association of Housing for Children. I spent quite a bit of time trying to get a read on a charity by that name and couldn't come up with anything.

"My guess is those donations constitute drug money that was originally driven to Mexico by one of Worthey's operatives then repatriated back to the United States through donations to the church from a phony organization. It's hard to prove, because once money crosses an international border, the trail gets obliterated. There's little to no cooperation from Mexican banking authorities, and enforcement across international borders is complicated and inconsistent. Sometimes impossible. Our federal agencies have no jurisdiction there."

Allie nodded. "I see."

"Then there's income from Internet sales of church logo items, religious books, prayer beads, things like that. That's income that's fairly easy to hide with the technology available today. Web site anonymizers installed on church computers could make their networks virtually impenetrable, blocking or concealing their actual Internet activity. Worthey can include large amounts of drug profits and overstate the income he generates from web site sales.

"Plus, the feds suspect Worthey creates fictitious contracts with fake companies, then sends invoices for overinflated amounts of money like, say, consulting services rendered from one of his fake organizations. The invoices are paid mostly in cash, of course. And by spreading his supposed income around through many business entities and avoiding large or too frequent deposits to financial institutions, it's fairly easy to avoid detection.

"Churches, like casinos, are good covers for money laundering operations, because they deal in a lot of cash. Freight and shipping companies are good too. And that's where Davy's father Norberto Lopez enters the picture."

Allie leaned in, listening intently.

"You've heard of C-Essel Freight Hauling?" Jason asked.

Allie shrugged. "Vaguely. I guess I've seen the trucks on the highway."

"Well, Worthey's church owns the company, or the company owns the church. The exact ownership structure is unclear, but they're connected somehow. They even tied the name in. C-Essel, get it? CSL? Church of Spiritual Light?"

"Clever," Beck said sarcastically, giving his head a disdainful shake.

"Yeah, well," said Jason, "to criminals, cleverness isn't as much a factor as luck. But the Reverend's luck might be running out. The feds are getting closer."

"Okay," Allie urged. "So, again, where does Davy's father fit in?"

"Norberto Lopez was one of Worthey's operatives, a freight hauler for C-Essel. Worthey thinks Lopez ripped him off."

"What?" Allie asked, surprised. "What did he steal?"

Jason turned down the corners of his mouth. "Don't know for sure. Could be documents. Could be money. Could be a shipment of drugs. All I've heard is something has gone missing, and the Reverend is desperate to get it back. And now Norberto's missing, too. No one has seen him in weeks."

Allie's gaze fixed on Beck. "The key," she said in a breathy whisper.

Beck dipped his head, nodding slowly, but said nothing.

Jason looked from one to the other expectantly, his expression inviting clarification. When neither she nor Beck answered his silent inquiry, he pressed. "What key?"

Beck looked at Allie. "Go ahead. Tell him."

Allie repeated Marie's warning, and filled him in on how she ended up at the ranch with Beck.

"Then last week we found a key Davy had hidden in his Monopoly game. He said his mother gave it to him."

Jason's eyes grew round, and he pursed his lips, intrigued. "Well now," he said. "Interesting." Allie could almost hear the wheels going around in his head, the cogs connecting, his investigator's mind fitting it all together.

"That must be what they're looking for," Beck said. "Norberto must have given the key to Marie, and Marie gave it to Davy. Now that Marie's dead, they're after Davy."

"And me," Allie added. "Remember? I told you someone else was in the house when Marie left the message on my answering machine. Whoever it was would have heard her tell me to take Davy and run. They know I have him. But they don't know where I am."

The silence that followed was palpable. Allie looked from Jason to Beck and back again.

"What?" she said.

"They do," said Jason. "They know where you are. The Reverend's wife knows."

"His wife?"

"That's why I came west. I'd been monitoring the Wortheys' activities in Michigan, trying to come up with some hard evidence I can use in my story and take to the feds. Then I heard Millie Worthey came to Durango. I drove out to see if I could find out what she was doing."

"What was she doing?"

"Mostly she sat in the saloons watching the street. But one day, she followed Beck's Hummer back here to the ranch."

Allie looked at Beck, then stared at Jason, trying to grasp his meaning. "You mean you followed her following Beck to the ranch?"

Jason shook his head solemnly. "Well, no, she wasn't following Beck. She was following you. Only, at the time, I didn't know it was you driving. Didn't recognize you." He tipped his head. "You know. You look so different like that.

"Anyway," Jason went on, "I wondered why Millie was interested in this place, so I came back later and drove around. I risked losing track of Millie, but I was curious, so I found a spot on the mesa where I could watch the cabin. I was hoping I'd be able to figure it out. Or that Millie would come back."

"So, did she come back?"

Jason nodded. "Yes. I saw her at the back door."

"That's not possible. Nobody's been here. Nobody ever comes here." She turned to Beck. "Isn't that right?"

When Beck didn't concur, a flicker of apprehension coursed through her.

"It was Millie," Jason insisted. "Big, husky woman. Bleached blonde hair. You stood on the porch talking to her."

Allie's mind went blank, and then a memory took form and she relaxed. "Oh, no, you're mistaken," she said. "That was the school guidance counselor. She was asking if Davy would be enrolling in . . ."

Her voice drifted off as realization took hold and understanding slid into place like pieces of a jigsaw puzzle. She'd let her guard down that day. She'd been thinking about Beck, worrying about his reaction to what she'd told him about his father. Instead of maintaining her unflagging vigilance, she'd lost her focus and allowed danger to catch up. That danger now took human form. A person. A woman.

Allie's chest tightened and burned. "She wasn't from the school."

"No," Jason confirmed, his eyes focused on her sharply. "That was Millie Worthey. And I have to tell you, I was damned shocked to see you come out that door. I'd heard talk that you'd run off with one of the kids, but I never expected to see you here. And then I couldn't figure out what your connection was to the Wortheys. So I've been watching the ranch hoping to get a clue about what was going on. That's what I was doing when Beck found me up on the mesa today."

Stunned, it took a few moments for the sound of Sadie's frantic barking to register in Allie's consciousness. Beck was out of his chair a split second before she was able to gather her feet under her. He flew out the front door, feet hammering down the porch steps, Allie close behind.

Davy wasn't there and neither was Sadie, but Allie could hear her agitated barking.

"Davy," Allie called. "Davy!"

"Davy!" Beck's voice, urgent, joined hers. "Davy, where are you?"

Allie stood in the center of the clearing, looking around. "He asked if he could go to Monica's to get one of Sadie's toys," she said. "I told him no, but maybe he went anyway."

At that moment, Sadie appeared, walking haltingly through the trees from the direction of Monica's house. Her nervous yipping dissolved into whimpering at the sight of them. Something was tied to her collar, and she dragged it through the dirt.

Beck went into a crouch and held out his hand, trying not to spook the already jittery dog. "Here, Sadie, come here, girl," he said. When she neared, he hooked a finger under her collar and gently pulled the trembling dog to him.

"What have you got there?" He checked her over to make sure she wasn't hurt, then removed the bag tied to her rhinestone collar. Inside was a cell phone, a handwritten note attached to it with a rubber band. He unfolded the note and read the terse message aloud. His voice was tight.

"I want what's mine or the boy dies. You'll receive delivery instructions on this cell phone. Keep it with you at all times. If it's not answered by the third ring, there will be no more phone calls. Don't contact the authorities."

"Oh, dear God, they took him," she breathed, covering her face with her hands.

Beck came to her, gathered her in his arms and held her against him. "Don't worry," he told her, tightening his arms. "We'll get him back."

A deep sob escaped from her throat, but she caught herself and fought it, then lowered her hands and looked into his eyes. Beck's strong presence was reassuring, but panic still rose inside her. She forced it down, knowing she had to maintain her self-control.

Jason held out his hand for the note, and Beck gave it to him. "Surely they don't think Davy has the key on him. Why would they take Davy instead of Allie?" Jason wondered aloud, reading it. "Or why not take both of them?"

"A child's easier to manage," Beck speculated. "And they know Allie will come for him."

Jason nodded at the cell phone Beck had taken from Sadie. "That's probably a disposable cell phone she bought at Wal-Mart. It can't be traced. She'll most likely toss hers after she calls with instructions. Either that or she'll call from her laptop using a blocking device. She's an extreme techie. Learned it in the military." He was silent a minute, thinking. "Better do as the note says. Wait for instructions."

"We don't have any other options," said Beck.

"None that I can see," Jason agreed. "But maybe Worthey won't hurt the boy. He wants what was stolen from him more than he wants the boy."

Allie glanced at him, uncertain. Though she recognized the lie intended to appease her, Jason's words held no comfort. She could tell by the furrow between his brows he didn't believe his own words. They both knew that if Davy could identify his kidnapper, he wouldn't be allowed to live.

Frightened, Sadie circled at their feet, whimpering, begging to be picked up. Beck bent down, took the dog in his arms, then led Allie back into the cabin where she collapsed onto the sofa. Jason followed. He took a seat in a hide covered armchair, and still studying the note, adjusted the light on a black iron floor lamp. Beck paced.

Allie sat taking slow, controlled breaths to keep panic at bay. No good ever came from hysteria. If she hadn't learned that by now, she never would.

A part of her, the part that still believed the good guys always won and the bad guys were always punished, demanded that she call the police immediately and report Davy missing. But gut wrenching reality forced her to reject such idealism.

She knew it would be a terrible mistake to call the police now. Better to follow instructions—no matter what was asked of her, she'd do it. Maybe that way there would be a chance she'd have Davy back unharmed. She avoided thinking about the alternative.

Beck stopped pacing, sat down next to her, and reached for her hand. His thumb brushed back and forth over the ridge of her knuckles. The cell phone lay on the coffee table in front of them, and Allie stared at it, willing it to ring. Minutes passed at an excruciatingly slow and painful pace.

Her eyes lifted to the rifle in the rack above the door where

Beck had put it only a short time before, and savage thoughts of retaliation and revenge against the woman who came to her door pretending to be someone she wasn't filled her mind. Allie remembered how overly interested Millie had seemed to be, staring at Davy, peering around the ranch, sneaking looks over Allie's shoulder taking in the layout of the cabin. Allie quelled the chaos of her thoughts, forcing a calm she did not feel.

When the phone rang, Allie's stomach somersaulted. She shot forward, reaching for it, but Beck snatched it up before she could.

"Hello? Hello?" he said, but the ringing continued. Across the room, Jason put his hand in the front of his jacket and took his phone from an inside pocket. He quickly thumbed it open and spoke into it.

"Jason Bright here," he said by way of greeting. His already serious expression intensified and his eyebrows slanted deeply as he listened to the voice on the other end.

"How do you know?" he said into the phone, but lifted his eyes to Allie. His gaze was grave. "You're sure?" he pressed the caller.

They were talking about her.

After a long moment, his eyes skittered away, and he spoke quietly to his caller, apparently resigned to the news he'd just received.

"Okay. Thanks for letting me know." He paused. "No, no, that's all right. Just keep me posted." With deliberation, he folded the phone and put it back in his pocket.

"That was one of my contacts," he explained, his voice grim. "Norberto Lopez has been murdered."

Allie gasped, and Jason cast her a sharp glance.

"Child Protective Services reported Davy missing. There's a warrant out for your arrest. For kidnapping." He paused. "And for the murder of Marie and Norberto Lopez."

Stunned, Allie opened her mouth to speak, but a lump of emotion closed her throat and no words came out.

"I don't have all the details," he continued, "but there's a massive manhunt on for you. Tomorrow your picture will be on the front page of every newspaper. The story is all over the cable news channels now."

Allie swallowed hard, dread pouring through her veins as Jason spoke.

"Even the governor has issued a statement. And you're going to be featured next Saturday night on America's Most Wanted."

CHAPTER NINETEEN

With one hand on the steering wheel and one eye on the road, Millie opened her laptop, which was mounted on a pedestal she'd had installed in her rental car within easy reach of the driver's seat. Terrorists had made it virtually impossible for her to travel with the tools of her trade, of which her laptop was the most important. That's why she drove everywhere she went, sometimes in her own car, but always in a rental car if she was traveling undercover. Driving, especially long distances, took more time and planning, but her laptop and its contents were too valuable to turn over to airport security, or anyone, even for a minute.

One of the problems with driving was that she often missed her gym workouts, forcing her to violate the first and foremost rule of her life, which was to stay physically fit, and by that, she meant strong, not trim. Trim was something she'd never be again. Most roadside motels didn't have workout rooms with the kind of equipment she required to keep her muscles toned. Also, the only food readily available along most major freeways was junk.

But driving was an absolute requirement of some of her jobs, and this was one of them.

She'd run into a little rain crossing La Veta Pass, but now that she was on the other side of the more than ninety-four-thousand-foot elevation, she was able to pick up her speed again. She applied steady pressure to the accelerator and slid a sidelong glance at Davy slumped against the passenger side door.

His head was dropped to his chest, and his eyelids hung at half-mast, but his eyes weren't fully closed. The only thing that kept him from pitching forward into the dash panel was the seatbelt.

She was pleased to see that he'd quickly succumbed to the sedative she'd slipped into his Dairy Queen shake in Pagosa Springs, even though she'd used it sparingly. She didn't want to put enough in to damage the kid or, God forbid, kill him. Hell, she liked kids, and now and then even wished she'd had some of her own.

No, all she wanted was to keep him quiet and compliant for the day and a half of straight driving it would take to reach the Reverend, and he wanted the child very much alive. Also, she wanted him capable of walking into public restrooms under his own power without arousing the suspicions of do-gooder by-standers.

She checked her watch. Soon she'd be in Walsenburg where she would shoot north on I-25 through Denver, then angle off on I-76. At Julesburg, she'd connect to I-80 and take it all the way to Toledo, after which it was a straight shot up the I-94 to Detroit. Once there, she'd unmount her laptop, dump the car, which she'd rented with a phony credit card, and meet up with the Reverend's driver who would take them two hours north to the Church of Spiritual Light children's camp.

But now, it was time to call Allie Hudson.

Millie had cleared the steep mountain canyons of the San Juans and was approaching the more populated areas where wireless connectivity would be available. She tapped some keys on her laptop and seconds later was on the Internet via cellular modem. Routing through the voice data equipment on her laptop, she dialed the number of the prepaid cell phone she'd left for Allie. It was answered on the first ring.

"Hello?" Allie's voice sounded rushed and breathless.

"Here are your instructions," Millie said, speaking into the computer's microphone.

"Where's Davy? Put him on!"

"He's fine. Calm down."

"Don't tell me to calm down! Where are you taking him?"

"Here are your instructions," Millie repeated, ignoring Allie's question and putting additional muscle into her voice. "Follow them to the letter. If you don't, I won't call you any more and you won't see Davy again. So, do as I say."

A pause, and a muffled sob. "Okay."

"Come to Detroit. Be there in three days. You'll receive further instructions after you arrive. I'd suggest you not lose that cell phone I left for you. I don't do call backs."

"But Davy—"

"You know what to bring."

"I want to talk to Davy—"

"By the way. Don't bother trying to trace this phone. There's a blocking device on it."

Beside her, Davy stirred and mumbled something. Allie's voice coming through the speaker had roused him, and he raised his head and looked at Millie. Confusion and fear swirled behind his half-closed eyes. He ran his tongue over his dry lips, and croaked, "Is that Allie?"

Quickly, Millie spoke again. "I'll call you in Detroit in three days with further instructions."

"Davy!" Allie shouted through the speaker. "I'm coming to—" But Millie disconnected the call, cutting her off.

Davy stared at her, expressionless, a blank look glazing his tired eyes.

"Are you hungry?" she asked him.

He nodded and licked his lips again.

She took a bottle of water from the cup holder in the console and handed it to him. He drank greedily.

"We'll stop for hamburgers in Castle Rock."

Davy didn't respond. He finished off the water and dropped into a twilight sleep.

Millie ordered burgers, fries, and apple pies at the drive-thru, and they ate in the car, staying on the move. Davy didn't say anything or ask any questions. He ate hungrily, but dozed off before he got to the apple pie. Late afternoon traffic on I-25 was beginning to pick up, so Millie settled into the left hand fast lane. Once at cruise speed, she tapped the keyboard again, accessing her e-mail account.

She had mail, a message from the Reverend asking for a progress report. She smiled to herself, another mission successfully accomplished. The Reverend would be proud of her. Holding the steering wheel with her left hand while keeping an eye on the road ahead, she typed a reply with her right.

"Delivery guaranteed. Temporary Mama will follow and pick up further instructions in Detroit."

Temporary Mama was the code name she used for Allie.

"ETA tomorrow evening," she typed. "Will call with specifics. Plan to pick us up."

After dark she stopped for gas and took Davy into the restroom with her, but she stood outside the door of the stall while he used the toilet and had him do the same when it was her turn. Because he believed he was going to see his mother, Millie knew he wouldn't run away. When finished, she performed an awkward hand washing routine, trying to clean him up, too, without touching too many surfaces in the cramped, grimy bathroom.

She paid for the gas, bought candy bars, coffee, and bottles of water, and left quickly. She needn't have worried about onlookers. No one in the station paid attention to them, least of all the cashier who argued over the phone with her boyfriend while ringing the cash register and making change.

In the car, Millie reclined the back of Davy's seat, and put a pillow under his head. She took the top off the coffee, blew on it and took a sip, then pushed the gear shift into drive and headed into the night.

CHAPTER TWENTY

Allie woke before daylight, surprised she'd slept at all. After hearing Davy's voice over Millie's phone yesterday, knowing he was alive, her panic had subsided the tiniest bit. Somehow she had managed to focus on preparations for the trip to Detroit.

Luckily, Beck had been able to get two plane reservations leaving at dawn from a regional airport an hour's drive away. They'd need to change planes in Denver, but then it was a direct flight to Detroit Metro.

She laid her clothes, purchased yesterday from the consignment shop on Second Avenue, on the bed. Baggy straight leg jeans, a blue and orange Denver Broncos visor cap, a too-big, laundry-faded tee shirt, and a stretched out cardigan to go over it.

She showered and stepped out of the tub, cringing a little when she caught her reflection in the mirror over the sink. Last night, her hair, thanks to Clairol's Nice 'n Easy Color Blend technology, had been transformed into a glossy dark chestnut brown. The dark color didn't go with her pale skin. It made her face look drawn and ghostly. Silently, she mourned her beautiful salon-created platinum highlights.

She dried herself and dressed, then peered at her face in the mirror. She picked up a newly purchased dark brown eyebrow pencil and carefully stroked color on her brows blending it in with her natural color. No lipstick, no mascara, no blush, only a smudge of grey shadow under each eye. Eyeglasses with black plastic frames purchased from Wal-Mart completed the look. She slipped on the dark blue cardigan sweater, pilled from wear and many washings, pulled the visor of her cap low, and checked her reflection again.

Now that she was being targeted, her picture in all the newspapers and on television, every police department in the country looking for her, this was the only way she could hope to go back to Detroit to get Davy without being recognized. It had to work. Davy's life, and hers, depended on it.

Beck was waiting in the kitchen, and looked her over when she came in carrying her travel bag.

"You don't look anything like your picture on television," he said, pouring coffee.

He was in khakis, cotton turtleneck, and hiking boots. No one was looking for him, so he didn't have to do much in the way of disguise, but he'd cut his hair short anyway. Her heart pinched a little at the sight.

"I'm sorry," she said, indicating his hair, which he'd covered with a backwards baseball cap. "You didn't have to do that." He didn't respond, and she added, "You don't have to do any of this, you know. I can go by myself."

"I know you can," he said, showing a reassuring grin over his coffee cup, "but I'm not going to let you."

She returned a brief smile, warm gratitude filling her heart, but she said nothing.

They finished their coffee, grabbed a bite to eat, and while Allie put the dirty dishes in the dishwasher, Beck opened a plastic shopping bag showing the logo of a local medical supply shop. He took out a foam-padded nylon leg brace and scooted a chair out from under the kitchen table.

"Sit down," he said. "Prop your foot on my knee."

Sitting in another chair facing her, he fitted the brace around her leg and adjusted the Velcro fasteners. "It's not hinged, so you won't be able to bend your knee. I rented a collapsible wheelchair from the medical supply place. I'll wheel you to the plane. If security gets too curious and starts poking around, just act like you're in pain and tell them you twisted your knee hiking."

She eyed the contraption on her leg. "I don't know," she said, dubiously.

"There won't be a problem. Once we get through security at the local airport, we're cleared for entry into the secured areas at Denver International. In Detroit, it won't matter. They'll let us deplane first with the mothers and babies and other wheelchair passengers."

Gently, he lowered her leg to the floor. He reached in the shopping bag again and pulled out a sling.

"Here," he said, holding it out for her. "You sprained your shoulder, too. Put your arm in here."

She bent her arm and placed her elbow in the pocket of the nylon mesh sling. Beck adjusted the hook-and-loop closure and fitted the padded strap over her shoulder. He sat back and looked at her sympathetically. "Okay?"

Forlorn, she nodded. She wanted to smile, but couldn't. Apparently, neither could he.

Looking solemn, he carried their bags out to the Hummer, then came back for her. With her arm over his shoulder and his arm around her waist, she hopped across the porch and down the steps. He helped her into the passenger seat, then got in the other side and turned the ignition, roaring the engine to life.

"Have you got the key?"

She nodded. "It's in my carry-on." She patted the bottom front of her sweater. "The cell phone's here in my pocket."

"Are you all right?"

"Yes," she lied. "I'm fine."

There were quite a few travelers in the terminal even at that

232

early hour, mostly pipe line workers, gas drilling engineers, or archeologists taking a break from their work in the desert. Beck parked her in the wheelchair against the wall in a corner, then went back out to the car for their bags.

The terminal was tiny with big windows, a small ticket counter, and a few benches in the waiting area. It was more of an airstrip than an airport, too small to accommodate jetliners. Instead, they'd be flying on a twelve-passenger prop driven express shuttle.

Nervous, Allie pulled her visor lower to cover more of her face, but the other travelers either ignored her or affected the usual disinterested notice reserved for people in wheelchairs. From where she sat, she could see passengers being screened at the door leading to the tarmac, and for a moment her courage faltered. The screeners, who also performed the duties of ticket agent and baggage handler, were vigilant in their security duties, thoroughly searching briefcases, sifting through the contents of carry-ons, occasionally pulling someone aside for a hand search. Allie closed her eyes, heart pounding. Oh, shit.

She'd wondered how she'd be able to board a plane without a driver's license or passport, and last night Beck had given her some authentic looking identity papers showing a fictitious name and an address in a Detroit suburb. When she'd asked where he got them, he said simply, "The same place millions of teenagers and illegal border crossers get them every day." His tone didn't invite further inquiry, so she shut up and let it go at that.

What did it matter now? When this was over, she was probably going to jail for the rest of her life anyway. Beck would undoubtedly do jail time for helping her.

Beck returned and took a casual stance beside her, their duffel bags slung over his shoulder. Outwardly, he appeared calm, but she could see the hardness in his eyes. When their flight was called, he wheeled her to the screening area. Nervous perspiration started in her armpits. She hoped it wouldn't smell.

At the boarding door, she winced and gritted her teeth when Beck removed her shoes so the screeners could run them through the x-ray machine. A plump, pleasant-faced security screener clucked sympathetically as she ran the hand-held scanner over Allie's body.

"What happened, hon? Car accident?" she asked.

"No. I fell. Hiking." Allie made her breath come fast and shallow as if she were in pain. "Tripped on a loose rock."

"Can you raise that arm any?" the screener asked, pointing to the sling.

Allie grimaced and lifted her elbow a little away from her side. "Only this much."

"Sorry, sweetie. I have to do this."

"I just want to go home," Allie whimpered.

"I know." The screener finished with her, but ordered Beck to take off his belt, watch, and shoes, then hold out his arms and turn around while she scanned him, too. Satisfied Allie was nothing more than an unfortunate hiker accompanied by her obliging boyfriend, the screener allowed them through.

Seated on the plane, Beck looked at her coolly. He took her hand and squeezed her fingers. "Good work," his eyes said. "Don't worry."

When the pilot came out of the cockpit and asked the passengers to move around to other seats, spreading out to help balance the plane for takeoff, Allie broke out into a full-on sweat.

Following a layover in Denver, they deplaned in Detroit, and Beck wheeled Allie to the car rental counter where he'd reserved a vehicle. A stab of panic sliced into her when she saw the missing child poster on the wall behind the counter. Davy's picture was on it, and a smaller picture of her taken from her driver's license. Her real driver's license from the Michigan Department of Motor Vehicles, not the phony one Beck had obtained for her. Davy wasn't very recognizable; he'd grown since the photo was taken. Hers was spot on except for the long red hair. Disconcerted, she hunched her shoulders and slouched further down, pretending to read the newspaper Beck had picked up at the newsstand.

Their rental SUV was brought around to the curb, and Beck made great pretense of helping Allie into the front seat. After he secured her seatbelt, he loaded the wheelchair into the back. Allie looked around uneasily at the bustling crowd, but none of the other travelers were paying any attention to them. They were too busy securing their luggage, schlepping off to airport parking, negotiating for a cab, or hunting down public transportation.

Overhead, cirrus clouds smeared a weak blue sky, the sun failing miserably in its attempt to burn through and warm the air. Beck drove, and since he was unfamiliar with the area, Allie directed him through the maze of airport traffic to I-94.

"When is Jason going to call?" she asked.

"Pretty soon. I told him what time our plane would be landing."

"Take this next exit coming up," she directed. "When we get downtown, we can check into one of the motels along Jefferson Avenue. They'll probably have a street map at the front desk. Maybe we can locate that address Davy had in his backpack."

Beck checked his rearview mirror before easing into the exit lane, merging onto I-96 heading toward Detroit. The time zone change made it late-afternoon rush hour. They found themselves caught in slow moving lanes of traffic passing along the roadway like a sluggish herd of cattle during round up. Allie angled away from the window to avoid the possibility of being recognized by someone in the next car.

235

Her nerves were raw, and she sat back, fighting off a grey haze of misery. She closed her eyes and conjured up pictures of Davy in happier days, a part of her hoping that by doing so she could somehow make them real again. Davy smiling big when he rode his new bike that first time, the way his eyes lit up when Jobby brought the saddle in for his birthday. Davy cuddling with Sadie, the shrewd serious look he got when he was winning at Monopoly.

Convulsively, she gripped the arm rest, beating back a burning sob that swelled her throat. *I'm coming, Davy. Just hold on, baby, wherever you are. I'm coming to get you.*

She snapped back to the present when Beck's phone rang. He took it off the car charger, spoke briefly, and hung up.

"That was Jason. He just drove through Chicago," Beck told her. "He should be in Detroit late tonight. He'll call tomorrow."

The outline of the city skyline appeared through a thick layer of haze, and they soon found themselves downtown. The once prosperous city, an international portal from Canada, had during the past forty years become a city of urban and industrial ruins. With the exception of the area around the convention center, which was bustling and vibrant, and some urban renewal along the waterfront, the rest of the city looked like it had been picked over and left for dead.

Here and there city booster organizations with grandiose aspirations were trying to help neighborhoods rise from the ashes—literally. Condominium and loft conversions in various states of development rose from the site of entire blocks that had either formerly burned to the ground or been bulldozed into a sort of urban prairie.

They passed the old, once glorious United Artists Building where graffiti artists had painted the windows of the towering hulk transforming the façade into an urban mosaic of Mayan symbols. Backlit from the setting sun, the windows glowed like stained glass.

By the time Beck pulled the SUV into a motel parking lot and got a room, Allie ached with weariness. Removing the sling and the leg brace, she watched the news, while Beck went out for food. An FBI spokesman came on and talked about her and Davy. Their pictures flashed on the screen. Someone from county family services deftly tried to spin the story in a way that absolved CPS of any responsibility for losing another child. Beck wasn't mentioned, and neither were the Wortheys.

Allie wondered where Millie Worthey had taken Davy, pictured him crying and afraid, her insides twisting with anger at the thought they might be hurting him. Later, she fell into bed exhausted, rage building until for the first time in her life she could imagine what it must feel like to want to kill someone. She felt a chill in the air as murderous intention filled the room. Instantly she cut herself off from the thought and prayed she'd find Davy in time.

"If you love burned out buildings, this is the place to be," Beck said the next day as they drove past block after block of low rent housing that had been devastated by combustion at various times during the last three decades. Concrete streets and weedy trash-filled sidewalks fronted more vacant lots than homes and businesses. The street looked as desperate as Allie felt. It was midmorning and still no call from Millie Worthey.

During the previous night, a cool wind from the north had rattled the windows, keeping Allie awake. The morning was unseasonably chilly, so Allie added a sweatshirt over her cotton tee and secured the Wal-Mart cell phone to a belt clip at her waist. Beck wore a black turtleneck sweater and a leather bomber jacket.

"I think it's near here," Allie said, alternately looking at the map in her lap and reading what corner street signs were still standing. They were searching for the address she found in Davy's backpack.

After a few blocks, the neighborhood changed somewhat for the better, though it still wasn't prime real estate. A few of the homes were still standing, mostly run down two-family attached houses with Big Wheels and tricycles tipped over in the dirt yard where grass had once grown. Meager attempts at revitalization had been made on a few of them; curtains in the front windows, flower pots on porch railings, fresh paint on the side facing the street, but everything looked unfinished, like the owners had lost heart or hope, or run out of money or time.

Beck drove slowly, peering at the numbers on the left side of the street. Allie looked on the right. Many of the structures didn't show street numbers, so it was hit and miss.

At the next intersection, dirt and trash littered the gas bays of what looked to be an abandoned gas station. Two of the three pumps were clearly broken. Other businesses were equally run down. A check cashing place, two bars, a tiny shoe repair shop, and a bakery with those old-fashioned slanted display windows but no baked goods on the shelves.

"Is this the address?" Beck asked, braking and pulling to the curb. He leaned across to get a better look on her side.

"No, but the number's close. It must be nearby."

The screen door of the station swung open, and an old black man shuffled out carrying a pack of cigarettes.

"Looks like they're open for quick-stop business. Maybe someone in there knows where this is." Beck took the slip of paper from Allie and got out. "Wait here and lock the doors," he warned.

She did. This was not a part of town she would have wanted to come to on her own, and was grateful to Beck for sticking by her one last time. Once she knew Davy was safe, she was going to turn herself in to the authorities and hope for the best. After that, she'd probably never see Beck again. Emotion swelled inside her.

Not many people were on the sidewalks, and only a few battered cars were parked at the curb. Allie waited nervously until Beck came back. She unlocked the door when he approached.

"That's it." He pointed. "That big building over there, across the street. Looks like an old warehouse."

Allie peered at the derelict building. At street level, a faded sign identified it as a former car repair garage. The upper floors looked like apartments bereft of tenants. The windows were thick with dirt, some were broken. Frayed weather-beaten lace curtains fluttered out one of them.

"The building belongs to the gas station owner," Beck said. "He rented it to a man who said his name was Norberto Lopez. He claimed to be a mechanic, was going to open an auto body and repair shop. Lopez paid three months rent in advance, but the current rent's a month overdue. The owner's waiting for Lopez to come back and pay him."

"He doesn't know Norberto's dead?"

Beck shook his head. "And I didn't mention it. I told him Lopez asked me to keep an eye on his space, but I'd lost the key. Apparently Lopez changed the locks, so the owner doesn't have a key, either. I caught him up on the rent with a little extra, and he said I could check it out, but if I had to break in or damaged anything, I'd owe him some more."

Beck locked the SUV and they crossed the street to stand on the sidewalk in front of the building, looking it over. It was three stories of grime encrusted brick, old, but with solid looking walls. Time had not been kind to what once had been a decent building, possibly even a prosperous location in its day.

On the street side ground floor, two large boarded up windows framed a set of sagging, weathered garage doors, the kind that opened out from the middle to admit a horse and car-

fascinating in a sick kind of way. She could almost feel the abandoned building's faint heartbeat. It smelled of growing things, moss blending with the rotting carpet, animals, insects, birds. The stale musty odor of the past.

Though deserted, it wasn't empty. Tenants had abandoned tables, chairs, dishes, lamps, and sofas. By now most of the fabric had rotted away. Magazines and newspapers, books with pages missing and torn, empty picture frames, and other forgotten items left behind were ghostly remnants of the life that once flourished there. It was almost like reading someone's diary.

They stepped over fallen plaster and holes in the floors, peering into decaying rooms. Pigeons roosted on cupboards, mice nested in upholstery, fungus grew on walls, weeds sprouted on windowsills or in dirt packed into the corners.

After Beck tested the stairway for sturdiness, they crept down to street level into what used to be an auto repair shop. At one time, vandals had had a field day in there. Greasy car parts, mostly broken, were strewn about, rubbish had been dumped around, workbenches tipped over, tools destroyed beyond usefulness then tossed into corners. Wall shelves showed round marks where cans of oil once were stacked. Sheets of paper littered the floor and desktop and every flat surface of what used to be a makeshift corner office. Invoices, letters, orders for car parts.

High up the wall, daylight barely filtered in through filthy windows near the ceiling. There was enough illumination to see a shiny, new looking cargo van, the kind with solid sliding side panels. The logo on the door said "Church of Spiritual Light."

The sight was so unexpected all Allie could do was stare at it, not blinking.

"Jesus," Beck said, the word blowing out of him on a breath. "What have we here?"

Warily, he approached the vehicle and tried the driver's door.

It was locked, and not surprisingly, the key didn't fit.

Allied cupped her hands and peered through the windows at the top of the rear doors. She saw shipping cartons, some of them with the tops open exposing their contents—candle holders, coffee cups, serving platters, and a variety of other CSL-logoed products.

"Beck, look here."

Beck joined her. After a moment, he stepped away and walked around the garage, looking for something. Finding a long, flat piece of metal, he went to work on the driver's door and managed to flip the lock. He opened it, reached into the back, and slid the lock lever on the side panel doors. Allie dragged them open and leaned inside.

"Looks like the kind of stuff they sell in a church gift shop," she said.

"Yeah," he said thoughtfully, his eyes narrowing. "It does. But what is it doing here?"

Together they went through the boxes. There were Bibles, religious art and jewelry, incense, chimes, crosses and crystals on leather cords, self-improvement books, CDs and DVDs.

Beck turned, reached over the front seat to pull the hood latch.

"Keep going through those boxes. I'm going to look under the hood."

Allie dug through the unsealed boxes and ripped the tops of others.

"If this is Davy's truckload of money," she speculated, "it's pretty meager. None of it appears to be particularly valuable. Do you think it might be worth more across the border?"

"Maybe, but not much. I'd say eight or ten thousand dollars, less on the black market." Beck looked under the hood while Allie continued to search in back.

"Then why would it be hidden here?"

"I dunno."

"What are we looking for?" she asked.

"I dunno. Just keep looking," Beck answered, his voice muffled in the engine compartment.

It was hard going. Perspiring, she pulled her sweatshirt off over her head and tied it around her waist. She opened a case of prayer cards. One of the boxes held books on healing and spiritual growth. Another had note paper and religious greeting cards. Methodically, she opened each box, sorted through and unpacked it looking for something that might give a clue to why it was there.

She shoved aside a carton of books. Behind it was a metal box with a hinged top, the kind available at office supply stores called safe deposit boxes. Only this one was the size of a picnic cooler on wheels, and too heavy for her to move.

"I found something," she said.

Beck's head popped up around the hood. "What?"

"I think I found what that key is for."

He came around and knelt beside her, taking the key from his pocket. The key eased into the lock and turned smoothly, releasing the mechanism. A combination of anticipation and dread settled in Allie's chest as she waited for him to lift the hinged top. When he did, she gasped in shock.

"Holy shit!" he said.

The box was filled with money, paper currency tied with twine, sorted into packets and labeled by denomination. The startling moment lengthened.

"How much do you think is there?" Allie asked.

"It's hard to tell," Beck said, his scrutiny long and hard. "It looks like they're all used bills, and in small denominations. Just the kind of money that's exchanged in drug deals. Used bills take up more space than new ones, so I'd guess . . ." Beck hesitated and riffled through the stacks of bills, lifting one up

244

and flipping the ends. He calculated in his head. "It could be several million dollars."

Allie's jaw dropped as realization struck. "Norberto stole this and hid it here intending to come back for it. Something must have happened to make him afraid he might not be able to, and he gave the key to Marie hoping she could get to it."

Beck nodded and continued pulling packets of money out, placing them on the floor of the van. On the bottom of the box was a Ziploc plastic freezer bag filled with computer disks and CDs. He pulled it out and held it up.

"This must be what Jason was talking about," Beck said, thoughtfully. "He said there was documentation incriminating enough to severely damage if not destroy Worthey and his church."

After a stretch of silence, Beck sat back on his heels. "You know what I think?"

"What?"

"I think this might be your bargaining chip."

The same thing had occurred to her, but she'd been afraid to give the thought free rein.

"This is not an inconsequential amount of money to the Reverend," he went on. "Without it, he can be set back financially to the point where his ability to make further deals is impaired. So he'll do anything to get it back. But I think he wants what's on these computer disks even more."

"But do you think he'll actually trade Davy for them?" she asked.

"Maybe. If he thinks you don't know what's on them," he said. "You could have the upper hand."

The Wal-Mart cell phone chirped and Allie grabbed it from her waist and answered it. Her hands were shaking and she willed them to stop, but they wouldn't cooperate.

"Hello."

"Is this Allie Hudson?" a man asked. The Reverend?

"Yes, this is Allie."

"Have you arrived in Detroit?" His voice was smooth, calm, in the tenor range, with a phony upper class intonation.

"Yes."

"Where are you?"

Allie's eyes darted around uncertainly. "I'm in Greektown looking for a place to have lunch," she lied, hoping Jason was right about these prepaid phones being untraceable.

"Are you ready to return what belongs to me?"

"Yes, if you return what belongs to me."

"You are in no position to set criteria, Miss Hudson." His voice suddenly had a sharp edge. "I thought Millie made that quite clear. I want what belongs to me and if I don't get it back, I'm prepared to exact appropriate retribution. The little boy's father stole something from me and, in turn, he paid a very large price for his mistake."

"I don't know what was stolen from you. All I have is a key. I don't know what it's for." Allie exchanged a hard look with Beck. He nodded, urging her to continue that line of conversation.

"That's a start," replied the Reverend.

"Can I have Davy back if I give you the key?"

There was a pause and Allie wasn't sure if he was thinking or waiting for her to say something more.

"Bring it to the church camp tomorrow morning," he said finally.

Allie shot Beck a look and tilted the phone away from her lips. "He wants me to go to the summer camp," she mouthed.

Beck shook his head, his eyes wide, mouth firm and tight.

"No," she said into the phone. "We'll make the exchange downtown."

This time there was such an extended silence, she was afraid the connection had been lost. Then she heard the release of a long exasperated breath.

"Where?" he asked in a tone that implied his gracious manner was deteriorating fast.

She thought quickly. "In front of the city hall on Jefferson Avenue. Tomorrow afternoon at five-thirty."

Another protracted silence on the other end caused Allie's heart to pound.

Finally the Reverend spoke again, his voice fraught with meaning. "Is it necessary for me to describe what will happen to the boy if you don't show up?"

Her stomach dropped and she swallowed hard. "No, it's not," she croaked. "Don't worry. I'll be there."

"You'd better be," he said before the phone went dead.

Fear bubbled into her throat, but Beck wrapped his arms around her and she was able to contain it.

"How are we going to find out what's on these CDs?" she asked him, straightening her shoulders and composing herself. She couldn't crumble now, they'd come too far. "There's no computer at the motel."

"Jason must be back in town by now. Let's take them to his office and he can look at them on his computer."

They left the way they'd come in. Luckily, the SUV was still parked where they'd left it and hadn't become a stolen car statistic.

Allie checked the city guide that had come with the rental car and found the location of the newspaper building. Jason wasn't in, so she left a message with the girl at the front desk telling him to call.

That night in bed, Beck reached out an arm to pull her close. He held her tight and put his lips to her hair. She turned around and flung her arms around his neck and hung on until the sun came up and it was time to start the day.

They met Jason for breakfast at Denny's, and Beck told him what they'd found in the old garage.

"Can you take a look at these on your computer?" he asked, showing Jason the CDs.

"I've got a meeting in an hour out in Bloomfield Hills," Jason said, hurrying through his meal. "But give them to me and I'll check them out as soon as I get back to the office."

CHAPTER TWENTY-ONE

Davy was stretched out on his stomach on the floor, his chin propped on his fists watching the activity in an ant colony. He'd never seen an ant colony like this one where instead of dirt the ants made trails through blue-green gel in a glass tank. It looked like an aquarium only with ants instead of fish. Lights in the base of the tank cast bluish green shadows around the room.

Davy, mesmerized, moved his finger on the glass, tracing the intersecting network of passageways the ants had made. What fascinated him most was the way the ants dug deep into the gel, and no matter what, they always managed to find their way back to the surface. He studied their movements, trying to discern a pattern to the ant logic that always allowed the insects to emerge unscathed through a complex series of tunnels. Sometimes they had to dig a new tunnel that branched out from the main one, but they always found their way.

Watching the success of the ants gave him hope, hope that he would soon be out of wherever this was the school board lady had brought him. He thought it might be a camp or school of some kind, because when he looked out a high window, he saw trees and fences and wooden buildings that looked like bunk houses. Once he saw other kids in the distance, sitting in a half circle in front of a grownup who seemed to be giving a lesson.

But mostly he saw grownups walking from one low slung building to another along white stone paths, or riding in pickups on dirt packed roads, or disappearing into the woods on ATV quads. They were like the quad Jobby used at Beck's ranch to haul the weeds and brush he cleared away from around the house and in the yard. Jobby had let him drive it once.

Though he wondered where he was, he wasn't afraid. He was used to being moved from place to place, living with strangers, and so far, this wasn't too bad. He had a room to himself with lots of pillows on the bed, plenty of toys to play with and books to read. He had just about anything he wanted to eat.

But, still, he was mad.

He was mad because the school board lady had tricked him. When he'd seen her standing in Monica's back yard, she'd told him she was going to take him to see his mother, but so far his mother hadn't shown up. He was disappointed because he'd wanted to tell his mother he was sorry for not keeping the secret about the key. If he'd known he wasn't going to see her, he'd have run away while the school board lady was in the bathroom at one of the rest stops.

And now, he was pretty sure he'd never see his mother again.

He'd been very sleepy while they were driving in the car, but not so sleepy he couldn't figure out some things on his own. He was pretty sure Millie had wanted him to be sleepy, and he thought she'd probably given him some medicine to make him that way.

Tears leaked out the corners of his eyes. Since there was nobody to see, he let them slide down his cheeks. He missed Allie and thought about how angry she probably was because he went to Monica's house after she told him not to. He wondered if Allie was so angry she wouldn't come get him. And then he wondered if Allie had asked the school board lady to come and take him away.

He wiped his face with the back of his hand and watched a line of ants march single file through a long subterranean passageway. Suddenly one of the ants stopped and began digging a new tunnel, dividing the trail into a Y. After some very hard work, this rebel ant connected his tunnel to another tunnel a few inches away, creating a shortcut. Davy thought that was very cool.

Just then, he heard footsteps outside his door. A key turned in the lock, and Millie came in carrying a tray.

"I brought you a snack to hold you over until dinner. Do you like chocolate chip cookies?"

Davy pushed himself up from the floor and took a seat at a little table. Millie set the tray in front of him and sat on the edge of the bed watching him eat.

Davy took a cookie from the plate and chewed thoughtfully, his eyes on Millie. "How long do I have to stay here?" he asked.

She smiled. "I don't know."

He stared at her and kept on chewing.

"Why can't I go outside?" he asked. "And play with those other kids?"

Millie gazed at him a long time, and she looked like she was thinking about something else. She looked at him with eyes that were nice, even if her voice was sort of rough and deep.

"When you finish your snack, I'll take you for a ride on the Ranger," she said.

"What's a Ranger?" He nibbled on a cookie, watching Millie's face.

"It's an ATV, like a quad only bigger. Would you like that?"

Davy nodded, but wondered if it was a trick.

It was the first time Millie had allowed him outside his room in two days. He barely remembered arriving, so now was surprised to see that his room opened onto a windowless hallway in a long narrow building. With her hand on his shoulder, Millie guided him down the hall and out the back door, down three wooden steps and across a patio between two buildings to a vehicle shed at the edge of the trees. Inside the shed was the coolest ATV he'd ever seen. It was shiny green with fat, knobby tires and a chrome roll bar, and a lot bigger than Jobby's quad.

Millie sat behind the wheel. He climbed in beside her and buckled himself in. With her foot on the brake, she turned the key and fired the engine, then shifted into gear and rolled out. In the distance, Davy saw some kids wearing shorts and hiking boots, carrying backpacks with sleeping bags rolled on top. They were coming out of the woods and filing into a bunkhouse. They were excited, calling out to each other and horsing around.

Millie quickly turned in the opposite direction, and steered down a trail into the woods where they bumped along a dirt path. From somewhere nearby, Davy heard the whine of a power saw. Someone was building something. Up ahead, through the trees, he saw water, a lake. At the water's edge, rowboats were anchored on shore, and rubber rafts were stacked and tied together above the high water mark.

They came to a stop on the sand, and Millie cut the engine. He thought about making a run for it, but he didn't know where he was. And besides, where would he go? He was only a kid.

"Why don't you take off your shoes and socks, and run around a while. Get some exercise. You can go wading in the lake if you want to."

Davy did want to, but held back, unsure. He shook his head no.

"Come on," Millie urged. She reached into the back and flipped up the lid on a cargo box. "I've got a Frisbee. Let's play."

At first he thought this might be another trick, but soon he started to have fun. No matter how hard or high he threw the Frisbee, Millie almost always caught it. And she threw it back hard, too. So hard, he had to run for it, and he hardly ever caught it. He wished there was a Monopoly game in his room. He'd beat the pants off her. But still, playing Frisbee was fun.

He was quick-stepping backwards, reaching up to catch a high flyer, when Millie's phone rang. She dug it out of her pocket and thumbed it on, then talked to someone for a minute. The Frisbee had landed in the shallow water, and he had to wade out to reach it. When Millie stopped talking on the phone, she wasn't smiling anymore. She came over to him and took the Frisbee out of his hand.

"We have to go," she said, taking his arm and hustling him into the Ranger. He barely had enough time to scoop up his shoes and socks.

"Where are we going?" They were moving before he finished buckling his seatbelt.

"The Reverend wants us ready to go in ten minutes."

He noticed Millie wasn't going back the way they'd come. Instead she drove into a thick stand of trees, bouncing over the rocky ground, tree limbs slapping at the roll bar. She entered an opening in the rock that looked like a cave. At first it was dark inside, but after his eyes adjusted, he saw they were in a concrete passageway dimly lit from overhead. It made him feel a little bit like being in the ant farm. The sound of the Ranger's motor reverberated on the walls, magnifying the sound.

"Don't mention that we went to the lake," she warned, speaking loudly over the sound of the engine. "The Reverend won't like it that I let you out of your room."

"But where are we going?" he asked again. It took real effort to stop newly rising fear from building inside him and giving him a stomachache. He didn't like the look on Millie's face, like she was afraid, too. "And why are we going this way?"

"Because it's a shortcut and we're in a hurry. The Reverend doesn't like to be kept waiting."

"Are we going someplace?"

"Yes. We're going to meet Allie."

CHAPTER TWENTY-TWO

Stepping over piles of bum trash and old construction debris, Beck walked across the sagging floorboards of a musty third floor room in an aged office building on which the renovations had long since been forsaken. Dust, mold, and animal droppings befouled the air.

Vandals and trespassers had destroyed everything. Broken glass was everywhere. Fast food containers, soft drink cans, and used condoms. Candy wrappers. Booze bottles. Dirty oil-soaked rags and old newspapers rotted into a layer of filth that looked like it had been veneered to the floor. Strangely, a chair with a folding writing surface, the old-fashioned kind used in elementary schools, was smack in the middle of the room. The whole place smelled like urine.

Avoiding some unidentifiable sticky spots on the floor, Beck made his way to the windows at the front wall overlooking the street below. Scaffolding erected on the exterior of the building hung loosely from bolts fixed in the outside brickwork. He looked around for something to use to wipe grime off the window, and finding nothing, used the sleeve of his shirt to clear a spot at eye level. It helped only a little, but he held the camera to it anyway, peered through the viewfinder, and focused the telephoto lens until Allie was framed in the viewfinder.

She was across the street, standing on the steps of the City County Building at the foot of Woodward Avenue where he'd dropped her, waiting for the Wortheys to bring Davy.

The sun had long ago disappeared behind the ragged edge of a low slung cloud shelf, and a sharp wind coming off the Detroit River had dipped the temperature considerably. Rain threatened.

Trash swirled along the sidewalk propelled by a gust of wind. Allie hunched her shoulders against the chill, holding the edges of her denim jacket together at the neck. Beck zoomed in and brought the image of her face close up. Worry lined her forehead and pulled at the corners of her mouth. Nervously she shifted her weight from one foot to the other as she watched the street, her eyes alert, darting, probing every passing vehicle.

Once she had Davy, she'd hustle him up the steps and into the building's main entrance. Beck would meet them in the lobby, and the three of them, along with Jason Bright, would dash over to the FBI field office on Michigan Avenue. Together, they'd tell their story and turn over the evidence they had collected against Reverend Worthey, including the pictures Beck was going to take of the exchange. The plan was a simple one. Maybe too simple, Beck thought now. There was no Plan B. No backup. The hell of it was, there were no options.

But even if their plan worked, even if they had Davy back and Worthey's operation came crashing down, they faced the very real possibility that Allie would go to jail for kidnapping. And him, too, for aiding and abetting.

The sky darkened, and a light rain fell, tiny drops that pattered and ticked against the windowpane. Across the street and below, it was quitting time. Civil service employees emerged from the City County Building and glanced up at the lowering sky before quickening their steps to the bus stop on the corner. Some of the men held folded newspapers over their heads as protection from the weather. Most of the women unfurled brightly colored umbrellas and held down skirts that blew up in the wind.

Beck sighted on Allie again, refocused, and widened the shot.

A panhandler approached and spoke to her. Instinctively, Beck tensed, but she waved the man away and he stalked off.

Beck's heart pinched. She looked tiny and vulnerable, dwarfed by the towering smoke glass high rises. Pedestrians swarmed around her, some of them accidentally bumping against her shoulder as they rushed by, but she ignored them, never taking her eyes from the street. He wanted to be down there with her, but feared the Reverend wouldn't give Davy up if she wasn't alone.

He lowered the camera to give his arm a rest, massaging the muscles strained from being flexed in one position for an extended time. Nearby, church bells chimed. He looked at his watch. The Reverend was fifteen minutes late. Nervous and impatient, Beck stretched his back and shoulders to relieve the tension. He re-checked the lens lock, then examined the telephoto lens to make sure it was free of dust. He lifted the camera and peered through the eyepiece.

The rain was picking up a little. Still, Allie waited, looking resolute, single-minded, and unconcerned about the weather. Time moved slowly by. His mind lulled itself into a mental rhythm in concert with the steady thrumming of the rain on the roof. His attention was caught by a freighter making its way down the Detroit River. Briefly, he zoomed in on the figure of a deckhand amidships at the rail, then swung back to focus on Allie.

She was standing near one of the city's landmark works of public art, and he filled the frame with it. The huge seated bronze figure held what looked like a globe in one hand and miniature people in the other. He wondered at the meaning and symbolism behind the work.

Suddenly he jumped, almost dropping the camera, when his cell phone rang unexpectedly loud in the empty space.

"Hello."

"It's Jason. Where are you?"

Beck told him. "Worthey's due any minute. Did you have a chance to look at those CDs?"

"Yes, and you'd better make sure you get Davy out of there today. Money laundering isn't the only thing Worthey's involved in. He's using that so-called children's camp of his to hide some pretty disgusting business. Those CDs are filled with pornography. Kiddie porn."

The impact of that knocked the breath from Beck's lungs, setting off something corrosive that churned in his gut and burned painfully.

"Oh, God," he breathed.

"I turned the CDs over to the FBI, but they were already on it. Apparently their investigation had turned up the same thing. They're preparing search and arrest warrants now. Worthey and the others are going to be served at the compound, tonight."

"How do you know that? About tonight, I mean."

"One of my contacts owns an ambulance service. He got a call from the FBI. They asked him to have some units on call ready to roll to the CSL compound."

"Oh, shit," Beck muttered. He couldn't help remembering the deadly outcome of an unsuccessful federal raid on a compound in Texas some years back.

"Yeah. I know," Jason offered quietly, his tone implying he was having the exact same thoughts. "But they're going to do everything they can to keep it peaceful. Their goal is to serve legal warrants and make arrests, search the premises, seize documents and other evidence. They don't want trouble, but if it looks like there's going to be some, they've got plenty of negotiators on hand. They don't want another Waco, either."

Beck blew a harsh breath.

"But," Jason went on, "the Reverend's got too much at stake to go down easily. He may decide to fight with everything he's

257

got. Thing is, no one's sure what he's got and how much."

"Do you know when?" Beck asked, after a pause. "What time they plan to go in?"

"Around three-thirty or four. You know how the FBI likes to use surprise to their advantage. I'll follow with a camera crew. I've already alerted some of the other media. Having reporters there with cameras may cause people to think twice before doing anything rash if they know it's going to be caught on video." He paused. " 'Course you can't count on that."

"No," said Beck. "You can't."

Just then, rain crashed down, whapping hard on the roof, making a hellish noise. Beck squinted through the watery curtain covering the windowpane, and during a momentary letup saw Allie running down the steps toward a black limousine at the curb.

"Gotta go," Beck told Jason. "Worthey just pulled up."

Beck jammed the phone into his pocket and raised the camera, pointing it out the window. Rain thrashed ferociously against the front of the building. Quarter-sized raindrops hit the glass so hard, he was surprised it didn't break. Fat rivulets ran down obscuring his view. Outside, the scaffolding swayed and creaked against the wind as metal support bolts worked their way out of concrete and brick. He expected to see it crash to the ground. All of a sudden, hail racketed on the roof, the sound ricocheting around the room like gunshots in an echo chamber.

Beck cursed and leaned forward, bracing his legs, frantic for a break in the downpour so he could zoom in and get a shot of Allie handing over the key, of Davy exiting Worthey's car, reuniting with Allie.

Thunder drummed overhead, and lightning split the brackish sky. He stood motionless, frozen in place, his finger hovering over the shutter waiting for a let-up in the storm when suddenly the camera flew out of his hands, and a white light exploded in his head bringing excruciating pain with it. Something had struck him from behind with the force of a sledgehammer. He stumbled and fell to the floor, but instinctively rolled on his back to see what it was.

Standing there was a man with no neck and massive shoulders. In his hand was a metal pipe. The son of a bitch had hit him. Beck tried to get up, but the pipe came down on him again. He collapsed and was instantly engulfed in a haze of agony.

After one last wallop that had rainwater washing up over the curbs, the leading edge of the fast-moving storm front passed over the river into Canada leaving behind fog and a miserable, misty drizzle.

Allie hurried down the marble steps toward the limousine where it had glided to a stop at the curb. The rear passenger window slid down, and she could see Davy sitting in the back-seat. He was peering over the shoulder of a heavyset man in a dark suit who was smiling at her, showing teeth almost as white as his shirt. It was Reverend Worthey. Millie sat on the other side of Davy, huddled in the far corner, the space between her brows bunched, looking like she'd eaten a bad grape.

Allie's step faltered. Her eyes probed Davy's pale face. Something was wrong with him. His eyelids drooped, his mouth was slack. He looked like he'd been drugged. Her stomach somersaulted, and fury erupted inside her.

What have you done to him, you prick?

Silent sobs heaved in her chest but she held them down and approached, stopping a few feet away. Slowly the door swung open. The Reverend, dressed in a black pinstripe suit with wide lapels, the crease in his pants sharp as a switchblade, held his hand out, palm open.

"May I have the key, please?" He was smiling a smile of pure evil, cunning and sly. "And the address where my belongings can be found so I may retrieve them." His voice was studied, deliberate and precise. A voice trained to first persuade, then intimidate.

She'd sealed the key and a note with the address in an envelope. She took it out of her pocket and held it just beyond his reach.

"Let Davy out," she demanded.

"The key first."

"No! Davy first!"

Allie glanced around at the people on the sidewalk. No one paid attention to them, and she realized she'd made a horrible mistake thinking a busy street corner provided any measure of safety. People hurried past, eyes averted, anxious to get where they were going, and she faced the wrenching reality that the busier the place, the less likely people were to notice what was going on around them.

The Reverend spoke quietly to someone out of sight. When he looked again at Allie, he was no longer smiling. Anger tightened the muscles in his face, narrowing his eyes to slits. He stared at her a long moment, then heaved an impatient sigh.

"Look, Miss Hudson. I'm tired of your games. I don't think you've thought this through. We have an innocent child here . . ." He motioned toward Davy, but didn't finish his statement, allowing a momentous pause to grow more significant.

"Now be reasonable. Give it to me, please." Though the request was spoken politely, she caught the undertone of warning in it.

Davy leaned forward, looking out, confusion swirling in his eyes. His gaze was riveted on hers, and she read the silent plea they imparted.

"Come on, Davy. Get out."

Davy made a move to climb over the Reverend's knees, but

the Reverend put a hand on his arm, holding him back.

"Give me the key," the Reverend repeated, his eyes boring into Allie. His tone was soft and insistent, but infinitely patient, as if he were speaking to a slow child. "When I have what belongs to me, you may have the boy."

"NO!" Allie screamed. Blinded by fury, she lunged toward the car. "You promised, you bastard!"

She tossed the envelope in the open door and reached for Davy, who was struggling against the Reverend's restraining hands. Just as she clasped Davy's outstretched arm, the Reverend moved like a striking snake and caught her wrist in a bone crushing grip, yanking her toward him, pulling her into the backseat. Other hands twisted in her clothing and helped haul her in. She fell hard, landing on her shoulder with a crunch.

The car door slammed shut. Somebody cried. Somebody screamed. She fought against the hands pushing her down, lashed out wildly with her fists and feet, yelling for help. Someone hit her hard in the face. She felt a pin prick in the soft flesh above her elbow.

Almost instantly, a heaviness came over her, a weight so intense she didn't think she could go on breathing. Voices sounding like they were buried under a mudslide penetrated her brain, which was quickly filling up with something thick and oozy.

"Don't give her too much," a woman's voice warned, alarmed.

The car began to move, and Allie felt like she was free-floating, swooshing up to the ceiling. A hand touched her cheek, a small hand. Davy. She scraped her eyes open and saw his face directly above hers. It was like she was looking at it through water. He was crying.

"You gave her too much!" the woman cried.

"She knows too much," the other voice said. Was it Worthey?

261

"I can't have her going to the authorities."

Hours later, Allie drifted to the surface, memories bubbling up alongside her, racing her to the top. The events of the day were rushing back to her, and she lay very still hoping they would overtake her. When she opened her eyes, all her injuries came to life. She tried to move, but let out a sobbing groan when hot needles tortured her shoulder. Someone was beating a drum in her head, and she wanted desperately to curl up against the onslaught of pain.

Vague memories materialized. The limousine stopping at a gate, a man shining a flashlight inside, then pointing it directly in her face, the bright beam hurting her eyes. She didn't remember getting out of the car. Someone must have carried her.

Moonlight streaming in through clerestory windows cast pale light into a grim, institutional looking room. She was in a narrow bed, like a folding cot.

Where was she?

Where was Davy?

She lifted her good arm and squinted at the lighted dial of her watch. Three-thirty, but it was dark, so it must be the middle of the night.

Careful not to jar her shoulder, she sat up and lowered her feet to the floor one foot at a time. She sat there a minute, waiting for pain to strike some new part of her body. Her muscles were stiff and she ached all over, but there was no major assault. If she held her arm just so, the ache in her shoulder was tolerable.

With effort, she slowed her breathing, and concentrated on listening, but all she heard was a ringing silence between beats of her heart. Gradually the fog cleared from her head and strength threaded back into her body.

She stood up, let a wave of dizziness pass, then moving gingerly, stepped up onto the mattress and peered out the high windows. In the clear full moonlight she could see a group of buildings situated at the base of a low hill in the distance. Two metal storage buildings. A big barn. A smaller barn. Several long buildings that looked like houses with porches, plain and boxy. Some of them were connected. Except for the prefab storage units, everything appeared to be constructed of weathered board and batten and had the look of a hunting lodge. She guessed she was at Reverend Worthey's church camp.

Suddenly, a flashlight beam traveled over the bumpy ground. Two men came into view, moving fast across the moonlit yard, and she ducked back from the window, but they didn't look her way. Clearly in a hurry, they disappeared along a stone path into the trees. Two more men followed, one of them talking, it sounded like arguing, into a cell phone. The other one carried a rifle. They, too, vanished into the trees.

Allie stepped down from the bed, fought off another dizzy spell, then looked around. The room was small, maybe ten by twelve, and it smelled like mildew, like her cottage in Caseville smelled when she opened it up for the season. There must be water nearby, a lake.

She stepped quietly to the door, put her ear against it and listened. Nothing, but that didn't mean no one was out there. She tried the handle, expecting it to be locked and it was.

But the door didn't fit snug in the doorjamb. There was space around the edges, and again she put her ear to the crack and held her breath, straining to hear. Still nothing. She tugged on the handle, rattling the door against the lockset.

When that brought no one running, she rapped her knuckles up and down the door panel. It sounded hollow. She took a step back, balanced on one booted foot, raised the other and thrust out with her heel, driving it just next to the knob. Once, and wood cracked. Twice, the doorframe splintered. The third time, the lock gave way.

Quickly, she took a step back and to the side, braced, ready to kick out violently if someone came in, but no one did. She waited a beat, then another, then peeked out into the dimly lit hallway. A straight backed wooden chair was shoved up against the wall, but, curiously, it was empty. Crushed cigarette butts on the floor next to it told her someone had been sitting there. It wasn't very long ago. She could still smell smoke in the air.

An exit sign glowed at the far end of the corridor. She trotted to the door, wincing at the pain in her shoulder, pushed the pressbar with her hip, and found herself outside. The sky was blue black and starry, the full moon falling away from apex. Daylight was beginning to bloom above the tree line to her left. Crickets and tree frogs were making a racket.

Quickly, she looked around, unable to get her bearings. She had a general impression of being surrounded by rolling land, but it was hard to tell because there were so many trees. The air was heavy with the scent of conifer. The smell of the lake was stronger, too. It must be nearby.

Flashlight beams climbed the trees, footsteps scrabbling in the dirt behind them. Allie ran around the end of the building, slipping into the shadows, out of the moon's light, and flattened herself against the wall. Men carrying battery operated lanterns, with weapons slung over their shoulders, ran into the trees in the direction the others had gone. Urgent voices carried on the breeze came to her from a distance, men calling to each other. The sound of engines starting, vehicles driving away.

She sensed a vibrancy in the air, an urgency, like something important was about to happen. It sent a deep unease through her, and she wondered chillingly why armed men were running around a children's camp.

She had to find Davy.

When it was quiet again, she stepped into the open and made a dash across a grassy area. Darting between a broken down school bus and a horse trailer, she headed for one of the buildings she'd seen from the window. Just as she reached the porch, a man slammed into her from behind, grabbing her around her upper body and throwing her off balance. She shrieked as pain radiated from her shoulder down her arm, but let herself be carried along with the forward momentum. Stopping abruptly, she dug in her heels and stepped back, tucking her head and ramming her hips and buttocks hard into his groin.

He wasn't expecting this, and the blow staggered him backwards. He went down still clinging to Allie and she fell with him, using him as a cushion as he hit the ground on his back with Allie on top of him. Quickly she sat up straddling him, made a fist, and swung a backward underhand into his groin. When his arms fell away from her, she bent her arm, gripped her fist, and thrust backward, ramming her elbow into his nose. He let out a howl.

She rolled off him and scrambled away on all fours, out of reach. She sneaked a quick look over her shoulder and saw he wasn't moving, then ran like hell up the porch and through a door under a sign that said CAMP OFFICE.

Inside, she leaned against the door, clutching her shoulder, catching her breath. She found herself in a wide central hallway that ran straight through to an identical entrance on the opposite end. Pine walls. Worn linoleum on the floor. Dim security lighting on the ceiling showed three doors on the right and three doors on the left. Some of the doors were marked. She saw ADMINISTRATION and JANITOR CLOSET and PRIVATE—NO ENTRANCE.

The administration office was unlocked, so she quickly slipped in and leaned her back against the door, listening for footsteps following. There were none. Breathing easier, she looked around. Three desks faced the door, each with a name plate facing out. Serena. Penny. Millie.

Millie!

Allie headed for Millie's desk and shuffled through the papers and file folders on top, finding nothing, then tried the drawer. It was locked. She grabbed a letter opener from the pen cup and jabbed at the lock. It gave way easily.

Inside the drawer were ballpoint pens, a small stapler, yellow highlighters, lip balm, breath mints. She shoved it all aside and reached to the back. Her heart took a leap as her fingers closed on a ring of keys the size of her wrist. She pulled it out, stuffed it in her pocket, and kept looking.

She spotted a tiny flashlight on a stretchy plastic wrist band in the pencil tray, and took that, too, using it to search the other desks. Disappointment burned deep when she found no clue to Davy's whereabouts.

She caught back a sob of frustration, tormented by thoughts that would not lie quiet in her mind. The memory of Davy's haunted, pleading eyes caused her chest to squeeze painfully. Please, God, let me find him. Don't let them hurt him.

Terrified that any minute someone would come in and find her, she scurried up and down the hall, using the keys to open the other doors and check the rooms. Davy wasn't in any of them.

She spotted a framed poster nailed to the wall, and shined the little flashlight on it. It was an overview of the camp, a map with line drawings showing where everything was and how to get there. A community center. A dining hall. A boathouse on the lake. Some of the structures were attached to each other forming a sort of fortress.

She stared at it, trying to impress the layout of the camp into her brain, memorizing the roads and walkways, where they led and where they intersected. Everything seemed oriented to a gatehouse at the highway entrance. She pinpointed the camp office, noting its position in relation to everything else, then left through the door opposite the one she'd entered.

Immediately her head shifted toward the sound of shouting somewhere in the distance, voices raised in anger. Headlights flickered through the trees, vehicles were arriving, converging in a rush on some central point. People were running, their excited voices slicing the night air. She closed her eyes and recreated the map in her head. As far as she could determine, the focal point of activity was at the front gate.

Was help arriving? She knew she couldn't count on it and was spurred to greater urgency in her search for Davy. She was going to find him or die trying.

Making sure the coast was clear, she jogged across a clearing, then dove into the shadows of a one-story building, cutting in low and fast. She looked around to get her bearings. If she remembered correctly, the community center was on the other side of the children's playground directly across from her. Quickly, she sprinted to the tall, boxy two-story that looked like an above ground bunker. A sign identified it as the Community Center.

She took the key ring from her pocket, wincing at the jingle as the huge handful of keys clinked together. She wrapped her fingers around them to muffle the sound, and tried them one by one until the door swung open. Quickly, she stepped inside and closed the door, releasing the knob very slowly to deaden the click of the latch.

The pain in her shoulder was growing more severe, so intense it felt like fire. She cradled her arm against her body and inhaled through her teeth. Fending off her attacker had damaged it further. After the worst of the pain passed, she eased out a breath and took note of the room. It was a little larger than a tennis court with wide plank flooring and white walls. High windows admitted the grey light of the coming day. The walls were hung with what looked to be hand loomed tapestries depicting religious themes woven into the fibers.

Rows of chairs were arranged auditorium style facing a lectern. She walked up the aisle to the front of the room and turned around. It was set up for a meeting or presentation with enough chairs to accommodate at least two hundred people.

In the corner to her left was a copy machine. Next to it, a worktable strewn with papers. She found copies of a meeting agenda from the week before, glossy camp brochures, a schedule of camp activities for the kids—hiking, swimming, row boating, handcrafts. There were staplers and paper clips, odds and ends of office supplies. A laptop computer, a calculator. There was a copy and collating station where bulletins and announcements or other communiqués were prepared for distribution.

To her right was another door, which she found to be unlike the flimsy hollow one she'd easily kicked in. This one was sturdy, made of metal, and it appeared to have a solid core. A substantial lock held it firmly in place.

With shaking hands, she used up precious minutes methodically trying each key. It was a slow and painstaking process, but that may have been because her heart was racing. Some of the keys didn't fit the keyhole. Others fit, but didn't turn. Then one of them stuck and she couldn't get it out.

"Come on, come on," she whispered in frustration. Frantically she tried to work it loose, but it wouldn't release.

Suddenly, she froze at the sound of voices coming from outside. The sound drew closer and stopped at the door through which she'd entered. Heart thumping, its beat pounding in her ears, she slid down the wall and huddled into the corner. Holding her breath, she covered her mouth with both hands to contain a terrified squeal.

A key rattled in the door across the room. Oh, God, someone

was coming in. Perspiration broke out on her forehead, running down her face, burning her eyes. She could smell her fear, sour and strong. It wafted off her, filling the room.

The door opened inward and a backlit man took a step inside, but he turned at the sound of someone outside calling his name.

"Hey, Murph! They need help at the front gate. They want you up there now! Take one of the Rangers. The key's in it."

Murph stopped in the doorway and turned to whoever had called his name. An outside light washed the shadows from his face, and Allie could see it was not the same man who'd attacked her.

"Yeah, right," he growled. "I'm on it." The door closed and his boots crunched gravel as he ran off.

Pressing her fist to her mouth to stifle a howl of fear, Allie lowered her head to her knees, and waited for her heart to settle down. When her breathing slowed, she stood and with trembling fingers went back to work on the stuck key. At last, she worked it free.

Eight more keys to go. Six more. Five. Finally, there was a click, a loud thunk, and the deadbolt released. Dry-mouthed and with pounding heart, she shoved the heavy door open and scurried through, quickly closing it behind her.

There were no windows in this room; with the door closed, it was pitch black. She couldn't see a thing, and felt along the wall for a light switch. She found one and flipped it on. Bright lights filled the cavernous space, and the sight that greeted her was startling. It almost looked like a television studio, or movie sound stage, and she wondered if this was where the Reverend taped his television specials.

At the opposite end of the room, the standard ceiling suddenly soared open, creating a vast space that rose right up into the roof's peak. Tracks of spotlights were attached to exposed rigging in the ceiling. Below, there was a raised platform three feet off the floor, draped in beige satin that puddled on the floor. Centered on the platform was a striking oversized canopy bed with clouds of filmy fabric spilling from the four corners of the canopy rack. Flood lights on rolling metal standards were positioned around the bed, and video cameras and more lights formed a semicircle around it. Four or five canvas chairs and stools were lined up slightly behind the cameras.

Off to the side, away from the platform, was a long conference table with armchairs around it. The shiny tabletop held a computer, a scanner, DVDs, a DVD player, a monitor, and a slide-sorting rack. As she approached, she saw plastic sheet protectors holding transparencies. Full color glossy eight-by-tens were scattered over the surface of the table. At first, the images looked like pictures of children playing; a second later, what her eyes told her caught up to her brain, but still she rejected it and stared, disbelieving.

Her heart thudded in her chest and she found she had to concentrate very hard on her breathing. When the ugly reality sank in, shock struck at the very center of her being, and she had a crazy mixture of hope and fear that she was going insane and not really seeing this.

The children in the photos weren't playing. Not like children are supposed to play. And they weren't all children.

She was looking at pornography.

Child pornography.

An all consuming fury let loose in her, beating back logic, crushing common sense.

Oh, Davy. Where are you?

Rage was a hot, hard ball in her gut that spread through her body, wiping out rational thought. If they had touched him, she'd kill them.

She turned and raced out of the room, out of the building, and found herself under a gunmetal grey sky, the beginning of the day. She halted and spun around, disoriented, not knowing which way to run. Frantically, she tried to recapture the image of the map, tried to remember what was where, tried to think of some logical place they'd put a little boy.

Her ears registered a sound, a crunch of stone to her right. Instinctively, she turned and out of the corner of her eye saw a fist coming toward her. The blow crashed into the side of her head, above her right ear. When it landed, her brain skidded away from the force. She could not draw breath, could not move, could not see. She fought to stay awake. She had to find Davy. Another blow sent consciousness spinning away, and her jaw smacked against the ground.

CHAPTER TWENTY-THREE

Christ, he hurt.

Beck groaned and rolled over, pain ripping through his chest and ribs. He grit his teeth, sucked a breath, and forced himself to his knees, then pushed up to his feet. His bladder was ready to burst. Looking around the room, he saw four walls and a bucket in the corner. He didn't know if that's what it was for, but he unbuttoned his pants and urinated into it.

Where had those bastards taken him?

Fog sluiced out of his brain allowing a vague recollection of driving a long way uninterrupted and at speed. A freeway. After that, the quiet of a curving two-lane, then gravel spitting against the undercarriage. He'd been in a sort of half-sleep, but a lighted sign resurrected in his mind, a sign with the words *camp* and *children.*

Allie had told him Worthey ran a summer camp for kids. Maybe this was it. A fleeting memory of brake lights flaring ahead, a limousine bobbing like a cruise ship at sea over undulating terrain. A gate closing behind. The truck in which he was riding was following, the two guys in front talking, their conversation cutting in and out of his consciousness like bad cell phone reception.

". . . the bitch and the boy . . ."

". . . where will . . . ?"

". . . don't know . . . wait for instructions from . . ."

That must mean Allie and Davy were here, too. He had to

get out and find them. Nothing else mattered.

He yanked ferociously on the doorknob.

"Let me out of here," he yelled. "Open the goddamn door." He pounded on it, the sound thundering in the stillness. He stumbled backwards when it flew open, and the man with the metal pipe burst in, the same man who'd bashed his head before.

"Shut up," he yelled at Beck. "Shut the fuck up!"

He raised the arm holding the pipe, winding up for a savage backhand, but Beck saw it coming and gave him a sidestep, slipping a punch into the boozy bloat of his midsection. Air whooshed out of the man's mouth in a sickening gush, and the pipe hit the floor with a loud clang. Beck followed up with an overhand left that sent pipe-man into the wall, but he rebounded from it, backing Beck up against the opposite wall. Beck managed to jam an elbow under his assailant's chin and shove him away just far enough to hit him again.

Incredibly, pipe-man didn't go down. Instead, he charged forward, hitting Beck in the face hard enough to split the skin over the bone under his eye. Beck felt blood running down his cheek, but he stayed close in, driving his fists into the man's middle, pounding the air out of his body.

Gradually, pipe-man began to weaken from lack of oxygen. He doubled over, and Beck brought his knee up hard under the man's chin. That sent him reeling backward onto the floor, and he stayed that way, dragging in air, trying to fill his lungs.

Beck stood over him, swaying, fists clenched, blood dripping from his chin. "Where's Allie?" he demanded. "And Davy? Where did they take them? Tell me now before I kick your head in!"

"I'll kill you," the man gasped, holding his stomach and trying to get up, trying to breathe.

"Not if I kill you first. Where are they?"

"Go to hell."

"I'm giving you one last chance to tell me before I beat the shit out of you. WHERE ARE THEY?"

When the man still didn't answer, Beck gave in to his rage, aiming a kick into the man's ribs, and a second one into the middle of his face. Bone crunched and blood exploded as the man fell back with a thud, holding his face and squealing like a pig. Beck hesitated a brief moment, tempted to carry through on his threat, but mindful of the FBI's approaching deadline, he took off, desperate to find Allie and Davy.

The widely spaced sodium yard lights provided sparse illumination, but created heavy shadows which Beck used to his advantage. He stopped in the murky gloom and looked around, breathing deeply, trying to get a handle on where to go next. A school bus was parked next to a telephone pole. A couple of older mobile homes sat at an angle to each other. Beyond was a tall, narrow square-sided building that soared three stories above the others. At the top, windows all around gave it the look of an observation tower. If he could make it there and inside, he'd have an overhead view of the compound, and maybe figure out where Allie and Davy were.

He made a run for it, dodging into shadows along the way, wishing he had a weapon. As he bounded around the corner heading for the tower, a barrel-chested man dressed like a woodsman, logger boots, jeans, and a tan canvas field coat, came out the main door carrying a semiautomatic rifle. Yelling into a hand held radio, he stopped under a yard light next to a picnic table, his back to Beck. He held the radio close to his lips while he talked, and looked around in confusion.

"No," he said into the handset, lowering his rifle slightly. "Don't let them in. I don't care how you do it, but keep them out."

Cursing, he dropped the radio into his coat pocket and started to jog away, and that's when Beck made his move. Knee to the middle of the back into the spine, and a double fist to the top of the head, and the man's knees gave way. He crashed to the ground face first, Beck on top of him, clinging to his back. The rifle skidded away over the stones.

The man rolled several times pulling Beck along, thrashing violently, trying to escape Beck's grasp. Beck caught the man's neck in the crook of his arm and squeezed, his bicep cutting off the airway. The man thrashed against Beck's grip, but Beck held fast until he rolled over a sharp rock half-buried in the dirt. A shock of pain raced up his spine, loosening his grasp.

With a grunt and a crazy lunge to the side, the man jerked free from Beck's grip, smashing Beck's ribs with an elbow. Burning pain tore through Beck's midsection, and he curled his knees to his chest, gasping for breath.

The man rolled away then jumped to his feet. Beck tried to get up, but the man pounced on him, punching his face over and over, ripping more flesh with a metal ring on his pinkie. He grabbed the front of Beck's shirt and tried to pull him up. Beck resisted, breaking free, and stayed on the ground, forcing the man to close in and reach for him again.

When he did, Beck swiveled in the dirt, yanked the man's forearm, pulling him off balance. With a quick movement, Beck hooked his thighs around the man's arm, squeezing hard. Putting all his weight behind it, he drove his hips up, and wrenched down on the arm, breaking it at the elbow. The man howled, writhing, the broken arm flopping. Beck double hammer-fisted him on the side of his head until he stopped moving.

Winded, Beck pushed himself to his feet, spread his legs and bent over, hands on thighs, and worked on getting his breath back. He thought he heard men shouting beyond the trees, but air was rattling so loud in his windpipe, he couldn't hear what they were saying.

When his breathing was close to normal, he picked up the

rifle and raced for the tower door. He yanked it open, stopping to listen, then stepped inside, bracing for an attack. None came, and he didn't see anyone, so made his way up the steps, holding the rifle ready. By the time he reached the landing at the top, he realized that though all the lights were on and doors hung open, no one was there. It was as if the inhabitants had suddenly rushed away.

He entered a room at the top, and found a half-played game of Solitaire laid out on a card table. A folding chair was overturned as if knocked back by someone in a hurry to leave. On a heavy metal rack attached to the wall were two rows of security monitors, four to a row. Beck stood there for a few minutes staring at the array of electronic equipment. It was a surveillance system, a black and white montage of the camp spread out before him—a baseball field, some structures that looked like bunkhouses, a giant barn, a kid's playground, numerous RVs and trailers.

A flurry of movement drew his attention to a monitor that was swarming with activity. People and vehicles were moving around near what he now realized was more of a security barrier than an entrance kiosk. Half a dozen cars were parked there. Men stood around in groups on both sides of the perimeter fence, and appeared to be conversing hotly. Some of them had weapons slung over their shoulders, but no one was shooting. Yet.

FBI agents, clearly identified by the logo on their jackets, had arrived to serve the warrants, but were meeting resistance. Beck squinted and leaned in closer. It looked like the agents were wearing bulletproof vests and other protective gear. Not a good sign, he thought with foreboding.

A television van with a tell-tale satellite on its roof pulled up and parked several yards away. A news crew jumped out. Two of them began setting up lights, another hefted a TV camera onto his shoulder. A woman smoothed her hand over her hair and positioned herself with a microphone. A second TV news crew arrived, followed by another, and then a car with the *Detroit News* emblazoned on the door skidded to a stop. Jason Bright got out from behind the wheel, and a woman carrying a camera and an equipment bag exited the other side.

It looked like Jason had misjudged. Despite the presence of a full court media press, trouble was brewing.

His gaze flicked over the other monitors, stopping briefly on each one before moving on to the next. He caught a skitter of movement, a figure passing quickly over a patch of gravel, ducking into the side door of what appeared to be a vehicle shed. Sure enough, a few seconds later, the corrugated metal garage door lifted, and a Ranger rolled out, then drove away from the camera.

In the next screen, he saw a massive two-story building, a half dozen air conditioning units and compressors on the roof. Two men loped along the perimeter of the structure, intermittently stopping to inspect its concrete block foundation. Or were they? They were doing something, but Beck couldn't tell what.

One of the men, small and wiry, turned his head briefly toward the camera as if startled by a sound. Beck had a brief glance at his ferret face and recognized him as the transient who had approached Allie in front of City Hall. Not a homeless person after all, but rather one of Worthey's men. When they finished, they jumped into an ATV and drove away, leaving something behind on the ground.

Beck ran his eyes over the control panel looking for an image enhancer switch. He found it and changed from quad view screen to single view, zooming in and adjusting the resolution, trying to make out what they'd left behind. The image cleared, and he immediately recognized Allie's slender form sprawled in the dirt.

"Oh, Christ, no."

He spun away from the monitors and ran for the landing. Beating back panic, he paced alongside the perimeter windows, studying the terrain to see if he could recognize the building and pinpoint its exact location. He hadn't been able to tell how badly Allie was hurt, but she wasn't moving. Cold dread raised goose bumps on his scalp.

The sun was still invisible, but he could see most of the cobbled-together complex spread out below. Odd-shaped added-on buildings, barns and sheds, a dozen tiny one-room cabins tucked into the trees, all enclosed in a border fence that disappeared out of sight over the rolling countryside.

Then he spotted it. There, rising above the treetops a hundred yards from where he stood in the tower, a sprawling building, cooling units on a rooftop. Beyond that, barely visible through the leafy trees, a lake with rowboats beached at the water's edge. He scrambled down three flights of stairs, stumbled and almost lost his grip on the rifle, but caught himself, and then he was outside. He halted, breathing deeply, spun a 360-degree sweep of the area, got his bearings, and took off at a run.

The wind had risen and the air had a brisk almost wild feel to it. Excitement was in the air and men were running past him calling to each other, barely acknowledging his presence in their haste. Gunshots came from the direction of the front gate. Spurred on by a fear-juiced mind, he cut through a stand of evergreens, then grappled up a rocky slope.

Allie was on the ground, her eyes closed, blood running from a cut on the side of her head and from a torn lip. He knelt beside her, slid his arm under her shoulders, and lifted gently. She moaned in pain, then opened her eyes. He started to wipe her face with the tail end of his shirt, but she clamped her hand around his arm, digging fingernails into his bicep.

"Beck! Thank God you're here. We have to get Davy out of here." Her voice was hoarse and ragged. "These people are evil."

"Yes, I know," he said, not letting her finish, not wanting her to say it and reinforce the reality of the malevolence.

"No, I mean really evil," she insisted. "They do unspeakable things—" Her words came out a terrified croak, and again he stopped her.

"I know," he assured her. "I know what they do. Jason told me. It's all on those CDs. The FBI is here now. They've come to arrest Worthey and the others. There's trouble at the entrance gate. We have to find Davy and get to safety. Do you know where he is?"

"No." He helped her to her feet, and she stood unsteadily against him. He held her until she regained her balance.

He heard the *whack! whack! whack!* of a helicopter approaching. It grumbled overhead, skimming the treetops, shining a spotlight over the ground.

Gunfire sounded, closer now, and he grabbed her hand.

"Come on. This way."

He pulled her into the community center, and she squatted in a corner next to him. He drew her close, positioning his body protectively over her. Urgent voices were raised outside, footsteps running. More gunfire was exchanged, not close by, but close enough. Allie pointed to the door in the corner and in a hushed voice began telling Beck what she'd found on the other side. The video cameras, the pictures. He tightened his arm around her, pulled her face to his shoulder and shushed her.

Men could be heard gathering on the porch and running around the building, yelling. Then there was a whistling sound and an explosion jolted the ground, sending vibrations into the soles of their feet. The folding chairs in the meeting hall shuddered out of place, scraping over the linoleum, slamming into each other, blown out of place by the force. The lectern at the front of the room skidded across the floor, breaking to pieces when it slammed into the wall.

"The feds are blowing it up!" Allie cried. Panic swirled in her eyes.

"No," Beck said, realizing with utter clarity what he'd seen in the tower. The ferret-faced man and his buddy had been planting explosives around the perimeter of this building.

"It's not the feds. It's Worthey's men destroying the evidence. We have to get out of here. Now!"

Before they could move, there was another whistling sound and a tremendous concussion accompanied by a horrible squeal, and the metal door leading into the studio was torn from its hinges and blown into the meeting hall. Folding chairs lifted from the floor, thrown into the air by the force. The movie screen broke away and crashed to the floor. A huge ceiling beam came down with a horrendous thud, just missing them. Plaster fell down in chunks. Sheets of paper flew through the air, smoking and on fire.

Suddenly, the whole room was ablaze, flames partially covering the exit. Smoke blocked out the weak light coming from the windows. Frantic, Beck looked around for an escape route.

"Follow me," he said, crawling behind a table that had been knocked over. Allie was right behind him, coughing from the black smoke rolling through the room. He felt her start to panic and move out from the table, but he pulled her back.

"Keep down close to the floor," he commanded. He put the rifle down and yanked at his shirt tearing off a piece. "Hold this over your nose and mouth." He pressed a piece of fabric into her hand and she held it to her face.

Through the dust and debris, Beck saw faint light. A hole

had been blown into a wall on the other side of the room. The smoke was thick. Charred debris drifted down. They weren't going to last long, not with the amount of smoke in the air. They had to get out.

He heard a burst of gunfire. "Keep down, no matter what."

When the shooting stopped, he picked up the rifle, grabbed her hand, and pulled her to her feet. "Come on, we can make a run for it. Let's go!"

He tried to lead her away, but his lungs burned and he couldn't breathe. He doubled over coughing. Stars appeared before his eyes. He faltered, and stumbled to his knees, but managed to hold on to the rifle.

She dropped the cloth from her face, grabbed his shoulders, and pulled him with both hands. His lungs were burning, he couldn't see, but he made it to his feet. Then Allie tripped and fell. Blindly, tears streaming from his eyes, he grabbed for her and tried to yank her up.

"My shoulder," she screamed.

He thrust his body under her and carried her.

The heat was horrible, the smoke turned from black to grey, and embers and soot flew everywhere, but they made their way outside, fell onto the grass, and rolled away from the flames. The air was sweet. They were both coughing and gagging.

An ATV roared over a rise, heading straight for them. Allie jumped away and fell on top of Beck. The Ranger skidded to a stop.

"Allie! It's me. Hey, guys. It's me."

Through the haze, Beck saw a tiny figure at the wheel of the Ranger. It was Davy. When Allie spotted him, she scrambled to her feet and pounced on him, crushing him with her good arm.

He sobbed, clinging to her. "I knew you'd come for me!"

Tears streamed down Allie's face, washing streaks through the dirt and soot. "It looks like *you* came for *me*," she said, squeezing him until he winced.

"Stop. You're hurting me."

Beck jumped into the Ranger and nudged Davy over with his hip. "Let's get out of here."

"No! Wait! The kids!" Davy yelled.

"What kids?"

"There." He pointed. "In the bunkhouse. We have to get the kids."

By the time the Ranger reached the bunkhouse complex, flames were crowning the trees, moving closer. Terrified children wearing only pajamas or underwear huddled together in the courtyard, crying and screaming for help.

Beck jumped out of the Ranger, Allie behind him, and sprinted to where they stood clustered together trembling with fear.

"We can't get all these kids in the back of the Ranger," Beck yelled, picking up a smaller boy and tucking him under his arm like a football. "You bigger boys, each take a little one and run to the lake. Do you know where it is?"

Heads bobbed wildly and fingers pointed. "Yeah. Over there."

"Then hurry," said Beck. "Do it now!"

Allie helped Beck carry a couple of kids to the rear stowage bed of the Ranger. The boys who were big enough snatched up a smaller child and fled through the woods.

"This way," Davy shouted, as Beck stomped the accelerator. "I know a shortcut. Go this way. There's a secret tunnel. I'll show you."

The Ranger reached the beach first. Allie, Beck, and Davy jumped out and dragged rowboats and rafts to the edge of the water. They slapped lifejackets on the little ones, then waited anxiously for the others. At last, the kids broke through the trees. They raced across the sand and piled into the waiting boats, launched themselves away from shore, and rowed and paddled to the middle of the small lake.

There they stopped and drifted with the current. The vessels floated and bobbed as everyone stared wide-eyed at the wall of flame and smoke cutting them off from the battle raging at the far end of the camp.

The flames reflected on the surface of the water making the lake look like it was made of molten lava. Away from the raging fire, safe on the water, the children's panic subsided, their sobs gradually diminishing to raggedy sniffles.

Beck's raft drifted toward Allie's rowboat. She grasped it and pulled it close. Drawn by the current or by an unseen hand, the other boats and rafts converged to the same spot, softly tapping against each other as they rose and fell with the swells. The children reached out across the water, holding hands with someone in an adjacent boat, silently watching the camp and everything in it burn to the ground.

CHAPTER TWENTY-FOUR

Allie found a parking space in front of Starbuck's, went in, ordered coffee and a maple oat-nut scone, and took a seat in one of the armchairs at a corner table. She was waiting for Monica Williams, though why Monica would call after all this time and ask to meet for coffee was a mystery. She hadn't seen Monica since she left the ranch.

One of Michigan's first wintry blasts had started to gust in the night, bringing a hint of the snow everyone expected to pile up by Thanksgiving. The afternoon wind had a nippy bite, and Allie had dressed in a turtleneck sweater under a down jacket. She unbuttoned it and slipped it off her shoulders. When her coffee was half gone, Monica came in.

"Hello, Allie."

The women embraced in the reserved manner of not-quite-friends-but-more-than-acquaintances greeting each other after an extended time apart.

"Monica, how nice to see you again. What brings you here?"

"I was in town to give a mystery writing seminar at the college and had a little extra time, so thought I'd call and see if you were free."

She was wearing a black knee length fitted wool coat, black slacks, black stilettos, and a black fur Cossack-style hat. She looked stunning, as usual, though Allie wondered how she was going to make it in the snow wearing those shoes.

Monica ordered at the counter, brought her latte tall to the table, and sat down. She smiled and gazed around the room as she removed her hat and gloves and unbuttoned her coat. She was having trouble meeting Allie's gaze.

"How are you doing?" she asked, when finally she did.

"Fine. Really. I'm fine now." Allie's injuries had healed with no more lasting effect than a tiny scar near her left eye. The memories, however, sometimes woke her in the night.

"And Davy? Is he well?"

"He's doing very well, thank you. He's caught up on all his subjects in school and getting good grades. The court approved my petition to have him with me in foster care. I've applied for adoption; it should be final in time for Christmas."

"Congratulations. What a wonderful Christmas present. I'm happy for you." Monica's smile eloquently conveyed the warmth and sincerity of her words.

"Thank you."

Monica fell into silence, and Allie studied her face. It was missing some of the haughty bravado usually displayed there. Something was on her mind. Allie wondered what it was.

"Sadie misses him," Monica said.

Allie smiled. "He misses Sadie."

The mention of Sadie and, by inference, their life at the ranch brought an uneasy moment that threatened to grow unabated, but Monica, in a cordial manner, stopped it from becoming overly uncomfortable.

"I saw you on Larry King last week," she said brightly, changing the subject. "You were talking about the child welfare system."

Allie nodded. "I've been invited to appear on quite a few talk shows since I came back. The system's been under intense criticism for some time, but after what happened with Davy, the governor stepped in and ordered an investigation into Child Protection Services."

Allie was gratified that as a result of the governor's involvement, the deficiencies at CPS had finally been exposed. Charges had been brought against Tiffany Day and other social workers for failing to fulfill their obligations in their positions of trust. Iris Neto, though good intentioned, had resigned in disgrace, and criminal charges were pending against her. Judge Berriman suddenly retired, whether by choice or by force, she wasn't sure. The scandal had hit the county hard. Law suits aplenty had been filed over falsified reports, lack of supervision of caseworkers, and other serious accountability problems. Unfortunately, some of the dedicated social workers in the department were undeservedly tainted by the wrongdoing of the others.

"The governor asked me for my input on a restructuring of CPS policies, and to write a report suggesting improvements."

There'd been a shakeup in the police department, too, she told Monica, resulting in the firing of several police officers who were also facing criminal charges. Tiffany, in an attempt to redeem herself to some small degree, told the investigators what she knew about Mark Medora. Apparently, Mark had told her about his past crimes, including his targeting of Allie as a whistleblower, just as Paul had told Allie about his misdeeds.

Why were men compelled to confess those kinds things to the women who loved them? Allie wondered. An attempt to alleviate their guilt, she supposed, by passing it on to someone else to bear when the burden became too much to endure.

"This time the bad cops are getting jail sentences instead of hand slaps," Allie said.

"I understand the charges against you were dropped."

"Yes, thankfully. I was quite worried about it, but after the whole story came out, it didn't take much to convince the district attorney I was justified in what I did. He agreed that necessity was a defense. In other words, my breaking the law resulted in less harm than not breaking the law. It kept Davy and other children safe from Worthey and his bunch."

"And uncovered a whole lot of other serious criminal activity. Thank God, those horrible people are in jail."

"The Church of Spiritual Light was a complete sham. The government suspects some of Worthey's illegal profits were going to finance terrorism. They're investigating that now. Can you imagine two hundred million dollars in the hands of terrorists?"

Monica shuddered. "Terrible. Thanks to you it's all come to an end." She sipped her latte. "Davy is one lucky boy. You'll be a wonderful mother." The corners of her mouth twitched up into a nervous little smile that didn't hold.

An awkward silence ensued, seconds sliding soundlessly into each other. Allie had done most of the talking while Monica listened politely, her fingers dancing in a nervous fidget on the tabletop and around her cup.

She searched Monica's face, wondering again at the reason for this visit. For an unguarded moment, an expression of unutterable sadness rearranged Monica's features, and it occurred to Allie that she was struggling to hold her emotions in check. She had never known Beck's sister to be anything but direct and in control.

Suddenly, Monica's rigid composure slipped, and her shoulders sagged as if they were melting inside her clothes. She shot Allie an uneasy glance, and cleared her throat.

"I lied," she blurted.

"What?"

"I didn't come to teach a seminar. I really came to talk to you."

Allie's eyebrows raised in question. "Oh?"

"We miss you at the ranch."

"Oh," said Allie, drawing out the word. She leaned back in

her chair, and lowered her eyes to her lap. Blank silence was all she could offer in reply to that.

"Beck tells me you won't be coming back." She paused. "Is that true?"

"Yes. It's true," Allie acknowledged.

"What are you going to do?"

"My law license will be reinstated after the first of the year. When it is, I'll return to family law. But only part time, since I have Davy now."

"Would you reconsider?" Monica asked after a long stretch of silence. "Coming back, I mean. Beck's miserable without you."

Allie blinked back sudden pain. "No. I can't. I've already discussed it with him."

But how could she make clear to Monica that it was Beck's seeming inability to reconcile the past that had created the insurmountable rift in their renewed relationship? Even though Allie had explained to him what happened all those years ago and why she left him, she sensed he'd continued to harbor uncertainty. He'd never doubted her before, when they were young. What had made him change now that he was an adult?

Inwardly, she cringed as realization was born on a breath slowly exhaled. By leaving the way she had, so suddenly, without a word, she'd planted in him the seed of distrust that had flourished with maturity.

"But Beck loves you."

"And I love him. More than I can say. But trust is part of love," said Allie. "And that's the missing piece with us."

Monica's eyes glistened with tears and grew distant as if surrendering to memories. "I blame myself for that."

She shook her head in dismay, her lips distorted in a wan smile. "I owe you an apology. I did a horribly wicked thing to you. It's taken me many years to realize how wrong I was. That failing has hurt a lot of people, including me."

"I've forgiven you," Allie began, but Monica raised her hand, forestalling Allie's pardon.

"No. I don't mean my boorish behavior toward you. Well, yes. That, too," she conceded. "But there's more."

Allie waited expectantly, her eyes unwavering, fixed on Monica's face, but Monica's gaze flitted around the room, stopping on the man with a laptop at the next table, then on the shelf display of coffee makers and mugs. Finally it came back to rest on Allie, and the corners of her mouth wobbled.

"I know what happened that night with . . . with my father. I was there."

The words lingered in the air, crackling like Fourth of July sparklers. Allie blinked a few times, beating back an onrush of sorrow.

"I saw what he was trying to do to you, but I ran away. I couldn't watch. Because I didn't want it to be true. So I went back to the party." Monica dropped her head to her hand, spread her fingers over her forehead, covering her eyes as if in shame.

"Did you tell your mother? Or Beck?" Allie asked, after a stunned moment.

"No. Not then." Monica lifted her head, and her eyes were red-rimmed and shining with held back tears. "I didn't want to tell anyone. It was my father, after all," she said, and shrugged as if that were explanation enough.

"Telling someone would have made it real. I just wanted it to go away. And later, after so much time had passed, it did go away. It was easy for me to forget it after you left. I . . . we . . . the family," she spread her hands, making the point, "was glad when you left. Just seeing you would have been a constant reminder of that night. We didn't want you around. That's why I wouldn't let you speak to Beck when you called and came over."

Allie closed her eyes, letting sorrow wash over her. She should have felt relief or joy that she was vindicated, should have felt a release of the remorse she had carried with her. Instead, she felt unutterable sadness for the lost years.

"My father was a son of a bitch," Monica went on, her voice harsh with regret. "Mother knew it, too." Monica shrugged. "But she loved him, and did everything she could to hide it from everyone. From Beck, who adored his father. And from herself, too, I suppose. She's a very proud woman. Back then, keeping up appearances meant everything to her."

Allie took a shuddering breath. "Does Beck know now?"

Monica nodded. "He will. Mother came up to the ranch for Thanksgiving. She's going to tell him. She actually sent me here to see you, because she was too ashamed to face you herself."

Allie lowered her head and inhaled deeply, trying to ward off a wave of regret sweeping up from her chest.

After a long pause, Monica spoke again. "Will you come back? Please?"

Allie looked up.

"No," she answered, softly. "I can't. I told Beck the truth, but he didn't believe me. Apparently, he has to hear it from someone else. I wanted him to believe because he trusted me, because he knew that anything I said to him would be the truth."

Monica took a tissue from her purse and wiped her eyes, being careful not to smudge her eye makeup. "Please don't be too hard on him." She sniffed into her tissue. "Losing you a second time would be almost more than he could bear. I'm not so sure he'd recover this time."

After Monica left, Allie sat alone, fighting off the disappointment that was making her sick in her heart. Why couldn't he have believed me? She felt battered and sad, suddenly very old and tired.

The outer door opened, and Allie's attention was pulled to

the sound of traffic. A young couple came in, each carrying their own Starbuck's mug. At the counter, he ordered for both of them, then smiled at his partner while they waited. She smiled back and leaned into him. He draped his arm over her shoulders, and they stood that way until their order came up.

Allie swallowed the lump that lingered in her throat, dried her eyes, and left to pick Davy up from school.

Abigail Emma Williams sat across from her son and dabbed at the dainty tears that had collected under her eyes. She was one of those women over whom age and experience seemed to have passed without leaving a scar, a line, a mark. Until now. Now, Beck could see his mother as what she really was—the long-suffering widow of a philandering husband, remorseful in her dotage about mistakes made in her past.

"What Allie told you happened with your father that night is true," she said again as though the first time hadn't had enough impact. "Monica was there. She saw."

Beck was reeling as his childhood came scrambling back at him, bringing previously squelched incidents rushing into his memory. His parents fighting long into the night. Raging arguments about his father's indiscretions. Fractious accusations thrown with the intent to not merely hurt, but to crush and destroy, followed by drunken half-hearted denials.

"I know what my husband was." Abigail drew her eyebrows together, unable to hold back a rush of tears. "I know what he did. He was an adulterer plain and simple. At first, I raised a ruckus about it. Then, after you and your sister were born, I tried, not always successfully I admit, to ignore it. Later, when you both got older, I did my best to hide it. I didn't want you children knowing your father was cheating on me. On the family."

She took a moment to dab at her eyes again. "Of course,

Monica caught on before she was in her teens, being a girl and sensitive to those matters."

Snapped back to his youth, Beck was held in the time warp of the past, a thousand memories clawing at him, repressed images, previously rejected, blooming at the back of his retinas. His father's hand sliding down the back of a woman not his wife. A lingering look into the eyes of a beautiful party guest. A smile bursting with secrets directed at someone in particular across a roomful of people, whispered phone calls immediately terminated when anyone came near. Late night, sometimes all night, meetings that were never discussed at breakfast, and finally, never discussed ever.

And Beck had to face another painful truth.

He realized now that, like Monica, he too would have caught on if he'd let himself. Instead, he'd spent his life trying to outrun the shameful truth about his father, and it had destroyed something precious in his life. Allie's love.

"But why didn't Monica tell me at the time?"

"I asked her not to."

"Why?"

"Because I was trying to protect you. You were so close to your father. And you were so like him. I didn't want you to think what he was doing was right."

Beck's heart wrenched. "I might have made mistakes, Mother, but they would never have been the ones he made."

Abigail reached out her hand and gently patted his knee, then left it there.

"And later I didn't tell you because I was angry. Angry at your father for dying and leaving me alone. Angry for all the things left unsaid. Angry at him for everything he'd done, and for everything he hadn't done. It was easy to blame Allie, so I did. Because in spite of everything, I still loved your father."

Beck was overtaken with a crush of mourning. He felt helpless, as if sand were shifting under his feet. A cry only he could hear filled his head. All those years. Lost forever. It must have shown on his face, because his mother held up her hand, feebly warding off his reproach.

"I know," she said sadly. "I know what I did to Allie, I know what I did to you. I'm sorry." She put her fingers to the bridge of her nose and closed her eyes, sinking into self-admonishment.

When she looked up, her eyes were sorrowful. "But maybe it can be salvaged," she offered. "Go to her now. Before you lose her again."

She began to weep once more. Beck rose and sat down next to his mother, embracing her. Her body was thin, her bones felt fragile under his hands. He held her until her shoulders stopped shaking and she collected herself.

"They say confession is good for the soul," she sniffed. "But all it's done is make me feel miserable." She sighed and then wilted against him. "Will you please take me back to Monica's so I can lie down a while?"

"Of course, Mother."

When Beck returned to the cabin, Jobby was sitting at the kitchen table, a cup of coffee in front of him.

"Are you goin' to get her?" he asked when Beck came in the door.

Beck shook his head sadly. "I can't. She won't see me. She won't even take my phone calls."

"Yeah. Well. She prob'ly wanted you to believe her without proof. Women are funny like that," he said and looked away.

Beck sat down across from Jobby, but didn't comment.

Jobby folded both hands around his cup and stared into it. A few moments passed, and he chuckled to himself. "I miss that kid," he said, with a slow shake of his head. "He was a smart one, all right. Sharp as a whip. I only had to show him one time how to drive that quad. He caught on right away."

Beck looked up in surprise. "You're the one who taught him?"

"Yeah."

The two men sat with their thoughts. After a while, Jobby stood.

"Well," he said, heading for the door. "I'll be getting back to work now. Got some chores need doin'." He stepped out on the porch, but stopped and looked back at Beck through the open door. "Oh, uh, what do you want me to do with Davy's bike?"

"Polish it up and put some air in the tires," Beck said with a sudden burst of hope and joy. "Then rub it for luck and make a wish. I'm going to get them and bring them back."

Jobby nodded and showed a crooked smile.

"Good luck, son. You're gonna need it."

It was close to midnight when the knock came on the front door. Allie got up from the computer and looked out the window to see who it was. A car was parked at the curb under the streetlight, and footsteps led from it through six inches of still falling snow up her front steps. A man was standing on the porch wearing a cowboy hat and boots, his hands shoved into the pockets of a thick sheepskin-lined jacket. She caught back a breath. It was Beck.

"I'd understand if you never spoke to me again," he said, the words spilling out in a rush when she opened the door. Before she could reply, he stepped into the foyer, backing her against the wall, then wrapped his arm around her waist and hauled her hard against him.

"Beck, I—"

His mouth came down stopping her words. All at once her heart was pounding, and when he parted her lips with his tongue, a sensuous movement that made her knees weak, she fell right into the kiss. He held her tight, and she became heady

294

with the scent of him. He smelled like cold and snow and winter. And Beck.

When she thought she might swoon from the thrill of it, he ended the kiss and looked at her, his eyes brilliant with desire. His hands held her face with exquisite tenderness, his eyes devouring her. Breathless, she stared back, not trusting herself to speak.

"I can't live without you," he said. "I don't want to live without you. I need you with me all the time, for real, not just in my thoughts. I want to walk with you beside me. I want to wake with you next to me. I want to see you every day and every night."

Struggling with his composure, he took both her hands in his, used his foot to close the door behind him, and led her to the sofa. He dropped into it, and she let herself be carried along to sit next to him. His eyes were brilliant with anticipation.

Allie gaped, speechless.

"Please don't make me go away. I want you. I've always wanted only you. I think of you day and night. I swear to God, Allie. Day and night, you've been in my thoughts. I see your face everywhere. Hear your voice, your laughter." There was a catch in his voice and a sob hitched out, but he caught it. It hurt her to hear it.

"Please forgive me," he whispered.

She watched the play of blinking lights from the Christmas tree on his face. The sensuous look in his eyes made her heart trip over itself. She placed her hand in the middle of his chest and felt the thundering of his heart.

He squeezed her hand and spoke earnestly.

"I know the truth now about my father," he said. "I don't know why I didn't see it then. I didn't want to, I guess. My parents always seemed a little in love and a little enraged. That's the way it was with them." His words choked off. "So many years, so much time gone by that we won't ever be able to get back, and it's all my fault."

He had never looked more handsome than he did at that moment, a charismatic mix of masculinity and sensitivity. Allie lifted her finger and put it to his lips.

"Shhhh," she said, but couldn't stop his onrush of words.

"Please come back to the ranch with me. I'll beg if I have to, if you want me to. I'll do anything for you. I just need you with me. You and Davy." His voice was coarse with raw emotion, his need of her shining clearly in his eyes.

Allie moved closer and threaded her fingers through his hair and kissed him tenderly. She scooted over and put her arms around him, curled up half in and half out of his lap, and hung on. She laid her head against his chest, and rocked back and forth, listening to the beat of his heart, feeling the intermittent shudder in his body when his breath caught.

She didn't let go and she didn't move away. She just rocked and held him tight in her arms. Slowly, he began to relax. She could feel the release as it moved through his body. When it passed, he rested his forehead against her shoulder.

"I'm sorry, Allie. I'm so, so sorry. Will you forgive me? I've been a damn idiot. None of this is your fault. It's all mine. I take full responsibility. Tell me how I can make it up to you."

She shifted position and drew his face into the hollow of her neck. "Shhhh," she said again, then put her lips to his ear and spoke.

"My darling Beck, there has never been anyone else but you for me. The most precious moments of my life were spent with you and I missed them more than I can say. I'm sorry about your father. I didn't mean for him to die. If I'd known he was having a heart attack, I would never have run off and left him there." A trapped sob quivered in her throat, making her voice come out high and shaky.

"After I left, there were times I thought I'd die without you. Sometimes I could read your thoughts in my mind, hear your voice, feel your touch. You're as necessary to me as my heartbeat." She fought back the tightness in her chest.

"Nothing, nothing in my life was ever complete, simply because you weren't there to share it with me. A day didn't go by that I didn't whisper to you in my head. I'd lie awake at night thinking of you. When I was at the cottage, I'd walk along the beach for miles writing your name in the sand with a stick, pretending we were kids again, having silly fantasies that somehow you'd fly over in an airplane and see what I'd written in the sand and that's how you'd find me."

She felt his lips move into a smile against her skin at her childish notion. Then he sucked in a breath, held it, and finally expelled the air slowly.

"Oh, Allie," he said. "I'm in so much trouble."

"Why?" she asked.

"Because I can't live without you."

She tightened her arms, and he clung to her.

"Will you and Davy come back to the ranch with me?" His voice held nothing back of what he felt. "Marry me and I promise I will never let anything come between us again." He lifted his head. His eyes were full of apology.

"You and I, both of us in our own way have been running from the truth. Let's stop it right now and not let any more time go by. We've both grown up now." He paused. "Well, you have. But if we love each other enough, we'll find a way to make it work. It might not be easy, but let's do it anyway. Okay? Please Allie. I can let go of the past. Can you?"

Allie took a little breath and held it.

"What about Jazzy?"

Unexpectedly, he chuckled. "She's getting married."

Allie pulled away and looked at him from arm's length, her

eyes searching his face. "What?"

Beck nodded. "Yep. She called to tell me. One of the guys on her excavation team up in Wyoming." He grinned. "She's pregnant."

Allie couldn't stop the laughter that burst from her throat. "She is?"

"Yes," Beck said. "She said that she'd been trying to tell me for weeks, but didn't know how. Finally she did."

Then his face clouded, and he shook his head. "She was only there to fill the void after I gave up on ever seeing you again."

He circled her in his arms, and with a sigh she let herself be gathered into his warmth, resting her head on his shoulder. He hugged her tight and held her that way, pulling her body in close. She was intensely aware of his touch, even his breath on her hair.

"So would you consider coming back with me?" he whispered, his voice hopeful.

She pulled his hand to her lips and kissed his fingertips. "I don't have to consider it." She looked at him and grinned. "The answer is yes."

Arms around each other's waist, they walked slowly up the stairs. They undressed in the bedroom and lay down on the bed, folding into each other. She closed her eyes and let herself melt into him while the room swirled around them.

He took her wrists, held them over her head, pressing them into the pillow. He put his mouth on her breast and moved his tongue sensuously on her nipple.

"Do you have any whipped cream and strawberries?" he asked her.

She opened her eyes. "No," she breathed. "Why?"

"So I can make a sundae out of you," he whispered, and closed his mouth on her again.

She let out a breathy little laugh. "I'll put it on my grocery list tomorrow," she managed to say before losing her breath completely.

They made love while an Arctic wind howled and snow collected in cottony drifts around the house. Before daybreak, she got up to put on flannel pajamas. When she returned to bed, Beck was asleep, snoring lightly. She climbed in, pulled the puffy quilts over them, and snuggled against his bulk, feeling safe again.

The next morning, Allie was in the kitchen putting on the coffee when Davy's voice called down the stairs.

"No school today! Look at the snow!" He burst into the kitchen and braked to a stop when he saw who was sitting at the kitchen table.

"Beck!" He flew across the room, flung himself onto Beck, burying his face in Beck's chest. "Oh, I'm so glad you're here. I missed you so much."

"How are you, big guy?" He held Davy in a bear hug. "I missed you, too."

Davy clung to Beck, ready to burst with joy. "How's Jobby? How's Sadie? Do you still have my saddle?"

"Jobby's fine, so is Sadie, and, yes, I still have your saddle."

He hugged Beck around the neck, squeezing hard. "Thank you for coming," he said.

"Thank Allie for letting me," Beck replied.

Davy released the hug and rocked back on his heels. "Oh, I knew she would eventually."

Face beaming, he reached out and pulled her into a three-way embrace. "But thank you, Allie." He kissed her cheek.

"How would you like to spend Christmas at the ranch?" she asked.

"Really?"

"Yes. Really."

"Can we go today?" Davy was practically levitating off the

floor with delight.

"Oh, damshuckems, no, not today," she said, smiling and looking at Beck, their eyes making sizzling contact. "Today we have to go grocery shopping."

ABOUT THE AUTHOR

C. C. Harrison lives in Anthem, Arizona. When she's not writing, reading, or working out at the gym, she can be found in the mountains of Colorado or some far-flung corner of the Southwest.